DEAD ERNEST

Books by Phoebe Atwood Taylor
available from Foul Play Press

Asey Mayo Cape Cod Mysteries

THE ANNULET OF GILT
THE ASEY MAYO TRIO
BANBURY BOG
THE CAPE COD MYSTERY
THE CRIMINAL C.O.D.
THE CRIMSON PATCH
THE DEADLY SUNSHADE
DEATH LIGHTS A CANDLE
DIPLOMATIC CORPSE
FIGURE AWAY
GOING, GOING, GONE
THE MYSTERY OF THE CAPE COD PLAYERS
THE MYSTERY OF THE CAPE COD TAVERN
OCTAGON HOUSE
OUT OF ORDER
THE PERENNIAL BOARDER
PROOF OF THE PUDDING
PUNCH WITH CARE
SANDBAR SINISTER
SPRING HARROWING
THE SIX IRON SPIDERS
THREE PLOTS FOR ASEY MAYO

Writing as Alice Tilton

BEGINNING WITH A BASH
DEAD ERNEST
FILE FOR RECORD
HOLLOW CHEST
THE LEFT LEG
THE IRON CLEW

PHOEBE ATWOOD TAYLOR

WRITING AS ALICE TILTON

DEAD
ERNEST

A Leonidas Witherall Mystery

A Foul Play Press Book

THE COUNTRYMAN PRESS
Woodstock, Vermont

Copyright © 1944 by Phoebe Atwood Taylor

This edition is published in 1992 by Foul Play Press, a division
of The Countryman Press, Woodstock, Vermont 05091.

ISBN 0-88150-242-1

Printed in the United States of America on recycled paper

10 9 8 7 6 5 4 3 2

DEAD ERNEST

I

" 'CLUTCHING the jewel-hilted sword of his departed ancestors, Admiral Yamaguchi, at bay at last, uttered a shrill yelp,' " Mr. Leonidas Witherall's pen hesitated no more than the fraction of a second as he became aware of the bulky figure of his charlady, Mrs. Mullet, looming for what seemed the millionth time in the doorway of his study, " 'like a wounded—' "

"Mr. Witherall." Mrs. Mullet said firmly.

" 'Cur.' " Leonidas wrote. " 'Our hero, Lieutenant Haseltine, bared his even white teeth in a smile of proud triumph. Now the foul fiend who had submitted the beautiful Lady Alicia—' "

"Mr. Witherall, in my candied opinion—"

Leonidas wearily raised his head, bade Mrs. Mullet a polite good night, and tried to think of a suitable and proper word with which to sum up Lady Alicia's fate. Considering that sometime in the next and final fifteen pages she was destined to drop into the lieutenant's arms by parachute—unharmed, and with every last golden curl in place—he shouldn't mislead his readers into expecting too much.

He wondered, as he drew a line through the unfinished sentence, if he'd remembered to have the rescue party bring along a fresh uniform for Haseltine, so that the grand finale wouldn't catch the fellow wearing his present disguise of a half-caste trader. The point ought to be checked, but he hated to waste a single moment looking back. This long overdue Haseltine epic *had* to be finished tonight. It *had* to be sent off at the crack of dawn tomorrow, before his publishers, now at the irritable telegram state, really began to get angry with him.

Glancing at the sheaf of yellow Western Union messages

which had been arriving at intervals all day, and which he hadn't even bothered to open, he dipped his pen into the tiny hollow bust of Shakespeare that served as an inkwell on his desk, and embarked on a pithy description of the evil admiral's gruesome demise.

"Mis-ter Witherall! In *my* candied opinion, you just *got* to stop long enough to *see* this here!"

Leonidas sighed at the Shakespeare inkwell.

For more years than he cared to remember, people had been telling him he resembled that inkwell, that he was the spitting image of old Bill Shakespeare, the Bard of Avon in the flesh. If only, he told himself grimly, he could suddenly turn into the Jimmy Cagney type, instead! For two blissful minutes, he would revel in being Cagney. To hurl the contents of that inkwell at Mrs. Mullet's face, to follow up with the copper bowl of chrysanthemums, and then to tell her exactly and specifically how he felt about idiotic interruptions!

Discretion forced him to turn around and assume an expression of polite interest. As the only charlady in Dalton who had not succumbed to the blandishments of the mills, Mrs. Mullet was a pearl of great price. Doubtless, in her own way, she also meant well.

"Yes, Mrs. Mullet?" he said.

"It's this *thing*." She held out for his inspection a baggy, shapeless garment of black cloth. "I mended all them moth holes as good as I could, but they show. And it shines, and honest, I don't dare try ironing it. It'll only fall apart, it's that old."

"Thank you," Leonidas said. "You're very kind to have taken so much trouble. Just put it on the chair, please. Good ni—"

"Mr. Witherall, is it like a *kimono*?"

"Er—no," Leonidas said. "It's my gown. Good ni—"

"Mr. Witherall!" Mrs. Mullet's eyes narrowed, and she looked at him coldly, "you ain't going to *wear* that thing!"

"It's an academic gown." Putting on his pince-nez, Leonidas surveyed the rusty black folds and concluded that there was considerable basis for Mrs. Mullet's openly expressed disgust. The tarnished gold tassel on his mortarboard was frayed and stringy, the gown was desperately shabby, the blue velvet bands around the sleeves looked as if they had been gnawed on by generations of famished mice. "Somewhat to my regret, I have to wear it tomorrow."

"In *public?*" Mrs. Mullet would have employed the same tone of voice had she spoken to Lady Godiva at the start of her famous ride. "What *for?*"

"Beginning tomorrow," Leonidas said, "I'm the headmaster of Meredith's Academy. It's necessary that on opening day I appear briefly in that—er—uniform, as you might call it."

"You'll appear briefly, all right!" Mrs. Mullet assured him. "Mr. Witherall, what you taking on *another* job for? Meredith's —that's the swell boys' school they been using to teach navy officers at, isn't it? What you want to teach *there* for?"

"Frankly, I don't," Leonidas said, "but I own it. Good night—"

"You *own* it?" Mrs. Mullet's eyes bulged. *"You?* You *do?"*

If he had made even the slightest attempt to satisfy her eager curiosity, Leonidas thought, if he told her that the school had been bequeathed him by his old friend Marcus Meredith, she would only ask how he happened to know old Senator Meredith so well. That would involve telling her of his teaching days at Meredith's, before he discovered that writing Haseltine was far more lucrative. It would necessitate explaining that as abruptly and as suddenly as the navy had requisitioned the school two years ago, so had they returned it two weeks ago.

"M'yes, I own it," he said aloud, "and because we've been handicapped in finding a staff on short notice, I decided to act as headmaster for a while. Now—"

"But you got so many jobs already, you get 'em mixed up!"

"They're all temporary. When the various directors and board chairmen come marching home, I'll fade back into oblivion. In the interim," he added with a smile, "I shall try not to inspect the Bide-a-Wee Animal Home again on bank-meeting day, or confuse the Greens Committee with the Bond Committee. Now, Mrs. Mullet, permit me to thank you for your solicitude, and to wish you a very pleasant good night!"

"You keep saying that, but it isn't time for me to go yet! It's not even four! And before you get all wrapped up in that stuff—Mis-ter Witherall! There's something else! In my candied opinion, I—Mis-ter *Witherall!*"

"Mmm," Leonidas picked up his pen.

"You're going to have terrible trouble with those Fingers, you mark my words!"

"They're merely stiff from writing, Mrs. Mullet." Leonidas dipped the pen into the ink. "They were quite all right until the typewriter broke."

"Not *your* fingers!" she raised her voice. "You're going to *rue* the day the Haverstraws moved away from next door! They was the best neighbors—"

Leonidas only half-listened as she launched into rhapsodic praises of the garden-mad Haverstraws, whom he had personally always regretted. For years they had bullied him unmercifully and without surcease, forcing rakes and hoes into his unwilling hands, compelling him to blend his flowers with theirs, to manicure his lawn into matching the contours of their land.

"*They* was neighbors!" Mrs. Mullet paused for breath.

"M'yes, quite so. Please, Mrs. M., now will you let me work?"

"Wait—what'll I do about all those people? And Bedford Scrim?"

"Bedford Scrim? Bedford Scrim," Leonidas said thoughtfully. "Oh, you refer to the guest-room curtains which shrank? *That* Bedford Scrim?"

"Not curtains! A man! A m-a-n!" she spelled out the word. "A man! What'll I do about him?"

"Man." Leonidas looked up. "Why, I hardly know how to advise you, really. If he's decent and honest and sober, and makes a living wage, and all that sort of thing, I suppose there's no reason why you shouldn't marry him. Providing, of course, that you wish to."

"Mr. Witherall, what are you *talking* about?"

"You asked me what to do about a man, and while I am no facsimile of Dorothy Dix—"

"You just got to put that pen down, Mr. Witherall, and *listen!* People been coming here to see you all day, fifty million of 'em, and you keep sitting there at that desk, scratching away, and telling me to leave you alone! And those Fingers, and those phone calls, and those telegrams you won't even open to see what's in 'em!"

"I know their contents," Leonidas said gently, "by heart. I've seen their equivalent many times before. They are iron-gloved messages from my publishers, who want this book. I point out to you that I cannot finish this book if I'm not permitted to work in peace, quiet, and without interruptions. In short, Mrs. Mullet, good night!"

"What'll I say to that Scrim?" she persisted.

"In all my wide acquaintance, I know no one named Bedford Scrim," Leonidas said with finality. "I have never heard of anyone named Bedford Scrim."

"But you do! You know his uncle! He—"

"I know no one who is the uncle of anyone named Bedford Scrim. I don't believe any man was *ever* named Bedford Scrim, Mrs. Mullet. It is obviously an alias. This—"

"But he—"

"This person," having decided to talk her down, Leonidas gave her no chance to protest, "is either an insurance man, an insulation salesman, or else he has designs on my silver. Bedford Scrim is a name fraught with villainous and sinister connotations. It is practically ballad material. 'Bedford Scrim was born to be hanged, Bedford Scrim was a crook, Bedford Scrim he languished in gaol—er—all for the life he took. Hey nonny nim for Bedford Scrim, the crook who took—'"

"He is *not* a villain, Mr. Witherall! He comes from my—"

"I depend upon you to foil him for me, Mrs. M." Leonidas got up. "If he returns again, inform him that I'm coming down with a malady diagnosed by my doctor as leprous mumps. Now!" he insinuated her into the hall, closed the door, and locked it. "Now," he called out, "go home early! Good night!"

As he returned to the grisly hara-kiri of the evil Yamaguchi, he heard her voice plaintively saying something that sounded, through the closed door, curiously like "Goldfish, Fingers, Mussels, Butter." She said it a number of times while Leonidas patiently waited for her to stop and go home.

Finally, after a terrific amount of banging about in the kitchen, he heard the front door slam behind her.

"Alone," he said with relief, "at last! Now, Haseltine—"

His pen bore down on the paper.

Simultaneously, a large red truck pulled noisily into his graveled driveway outside the window.

Two men jumped out, and with almost prewar dispatch, proceeded to roll down the inclined truck tail a large, cabinet-like object which vaguely reminded Leonidas of a drugstore ice-cream storage container. Oozing efficiency, the pair slid the cabinet onto a wheeled platform, aimed it, and sped it forward as if they were the van of a panzer attack.

Somewhat belatedly, it occurred to Leonidas that his own back door was their target.

Unlocking his study door, he raced to the kitchen to find that the two men and the cabinet were already there.

For such agile workmen, Leonidas noted as he surveyed them in bewilderment, they were two of the most slovenly individuals he had ever seen outside of a sewer. Their ill-fitting dungarees were stiff with dirt, their greasy sweat shirts hung halfway to their knees, their faces were virtually camouflaged with grime.

"Here, chum!" The taller man produced a slip of paper from the lining of his checked cap. "Sign here. Where's she want it?"

"Er—where," Leonidas returned, "does—er—who want what?"

"We ain't got all day, chum!" he thrust the slip at Leonidas and waggled it impatiently. "Where's the lady of the house want this put? It ought to get connected right away, so as—"

"There is no lady of the house," Leonidas informed him, "and whatever that object is, I don't want it!"

"If you din't want it," the short man demanded truculently, "why'd you buy it, huh?"

"I didn't buy it!" Leonidas felt a little absurd at being put on the defensive when this misdelivery was none of his fault. "I did not—"

"Listen, chum, a deep freeze *this* type ain't nothin' to blow hot and cold about these days!" the tall man told him severely. "You wanted it this morning, all right, and you bought it, and you paid for it! *We* know you paid for it, see? We ain't tryin' to collect nothin', see? All we want is you should sign and tell us where you want it, see? We—"

"If," Leonidas interrupted, "you will permit me to—er—insert a word, what is the name of the consignee on that slip of yours? Is it Witherall?"

"There ain't no name. It just says Forty Birch Hill Road, that's all!" he waved the slip under Leonidas' nose. "See for yourself, chum. That's Forty, ain't it? And this's Forty, ain't it?"

"Indisputably," Leonidas agreed. "But the fact remains that I neither ordered nor purchased a deep freeze. It isn't mine. I don't—"

"It *says* Forty, chum!"

"If Forty Birch Hill Road were inlaid in rubies on the lid of that thing," Leonidas said, "I still should not wish it. It is not mine."

"Well, if it ain't yours," the short man said, "then whose is it, huh?"

Leonidas swung his pince-nez on their broad black ribbon. "I wonder—m'yes, I wonder if this isn't perhaps destined for One-forty, next door?"

"One-forty, next door? You mean One-forty's next to Forty, chum?"

"The eccentricities of the street numbering of Birch Hill Road," Leonidas said, "are no fault of mine, I assure you. Forty is flanked by One-forty, and by Six. I suggest that you wheel this thing to One-forty. A new family is moving in, and this is doubtless theirs."

For some reason not at all clear to Leonidas, both men appeared to view such a transfer with the utmost suspicion.

"What's the name there, huh?" the short man demanded.

Leonidas shrugged. "The name *was* Haverstraw, but the new owners are strangers to me." He tried to recall if Mrs. Mullet had mentioned their name. She must have, in the course of the day, but he hadn't been paying attention. "I might—er —bring to your notice the fact that if you don't possess the name of your consignee, the name of the new occupants of One-forty should hardly concern you to any extent. I'm sure One-forty is your goal."

"If you was so sure," the short man said bitterly, "whyn't you tell us before we went and gone to all the work getting this in here, huh? Come on, Matt, roll her out!"

They rolled the deep freeze out, maneuvered it back onto the truck, and almost before Leonidas had prudently turned the key in the kitchen door—Mrs. Mullet must have been very annoyed with him to have left that open, he thought in passing —the truck had taken its noisy departure. A moment later, he heard it entering the driveway of One-forty.

"What *was* the name of those new people?" he murmured as he returned to his study. "Ah, well, I'll find out after Haseltine's done and Meredith's is started, and make a formal call!"

On his way to his desk, he paused, picked up the shabby gown, slipped it on over his gray-tweed suit, and clapped the mortarboard on his head. While the effect was admittedly more raffish than academic, he decided as he surveyed himself in the mirror, the outfit should at least last through tomorrow's opening exercises without disintegrating.

The front-door bell chimes rang out as he turned away from the mirror, and with a muttered exclamation of annoyance, Leonidas strode to the door and opened it.

A chubby, barefooted, fat little girl in blue shorts and a middy blouse looked up at him seriously through tortoise-shell rimmed glasses.

"Er—yes?" Leonidas said encouragingly.

Her smile disclosed what appeared to be a fretwork of gold bands on her teeth.

"Mother wants goldfish now," she said in a rush of words.

"Does she, indeed!" Leonidas returned. "I've never particularly pined for them, myself, but I dare say that if your mother wishes goldfish, she will doubtless derive much pleasure and happiness from the—er—little things. Was there any other tidbit you had in mind to divulge to me?"

"Mother thinks the worst is over, now. She—"

"Fine!" Leonidas said heartily. "Capital! I'm delighted to hear it. And now, will you excuse me? I'm rather busy."

He had Yamaguchi's dying speech well under way when the back-door chimes sounded.

It was the grimy pair again, and beside them on the doorstep stood the deep freeze, resting on its wheeled platform.

Both men, on beholding him, started to laugh. They didn't say anything, they just stood there, laughing raucously.

"To what," Leonidas inquired crisply, "do I owe the dubious pleasure of this return visitation?"

"Wow, chum, that's some hat you got there! That's a lid, boy!"

"Hat? *Hat?*" For the first time, Leonidas realized that he had forgotten to remove the raffish mortarboard. And the baggy gown. "Ah, yes. Possibly it's a bit out of your world, but permit me to say that I should not care to trade it for the repulsive checked object on your own noggin. Er—what do you want?"

The tall man cleared his throat. "Next door they won't take it, chum."

"Take what?"

"The deep freeze, what else? They say *they* don't want it."

"What'll *we* do with it?" the short man asked in a doleful voice.

"Take it back where you got it," Leonidas started to draw the door to. "Perhaps you'll be good enough to remove your large foot from this door sill?"

"Wait, chum!" the tall man said persuasively. "Hold it! We *can't* take it back."

"Why not? You got that thing somewhere," Leonidas said, "certainly you can return it to the same place, can't you?"

"Listen, chum," the tall man edged into the kitchen, "it's like this, see? This guy, he's got this freeze on a beachwagon, see? And he's got a flat, see, and no spare. So he stops me and Shorty on the pike, and says how's for maybe we deliver this freeze for him, see? And it's on our way, so we say sure, we'll deliver it, see? So we do, only we can't, on account of you don't want it, and they don't want it to One-forty, see?"

"Return it!" Leonidas said wearily. "Return it to the individual in the beachwagon! Now, please remove yourself from my—"

"We can't return it, chum. We don't know who he was, see?"

"You mean that you neglected to ascertain his name?" Leonidas inquired. "Or the license number of his beachwagon?"

"We don't know who he was from nobody!" Shorty said. "We was just pickin' up a couple bucks on the side, wasn't we, Matt?"

Matt agreed that they was just picking up a couple bucks. "You can't blame us none," he added. "It was on our way, see? And we can't take this back with us, see, on account of the boss, he wouldn't stand for it. He gets sore when he finds out we tried to pick up a couple bucks on the side. He says we waste too much gas. So you see how it is, chum!"

"While I feel for you deeply," Leonidas said, "I have neither the time nor the inclination to offer any constructive suggestions. You—er—picked up a couple of bucks, and you also reaped a deep freeze. Let it be a lesson to you both."

"Chum," Matt said, "chum, wouldn't you just keep it overnight, till we find out who it belongs to?"

"I fail to see," Leonidas said, "how you can expect to ascertain the ownership of that object when you have, according to your own statement, absolutely no basis on which to work. As I have repeatedly informed you, I personally do *not* want that deep freeze! Not even temporarily!"

"Wouldn't you be a sport and ask around the neighborhood who was *expecting* a deep freeze, huh?" Shorty asked in a wheedling voice.

"I am altogether too cluttered with my own problems—" Leonidas paused as he heard his front-door chimes pealing again.

"Doorbell's ringing, chum!" Matt told him.

"I hear it." Leonidas reached out for the doorknob. "Gentlemen, I shall think of you in the days to come, wandering from pillar to post with that poor, homeless deep freeze. Good-by!"

He shoved the door closed over their protests, turned the key in the lock, and ran to the front of the house while the chimes continued to ring out like a fire alarm.

He flung the door open wide, then stopped short and whipped on his pince-nez.

Standing on the top step was a girl, but a girl so different from the fat, chatty moppet that the two hardly seemed to belong to the same sex.

This one was blonde, dressed in a long, shimmering white evening gown, with a cluster of orchids pinned on her shoulder. Over her arm was a velvet evening wrap of royal purple.

Leonidas blinked, noted that her eyes matched her wrap, and blinked again. He had never seen anything like her except on a magazine cover, or in an advertisement for sable capes.

"Er—" he found his voice, "er—by any chance, are *you* Bedford Scrim?"

The girl shook her head slowly. Leonidas got the impression that she was as surprised to see him as he was to see her.

"Then perhaps you will forgive my—er—rushing off. I am

sorry," Leonidas said sincerely, "that I'm busy, but honesty compels me to add that even in a state of comparative calm, I should regretfully not be in the market for either perfume or sables, one or the other of which I assume you—er—dispense."

"Ready?" the girl said.

"Er—*what?*"

Cocking her head on one side, the girl opened her mouth and began to sing.

"Hap-py birth-day to you, hap-py *birth*-day to you! Hap-py birth-day, dear—" she stopped. "Damn!" she said blankly, "I've gone and forgotten the name! Something like Marmaduke, wasn't it? Or Leffingwell? Or Strawbridge?"

Before Leonidas could manage to extricate himself sufficiently from his state of bewilderment to tell her that he was none of those people, she resumed her blithe caroling.

"Hap-py BIRTH-day to you!" she wound up. Then, pointing to his academic gown, she added conversationally, "Fancy dress?"

"I might," Leonidas said in a choked voice, "ask the same of you! While I have enjoyed your little musical interlude—"

He broke off as the red truck roared out of his driveway, caromed off the curb, and sped away up the street like a patrol wagon answering a riot call.

"I must nevertheless confess," he continued, "that I am not Marmaduke, or any of the others, and that my birthday is next July. In a nutshell, you probably want One-forty Birch Hill Road. Not Forty. Good evening!"

He closed the door with polite firmness.

"Dear Smith and Beston," he murmured as he turned away, "I am desolated to think that the reopening of Meredith's Academy delayed this new Haseltine during its formative stages. Owing to the manpower shortage, I was compelled to walk the streets of Boston in my desperate search for a staff. I combed alleys for an athletic coach. I visited old men's homes for Latin teachers. I rang doorbells canvassing material for the French department. Having garnered in a motley lot, I then applied myself to Haseltine as I never applied myself to any-thing else in this wide world."

He sighed. It was all gospel truth, and his publishers never would believe a single word of it.

"But interruptions abounded, dear Smith and Beston. I was tormented continuously. By charladies. By moppets wish-ing goldfish. By orchid-strewn glamor girls who sang to me. By a couple guys wid a deep freeze who wanted I should take it for free—hm! I wonder why in the world that grubby pair raced away in such a cloud of dust?"

He stopped in the doorway of the study as a sudden dark suspicion flitted through his mind.

Then he relaxed. He'd locked the kitchen door. He definitely remembered turning the key. They couldn't possibly have got in. Besides, it was idiotic to think that they'd ever leave that deep freeze anywhere. Not when they could dispose of it, and doubtless pick up a couple of bucks in the process!

Still and all, he found himself walking slowly toward the kitchen, although his thoughts were still largely occupied with the finale of Haseltine. What medal should a grateful govern-ment bestow on the gallant young hero this time? His manly chest was already bedecked like Goering's—

A little gust of wind in the hall set the skirts of his gown billowing around his legs.

Wind?

A *gust* of wind?

"No!" Leonidas said, and dove for the kitchen. "No! I locked it! I know I locked it!"

But the back door was open, wide open.

His gaze went from it to the open casement window over the

sink, to the streaks of dirt on the white porcelain ledges, to the dirty, muddy footprints on the waxed linoleum floor.

Finally, he forced himself to acknowledge the presence of the deep freeze, standing there next to the refrigerator in a sort of passive triumph.

Beside it sat a bowlful of goldfish.

Leonidas, watching the fish streak around and around a decorative chunk of coral, decided for a numbed moment of confusion that he had probably written too much Haseltine. This was just the type of thing he kept dreaming when he'd banged out too much heroic blood-letting, thunderous violence, and sudden death. There was the same aura of lunatic disorder, the same fantastic twist to what should have been normal, sensible objects.

Goldfish, forsooth, goldfish swimming by a homeless deep freeze, left to him for no reason by two strange men named Matt and Shorty, with faces that looked like illustrations out of a camouflage book!

And to think that that pair had even connected the freeze by plugging it into the iron socket!

"*Why?*" Leonidas said. "Why? Certainly it isn't full of rib roasts!"

He raised up the heavy oblong lid.

Then he let it fall.

Drawing a long breath, he held out his pince-nez and breathed on them. Then, with a clean handkerchief and shaking fingers, he polished them elaborately.

At last he carefully affixed the pince-nez, and lifted up the lid again.

His eyes had not deceived him.

There was the leg of lamb. There were the frozen fillets of haddock.

Leonidas shook his head.

No, his eyes hadn't deceived him on any detail.

There was still that body of a man lying there, too.

And still that crimson patch on the left breast of the man's gray-flannel suit.

II

His discovery that what he had brought to light was not an optical illusion or a figment of his tired imagination somehow had the effect of steadying Leonidas at once.

An actual body with an evident wound which obviously couldn't have been self-inflicted was not without its share of accompanying shock.

But it was real.

It was a fact.

And however distasteful they might be to one's personal predilections, reality and fact were things with which one could at least attempt to cope.

"I should summon the police," he said firmly, and stood there slowly twirling his pince-nez on their broad black ribbon. "I should summon the police immediately. M'yes. I should."

In spite of his natural feeling of mingled horror and bewilderment, he found his professional attitude somewhat crassly coming to the fore.

What a magnificent method by which to dispose of a body!

What a thoroughly masterly piece of work!

Like the splendid aura of villainy surrounding the very name of the unknown Bedford Scrim, this exquisitely clever means of getting rid of an unwanted corpse filled him with a sense of envious inadequacy. If only *he* had the creative wit to enliven the assorted adventures of Haseltine with such a brilliant villain-name, and such skillful evidence-abandoning! While he muddled about with drab Japanese admirals, with commonplace thefts of The Jewels, or The Papers, or The Formulae, while he lacerated his brain inventing laboriously intricate murder devices, here, here in the smug suburban town of Dalton, real melodrama took place with artless ease!

He glanced suddenly at the open doorway, listened a moment, and frowned. Then, after stepping gingerly around the deep freeze and the bowl of goldfish, he closed the door and locked it.

That nervous sensation of being watched was probably perfectly natural, he told himself. Under similar circumstances, Haseltine and the beautiful Lady Alicia often clutched each other tremulously and said hist, were they being observed by hostile eyes?

It was all so pellucid, so crystal clear to him now, he thought as he leaned back against the broom closet. It was all so very simple! So very Columbus-and-the-egg!

Matt and Shorty had been snakes in the grass, wolves in sheep's clothing.

In short, fakes.

Their ill-fitting garments were costumes. Their grubby camouflage had been a disguise which shouldn't for a minute have taken in anyone whose mind wasn't imbedded and immersed in Yamaguchi's hara-kiri and in Haseltine's Garrison finish.

From the very onset, Matt and Shorty had intended to leave that deep freeze at his house.

Almost their first words, he recalled, had been an assurance that no payment was due, that they were asking him for no money, that they had already been paid in full.

They expected him to bite, to tell them to leave the deep freeze and begone. It wasn't an unnatural or a far-fetched assumption on their parts, either. Many good respectable people in Dalton's Oak Hill section would have jumped from their skins at the opportunity thus to achieve a deep freeze for nothing.

When he hadn't risen to their bait, they tried wheedling him. When wheedling failed, they sneaked in by the window, unlocked the door, and left the thing in his kitchen anyway.

"Superlative acting!" he commented appreciatively. "Sheer genius!"

With a wry smile, he remembered how sharply he'd retorted to Matt's plaint that they knew neither the name nor the license-plate number of the nebulous man-in-the-beachwagon from whom they claimed to have acquired the deep freeze.

How could he have had the audacity to smirk pityingly at their apparent stupidity, he wondered! He, himself, had noticed absolutely nothing about their red truck other than its color, and the fact that it was a truck as opposed to a pleasure vehicle. It might or it might not have possessed marks of identification, like number plates or common carrier plates, a lettered company name, a battered fender, a missing bumper.

All he could possibly tell the police was that the two men arrived in a red truck. A truck that was not scarlet, vermilion, carmine, crimson lake, ruby, rose, claret or cherry colored. Just plain, everyday red!

And as for conjuring up for the ears of officialdom any lucid and informative description of that pair!

Leonidas sighed.

"Their height, officer? Ah, well," he murmured with irony, "Matt was taller than Shorty, and Shorty was shorter than Matt. Each man had two arms and two legs. Each had a face. Washed, they might be a couple of youthful Apollos. They might, on the other hand, be middle-aged. Their weight? With those floppy clothes, one could not even venture a surmise at their poundage."

However idiotic his explanations might sound, he must summon the police!

He must turn his thoughts away from the headlines which

tomorrow morning, on the grand reopening of Meredith's Academy, would scream to Dalton and vicinity that the owner and new headmaster of that fine, renowned old school had been presented with a leg of lamb, some fillets of haddock, a deep freeze, and a murdered man. He should not consider the resultant shrinkage of the pupil roster. Such considerations were selfish, and unworthy of him. The police must be called in!

After all, the Dalton police were splendid fellows, as he had publicly announced only last week at a committee luncheon of the Police Widows and Orphans Benevolent and Protective Association. Tactfully, he had ignored the bitter truth that the majority of Dalton's finest were off to the wars, that the present incumbents were for the most part retired cops of another era whose standards—if they could be termed such—were not of the highest.

In all honesty, *could* he ever explain to these paunchy, dull-witted duffers that two strangers had broken in and left behind a deep freeze containing an indisputable body?

He could try, Leonidas told himself stoutly. He *had* to!

He must, even though he could write the ensuing scene in his mind, right now!

"Whatcher doin' when they busted in, Mr. Withrell, huh?"

"Er—as a matter of fact, a rather beautiful blonde girl with violet eyes was caroling 'Happy Birthday' to me on my front steps."

"This your birthday, huh?"

"Er—no."

"Then what was she singin' 'Happy Birthday' to you for, huh?" Deep suspicion.

"I can't imagine."

"Who *was* she, huh?" Deeper suspicion.

"I don't know."

Impasse.

It was going to be very, very difficult!

Of course, Sergeant MacCobble might possibly take a more intelligent view of the situation. One might almost hope that the sergeant would pass lightly over the minor impediments, like the girl singing "Happy Birthday" when it wasn't, and concentrate his fire on the core, the raison d'être, the Why.

But Leonidas couldn't tell him why. He didn't know why.

For the last ten minutes he had been asking himself why that body had been left here, in his kitchen, and why anyone should have the remotest desire to implicate him in a murder.

As yet, no hint of an answer had presented itself to him.

That deep freeze could have been deposited in any other kitchen in any other house in Dalton or in any of the surrounding towns of Pomfret, Carnavon, Framfield, or Wemberley.

More accurately, it could have been left in any field, or on any street corner.

Anywhere!

Why here?

Leonidas shrugged.

"It is not," he said aloud, "as if it were anyone I knew!"

Surrendering his disinclination to his common sense, he again lifted up the lid of the deep freeze, and looked long and thoughtfully at the man inside.

His face was long, narrow, and lined. His hair, not in the least disarranged, was black. His gray suit was neither cheap nor badly cut, although for Leonidas' own conservative taste, it was rather on the light side, and far too sharply padded around the shoulders. But then this man was a lot younger, Leonidas thought charitably. Perhaps in his late twenties. In his early thirties at most.

He tried to dismiss his growing suspicion that he had seen the man somewhere before by telling himself that if one studied any face steadily for any length of time, certain features of it were bound to achieve a reminiscent familiarity.

Or was it that he had known the man in different clothes?

On countless occasions, Leonidas had admittedly failed to recognize his butcher or his barber or his milkman when he met them in their everyday civilian raiment, and away from their own bailiwicks.

Mentally, he redressed the fellow. In white coats, tweed suits, blue serge, work coveralls, overalls. Even in a bathing suit, and clerical garb.

It didn't help.

Hats were no better. Uniforms elicited no shrill scream of recognition. Glasses, from gold rims to monocles, rang no bell within him.

A beard, maybe?

"A mustache!" he let the lid fall. "He wore a mustache! Eureka!"

But gratification at his belated success gave way almost at once to that nervous feeling that someone was furtively peering in at him. He very nearly tripped over the bowl of goldfish in his haste to jerk down the kitchen shades.

He moved the fish over to a corner. He wasn't even going to consider those fish yet!

"Now!" he snapped on the light. "When you saw that fellow before, he wore a mustache. A small black mustache with waxed tips. Where was it? And who is he? Who—oh, dear!"

The pince-nez began to twirl like a dynamo at the end of their ribbon.

"Oh, dear me! How fortunate that Dalton's finest were *not* summoned at once! But how exceedingly fortunate all around!"

For with a small waxed mustache, the man was undeniably the newly hired French master of Meredith's Academy!

His name? Leonidas prodded around in the depths of his

memory. What was the fellow's name, now? A part of the body. Head? Not Head. Nor Legge. Nor Hand.

Finger!

That was it. Ernest Finger. Ernest Bostwick Finger, to be exact.

In other and more selective days, Ernest Bostwick Finger was probably the last person whom any headmaster of Meredith's would have considered hiring as a teacher of French or anything else. He was definitely not the Meredith type. Meredith's preferred tweedier masters, preferably pipe smokers, who could rush out and substitute as coach of the football team without any more effort than changing their shoes. On the day Leonidas had interviewed him, Ernest Finger had smoked cigarettes in a longish amber holder, and he had worn a dark-green suit with a wide pencil stripe, and his shoulders were even sharper than those of the gray model he had on now.

But in spite of his clothes and his lack of previous teaching experience, Finger possessed several bona fide degrees from excellent colleges and universities, he spoke French fluently and well, he had an intimate knowledge of the country, and his character references had been unimpeachable.

After that one brief interview with the man, Leonidas had turned him over to old Professor Skellings, who was acting as general factotum during the preopening days, and told Skellings to show him the ropes and help him plan some sort of curriculum on the basis of the former French master's notes and outlines.

Before leaving, Leonidas remembered carelessly tossing out a few subtle hints concerning the standards and the appearance of Meredith masters—could the missing mustache and the comparatively quiet gray suit be the result of those comments, he wondered?

At all events, after shaking hands and wishing the fellow

luck and Godspeed with his little charges, Leonidas had plunged back into Haseltine. From that moment until now, he had never given Ernest Bostwick Finger another thought.

No question about it, his identity was going to complicate a situation already far from simple. What the Dalton cops would make of—

He crossed over to the kitchen door, unlocked it noiselessly, and threw the door wide open.

That time he really *had* heard the sounds of someone lurking out there!

Standing on the top step, he peered around in the gathering dusk and tried to catch some sight of something—even a dog—which might have been responsible for the peculiar creaking and tapping that had caught his attention.

But there was only the wind rustling through the oak leaves, and the distant wail of the Abercrombie boy's saxophone over on the next street.

Leonidas stepped down to the flagstone path and tentatively walked to the corner of the garage, then to the opposite corner of the house.

There was no trace of any prowler, or of anyone skulking in the bushes, nor had he heard the footsteps of anyone running away.

Probably squirrels, he decided as he returned slowly to the kitchen and locked the door again. Or that indomitable skunk that could remove the patent garbage-pail top which foiled everyone else in the world, including Mrs. Mullet and the garbage man.

He was adjusting his pince-nez as he turned around from the door, and for a full minute he stood there with his right hand glued to the nose piece.

The glamor girl was perched on the kitchen table, her purple wrap in a heap beside her.

"Hullo!" she said pleasantly.

Leonidas drew a long breath. "My dear young woman, I'm afraid I must ask you to leave—"

"Leave? *Leave?* After all the trouble I've had getting in here?"

After all the trouble she'd had getting *in?* What did she mean? Leonidas all but screamed the question at himself, and hoped that none of the sound would break forth and issue from his lips. Had she been wandering around all this time, ever since her caroling? Had she—was it possible that she could have peeked through the window and seen Ernest Finger lying there inside the deep freeze?

Leonidas swallowed hard. He had the sensation that a golf ball was stuck in his throat.

Reason came to his rescue and told him that no woman, glamor girl or otherwise, could have seen that body while he had the lid lifted and not have given vent to some audible reaction. No woman, having seen it, could remain as entirely cool and collected as this beautiful blonde creature.

Conversely, anyone so completely poised and self-possessed would have taken the practical approach, and sent for the police.

"It is my impression," Leonidas said with all the blandness he could summon up, "that there has been some misunderstanding. I—"

"Misunderstanding is right!" the girl said, nodding her head in violent agreement. "No one bothered to break it to me that you look like Shakespeare, and if you only knew the shock you gave me! Shakespeare the Scholar, complete with cap and gown! It took my voice away. I suppose," she added, "that everyone calls you Bill, don't they?"

"The less reverent," Leonidas said, "are so inclined to address me. Now, my dear young—"

"My name's Hall. Terpsichore Hall. To you," she said with

a grin, "I can confess the Terpsichore. But since I was old enough to use my fists, I've been called Terry. I hope you have a thick steak in that deep freeze, Bill. Chasing you has whetted my appetite. I am but definitely starved!"

"Chasing me?" Leonidas inquired. "You are—er—chasing *me*?"

She looked at him curiously, and then she leaned back against the wall and laughed.

"So you haven't been told! And me thinking of course you'd been tipped off! Oh, you poor dear, what a blow I must be to you!"

"I'm afraid," Leonidas said, "that I still don't quite understand. What wasn't I told?"

She slipped off the table, crossed over to where he stood, and held out her right arm.

Tied around her wrist was an enormous and elaborate bow of lavender satin ribbon, from the center of which a card dangled.

"Read it!" she said. "I was so shattered by your turning out to be Shakespeare, I forgot to take my wrap off my arm and display this to you. I suppose it's really all my fault, your not catching on sooner. Read it!"

Leonidas read it, and the golf ball started to return to his throat.

"Happy Birthday, darling!" it said in a neat handwriting. "I am what you wanted!"

Terry removed the lavender bow and thrust it into his hand.

"For a man whose only wish for his birthday present has always been a beautiful blonde with violet eyes," Terry remarked, "you don't look a bit happy! You don't look as if I were what you wanted at all!"

"Miss Hall," Leonidas said firmly, "my birthday is next July. There has been some misunderstanding. There has—er—I regret sounding like a parrot, but let me assure you that there has been some misunderstanding!"

"Isn't this Forty Birch Hill Road?"

Leonidas nodded. "It is. I have never attempted to pretend otherwise, although," he cast a sideways glance at the deep freeze, "I'm beginning to feel it might possibly have been better if I had. This is Forty Birch Hill Road. But it is not my birthday."

"Didn't you ever go around telling people that all you wanted for your birthday was a beautiful blonde with violet eyes?"

"Er—not out loud," Leonidas returned. "Now, a new family has just moved into One-forty Birch Hill, next door, and I'm convinced that you must be a—er—a present for someone there."

"Forty," Terry said. "I was ordered to Forty, Forty is where I am, and Forty is where I stay till the stroke of twelve."

"You can't!" Leonidas said. "Circumstances over which I have no control make it thoroughly and utterly impossible for you even to contemplate staying here!"

"I've got to stay." She smiled. "Circumstances over which *I* have no control make it thoroughly and utterly impossible for me even to contemplate leaving here!"

"I should regret," Leonidas said, "the necessity of requesting the police to remove you by force, Miss Hall! I should regret it deeply!"

"I'm sure you would, Bill."

It was a simple statement, simply said, but Leonidas sensed the underlying threat.

He tried another tack.

"Miss Hall, I will be quite honest with you. Your continued presence here will be the source of considerable embarrassment, both to me and to yourself. I am the headmaster of Meredith's Academy—er—did you speak?"

"D'you have a match? Thanks," she said as he lighted her cigarette. "So you're the head of Meredith's! No one told me that, either."

"I expect some of my colleagues here tonight," he indicated his gown, "on academic business, and—er—I believe you see my point."

"I'll just trot upstairs and keep out of sight," Terry said cheerfully. "Maybe you've got a good book I can read."

"Miss Hall! Please!"

"I'm sorry to discommode you, Bill, but it's a contract. I said I'd be your birthday present, and I've been paid, and there's nothing I can do about it. My job," she added quickly, "as outlined to me, is to sit and let you look at me till midnight. Then I leap into a Coach-and-Four—really it'll be LeBlang's taxi—and go out of your life forever. So—"

"Don't!" Leonidas said suddenly. *"Don't* sit on that deep freeze!"

"Why not?"

"It's out of order," Leonidas told her glibly. "You might be electrocuted. Miss Hall, who ordered you to come here?"

She shrugged her beautiful shoulders.

"Don't you *know?"* Leonidas demanded.

"No."

"Who paid you?"

"Well, it's a little involved, Bill. I mean, it's all on the up-and-up, and perfectly proper and respectable and legitimate, and all that sort of thing. I *was* hired, and I *was* paid. Only by proxy."

"Indeed?"

For the first time, the girl seemed to lose a little of her poise and self-possession.

"I didn't think this angle would crop up," she said. "I assumed you'd know who made you the present of me. Because I don't really know. I'm substituting for a friend, you see. I—oh, I suppose I might as well tell you all about it! When I came home from work this afternoon, I found a note from my roommate pinned up on the door."

"How very painful for the poor girl!" Leonidas said sympathetically.

"*Painful?* All right, all right! A note pinned on the door, comma, penned by—oh, it's not right that way either, is it? Anyway, you get the gist. Franny left a message, and forty dollars. She'd kept ten. Of course, it was really fifty."

"Er—what was really fifty?" Leonidas wanted to know.

"The fee. Franny's a model," Terry explained, "and she'd been given this job of being a birthday present for fifty dollars. Cash. Her boss frowns on such extracurricular activities, but Franny happened to answer the phone, and picked up the job herself. After the messenger brought the money, she came home to dress, and found a telegram from her fiancé, who's in the air corps. Seems he was being here tonight en route from somewhere to somewhere else. So she turned the job over to me. I'm duty-bound, as you might say, to stay here. I owe it to Franny. You're going to get your money's worth, Bill!"

"I see." Leonidas had no doubt that she meant it. "M'yes, I see, and I'm sure it's very conscientious of you. Er—I don't suppose you'd possibly be willing to—er—acquire another fifty by departing forthwith?"

A smile curled around Terry's lips as she stubbed out her cigarette.

"I'll admit I anticipated some slight hitch in my getting away from here," she said, "but I hardly foresaw any trouble in just *staying!* No, Bill, it's a matter of honor. If I go, and if whoever paid that fifty finds out that I went, they'll call Franny's office, and Franny will probably get fired. For taking on the job at all, if Rivers is in that sort of mood, or for taking it and then not going through with it, if he's in another mood. I'm seeing this through to the bitter end, Bill. Franny said in her note that it was a matter of life and death."

Leonidas looked at her sharply as she rearranged the cluster of orchids on her shoulder.

"Er—a hundred?" he asked tentatively. "Two hundred? Or should you care to name your own price for leaving?"

Terry's chin went up in the air.

It was a small chin, Leonidas noted, but it was a very firm little affair.

"Here I am," she said. "Here I stay. J'y suis, j'y reste, as the French put it. Now, *will* you open up that indecently large deep freeze and produce a steak for my dinner, or anyway a hamburg? I'm ravenous."

"Don't!" Leonidas said as her hand went out toward the lid. "Don't! Don't *touch* that! Don't lift up that lid! Don't—"

He broke off abruptly at the sound of someone knocking vigorously at the kitchen door.

Life, he thought unhappily as he looked from the door to the girl—whose beautiful hand was still resting ominously on the lid of the deep freeze—life had seemed complicated enough when he had only Haseltine to finish!

Now, with Ernest Bostwick Finger lying there murdered in that repulsive cabinet, with this stubborn glamor girl attaching herself to him like a starved leech, he could look back on his efforts to complete the Haseltine manuscript in peace and quiet as practically The Good Old Days!

"The Golden Era!" he murmured. "Utopia!"

"Why don't you open that door?" Terry's question was almost a challenge. "If you don't let 'em in pretty soon, someone's certainly going to knock that door off its hinges!"

Hurriedly stuffing into the cakebox the lavender satin bow

that Terry had forced on him, he walked over and resignedly opened the door.

A motherly-looking woman with white hair—instantly, Leonidas corrected his first mental impression of the woman outside on the step.

Aside from her white hair, there was nothing the least bit motherly about her. Nothing could be less motherly, in the classic sense, than those flashing black eyes. Or her vividly plaid slacks and scarlet sweater. Or her very slim, trim figure.

"Good evening, Mr. Witherall!" she said brightly, and pushed her way past him into the kitchen. "It's *so* nice to meet you at las—oh. Oh, *good* evening!"

She smiled at Terry, but the tone of her second good evening was very different from her first cheery greeting to Leonidas.

So, it seemed to him, was her manner when she turned back and addressed him.

"Goodness, Mr. Witherall, *don't* you look like Shakespeare!"

Leonidas bowed politely and wondered if her changed attitude might be described as a sudden chill.

He also wondered who the woman was. She might have his name on the tip of her tongue, but he had never seen her before in his life.

"It's *simply* phenomenal!" she went on. "You're the *image* of my little Pierian marble bust! No *wonder* you dazed Cupcake so!"

"*Cupcake?*" Leonidas inquired, and stifled his inclination to shout at her that he was beset by too many baffling problems to concern himself with the cupcakes of a strange woman who barged without invitation into his house.

"My little girl. She came for the goldfish," the woman explained, "but I guess she didn't manage to make herself clear. She's *so* dreamy!"

Leonidas thought back to the chubby moppet in the middy blouse, with all those gold bands on her teeth. In his private estimation, not even the blindest and most biased of parents could honestly sum that child up as the dreamy type!

The woman appeared to sense his reaction.

"You might *never* suspect it," she said, "but Cupcake's a poet. She writes sonnets and blank verse, and she's started two different novels—are they all right?"

"Er—the novels?" Leonidas couldn't entirely prevent some of the confusion he felt from creeping into his voice.

"No, no, the goldfish! Are they all right?"

"Oh, the goldfish!" Leonidas extricated the bowl from the corner. "Er—are these yours?"

"Didn't Mrs. Mullet tell you? Oh, I'm so sorry! I explained to her all about the moving. They're *awfully* nervous about moving, you see."

"Who isn't?" Leonidas said courteously, inwardly delighted at being able finally to place this extraordinary stranger as his new next-door neighbor. "I know of no more trying experience for man or beast."

"The dogs never mind it a bit, but the fish simply *hate* it! So I asked Mrs. Mullet if she wouldn't take care of them till the worst was over. Haig and Johnnie Walker jump out when things *bang,* and Ballantine won't eat for days."

"Indeed!" Leonidas peered at the three fish. "To an impartial observer, the little fellows would seem to be in excellent spirits and—er—fine fettle at the moment. Let us trust that they have suffered no ill effects from their ordeal."

He put a stop to Terry's giggles by glaring at her severely.

"They *look* all right," the woman surveyed them critically, "but of course you can never really tell till the next day. Time before last, it was nearly a week before they reacted. Well," she picked up the bowl, "it's been very kind of you, Mr. Witherall, and I'm awfully grateful. I *do* hope you'll come see us after we're settled a bit, you and Miss—Miss um—"

"Uncle Bill!" Terry's voice dripped reproach as the woman paused. "You forgot to introduce me! He's *so* absent-minded!" she added with a charming smile.

"Oh!" the woman's answering smile was equally charming. "So you are his *niece?*"

"How very remiss of me!" Leonidas said contritely. "My niece, of course—er—my brother's older girl. His younger child," he went on, feeling that if one were forced to invent an imaginary brother, one should at least endow the fellow with a substantial family, "is about the age of your—er—Cupcake. She paints rather well, and experts feel she has quite a future on the oboe."

"Really?" the woman said. "How interesting! Mrs. Mullet told me you were a bachelor who lived all alone, and hadn't a relation in the world!"

Leonidas put on his pince-nez and wondered why he had the impression that he was racing wildly to the base line to pick up a high lob. Why had this woman dropped her idle chatter about goldfish and started in to play verbal tennis with him?

"As the mother of twelve children," he said with a forced smile, "Mrs. Mullet refers to anyone possessing a lesser brood as childless, and utterly lacking in kith or kin."

"Twelve? But she only mentioned *one* daughter to *me!*"

"Mrs. Mullet," Leonidas felt breathless, "is not a woman to —er—brag. And now, I mustn't keep you any longer. I'm sure you'll be very happy at the Haverstraws'. They kept their place up, as the saying goes."

"Everything's in wonderful condition, except for the refrigerator—that reminds me, what a perfectly *lovely* great big deep freeze you have, Mr. Witherall!"

"Er—don't I," Leonidas said without enthusiasm, and found

himself remembering "What great big EYES you have, grandmother! What great big TEETH!"

"Two·frightfully dirty men tried to deliver one at our house today," the woman went on, "and I simply could have *choked* my son for not letting them leave it! Of course, it *was* a mistake, but he knows how I've wanted to get one of these things in my clutches—why, this must hold *oodles!*"

"It does. I do hope," Leonidas tried unobtrusively to get between her and the deep freeze, toward which she was definitely heading, "that you will find the Haverstraws' pleasant and comfortable, and all that sort of thing. We are a very quiet neighborhood, as neighborhoods go, and nothing very untoward ever happens—"

His words nearly choked him, and short of giving her a good solid shove, he couldn't maneuver that woman away from the vicinity of the deep freeze.

"Oh, I'm sure we'll like it. We always love change. You know," she said, "I never saw a freeze with a long lid like this before. Usually they have holes, or drawers, and you have to *grope* so! Is it hard to open? I mean, is it heavy to lift?"

"That's absolutely the *one* drawback!" To his amazement, Terry flung herself into the breach before Leonidas had a chance to answer. "It's *fright*fully heavy! I've never been able to move it an inch, myself."

Somehow, in some indescribable feminine fashion, she was also successfully insinuating the woman toward the door.

"And of course, it does get out of order a lot," Terry added. "It fuses, or something. Uncle just got a terrific shock from it a little while ago, didn't you, Uncle Bill?"

"One of the worst shocks I ever experienced," Leonidas said with perfect truth. "M'yes, I must confess that the freeze has proved a disappointment. Almost a body blow. We lost all the green beans Mrs. Mullet laboriously put up from our Victory

Garden—perhaps Mrs. Mullet also told you about that? She felt the loss keenly."

Now that the woman was actually back on the doorstep, Leonidas felt as fluent as a campaign orator.

"Don't hesitate, now, to call on me for any information— the garbage man comes Tuesdays, the trash man on Wednesdays, and the egg lady on Thursdays. If you wish chickens, you must speak for them in advance, and she will deliver them Saturday mornings. Good night! I do hope you'll like it here! Good—"

"Mother!"

A young man with black hair, flashing black eyes, and the general vitality of a vitamin ad, burst up the flagstone walk.

"Hello, darling," the woman said. "Found the Lowestoft?"

"No, but Cupcake's unearthed the ash trays. They were in with the hoarded pineapple juice. And the curtain rods were in my golf clubs. Mother, did you remember to retrieve—oh!" he noticed Terry. "Oh, good *eve*ning! Mother, have you got the mussels and the butter?"

"I knew I'd forgotten *some*thing!"

Suddenly she was back in the kitchen, and the young man with her.

"Are they in the deep freeze here?"

It was probably a mercy, Leonidas thought, that the young man couldn't keep his eyes off Terry, for his outstretched hand didn't quite come to rest on the lid handle.

"Don't touch that thing!" Terry said quickly. "It's out of order, and you'll get a shock—the mussels and the butter are in the refrigerator, aren't they, uncle?"

"I'll get them." The meaning of Mrs. Mullet's garble about "Goldfish, Mussels, Butter" was beginning at last to filter through his mind. No wonder the poor soul had been so distraught, if she'd been subjected to these people all day long!

No wonder she mourned the Haverstraws and thought of them as such lovely people!

While he hunted for the two items among the contents of the icebox, Terry stood in front of the deep freeze like Horatius at the bridge.

He could *never* pry that young man away from Terry, Leonidas thought sadly. He could *never* pry Terry away from the house!

He'd *never* get to solving the problem of Ernest Finger, which he'd decided some half hour ago to tackle by himself, without recourse to the police!

But Terry again flew to the rescue. Within five minutes she had the pair back on the doorstep, and after another minute of fervent you-*must*-come-over-ing on the part of the young man, the two started down the walk with the goldfish, the mussels, and the butter.

"By the way," the woman called back brightly, "I hope Mrs. Mullet remembered to tell you that our name was Finger! F-i-n-g-e-r!" she spelled it out. "I'm Louise, and this is Jay! Good night, and thanks *so* much!"

III

"FINGER!" Leonidas whispered the name to himself. *"Finger!"*

How idiotically stupid of him not to have caught on! Finger was the other word of Mrs. Mullet's garble—"Goldfish, Finger, Mussels, Butter." She'd talked interminably of trouble with Fingers—and he'd thought the while that she was referring to his own fingers, with a small *f*.

He should have known it all along! Just as he should have realized that Terry's poise and coolness and self-assurance were assumed. The manner in which she had fended off the combined Finger sorties against the deep freeze proved that Terry knew.

Indubitably, Terry knew about the presence of the other Finger!

He turned from his task of locking the door, and faced her.

"So you have been aware all the time that—my dear child, what's the matter with you?"

The girl's face was as white as her gown, and she was trembling from head to foot.

"It's this!" she waved her hand in a vague gesture. "All of it!"

"After your efficient flanking of the Finger attacks," Leonidas said, "it somewhat tardily dawned on me that you knew. Er —you *do* know what's in the freeze, don't you?"

"Yes, but I didn't know those two were *Fingers!*" Terry said a little hysterically. "Oh, Bill, this is perfectly awful! What're we going to *do?* It's too incredibly *aw*ful, and I can't pretend any longer that it *isn't!*"

Leonidas led her gently to a kitchen chair, sat her down, and gave her a white-linen handkerchief from his breast pocket to replace the crumpled bit of lace she was nervously dabbing at her eyes.

"I share your feelings, Terry," he said, "but we hardly have time to salve ourselves with regretful comment. How did you find out? Were you peeking in through the window when I lifted up the lid?"

"I knew before you did," she said, "although I *did* sort of check up by peeking in later, when you had the lid up. You see, Bill, after you closed the front door on me, after I'd finished singing, I rushed around back here, and came in. The door was wide open, and the freeze was sitting here—Bill, what *happened*? How did Ernest get *in* there?"

Briefly, Leonidas told her what he knew.

"*Never,* Bill! It couldn't just have been *left* here with him in it!"

"On the contrariwise, it was," Leonidas returned. "We can but regard the freeze and its contents as a diabolic gift from those two cards, Matt and Shorty, as they laughingly called themselves. So you saw the freeze, and looked inside?"

"No. That is, I looked, but I didn't do it on purpose," Terry said. "At that point, I was frankly chasing you, and as I rushed past the freeze, the lavender bow on my wrist caught on that metal gadget—see, that chromium thing on the corner of the lid? I had to lift it up to free the ribbon, and I couldn't help seeing what was in there. I went out of this kitchen," she added grimly, "like a couple of hawks on the wing. But by the time I reached your lilac bushes, I was jelly around the knees. I just crumpled into a heap, and you couldn't have scooped me to my feet with a steam shovel! While I cowered out there, too scared even to whimper, you shut the kitchen door."

"What prevented you from calling the police?" Leonidas asked curiously.

"I had a certain aversion to being known for the rest of my life as the 'Beautiful Blonde Birthday Present,'" Terry said simply. "My role would make a pretty complex tale. What prevents you from calling 'em, Bill?"

"Touché!" Leonidas said. "I doubt if the police would even taste my epic of Matt and Shorty, let alone swallow it in toto. I also doubt if they'd approve of your pinned-up roommate—was she true, by the way?"

"It's all true, Bill." She looked him straight in the eye. "Everything I told you is true."

"But," Leonidas swung his pince-nez, "but you knew I was not the person to whom you'd been hired to sing, didn't you?"

"Not till after I talked with you. When I realized it was the wrong address—well, Franny's note *said* Forty Birch Hill Road!" Terry said defensively. "So I decided to stay where I'd been told to go, to justify my taking the forty dollars. And I *wanted* to stay with you." She hesitated. "I—well, I wasn't too keen on this job!"

"And I was—er—safe?"

"You're an old dear!" Terry said with something suspiciously like a sob in her voice. "If I hadn't thought so, I should have cut and run, way back there— Bill, I'm sorry, but I simply can't stay in this kitchen another minute! D'you mind?"

"Of course not! It was thoughtless of me to remain here." Leonidas reassured himself that the door was locked, and he took the trouble to flip the window catches in place. "We'll adjourn to my study. Along this hall," he added as he snapped out the kitchen light. "This second door—"

He stood aside to let her enter the study, where his desk light was still burning, and then he prudently crossed over and drew the Venetian blinds.

"So *many* books!" Terry said.

"M'yes. Now, how—" he had been going to ask her how well she knew Ernest Finger when his eyes lighted on the Shakespeare inkwell, lying on its side.

"What's the matter?" Terry asked quickly.

He pointed to his desk.

"The inkwell's been tipped over!" he said. "And look—the desk drawers! Terry, someone's been in here! Someone's been rifling my desk!"

He followed the course of the inky rivulet, which had mercifully missed his box of manuscript by something less than a sixteenth of an inch. From the backstrip of the Roget Thesaurus, it ran along the corner of the blue blotter to the edge of the desk.

It was still dripping down on his favorite Kabistan rug.

Someone had been at his desk very recently indeed!

The pince-nez began to twirl as Leonidas' mind raced into action.

Could it be possible that the intruder had been disturbed by their sudden entry from the kitchen?

It was very likely, Leonidas thought.

Where could the person be now?

He couldn't have gone out the front door without being heard. That was not a door which opened or closed silently. The back door was out of the question. So was the cellar door, which led out of the hall.

Up the stairs? Leonidas looked tentatively up at the ceiling, and shook his head. No. Those loose floor boards at the head of the stairs would have made their characteristic clatter.

There was only one solution. If they had disturbed the intruder, he must have darted across the hall to the living room.

Leonidas began to smile.

While it was no trap in Haseltine's sense of the word, that living room could at least be considered a dead end. The metal screens had been on since his handy man went to war. No one else in the town of Dalton had been able to budge them. And since Mrs. Mullet misplaced the French-door key a month ago, that handy exit had remained locked tighter than the well-known drum.

"Bill!"

Leonidas, rapidly assessing the liability side of the situation, waved her to be silent.

Assuming that the intruder was bottled up in the living room, there still remained the unpleasant task of subduing him. And the only lethal weapon in his possession was an antique derringer pistol, rust-coated and triggerless, packed away somewhere in his attic.

And his own jujitsu, so deadly efficient on paper, was virtually untested in actual combat.

"Bill!" Terry was thrusting something into his right hand.

Leonidas looked down at a little twenty-two Colt revolver, and smiled.

A moment later, he was creeping toward the light switch in the living room.

As his fingers groped for the button, a hand grabbed his wrist.

Deftly, Leonidas freed himself.

Too many stray hands had grabbed at one or the other of the heroic lieutenant's wrists for his creator to be caught that way!

Experimentally, he lunged and kicked violently ahead into the darkness.

To his infinite surprise, he heard someone fall to the floor with a thud. That was the way he always wrote it, to be sure. Haseltine always lunged quickly, kicked violently, and his adversary invariably fell to the floor with an obliging thud. But in his own innermost heart, Leonidas had never believed a word of it!

"I've got you covered!" Hampered by the baggy sleeve of his gown, Leonidas' left hand groped again for the light switch. "Be still, or I'll shoot!"

The more he groped, the more his hand became involved with the sleeve.

And the man on the floor somewhere beyond him was not being still at all! He was hurriedly and noisily scrambling to his feet.

As he struggled to free his hand from the voluminous folds of robe, Leonidas could see the man's figure silhouetted against the French door.

"Stop!" Leonidas couldn't just drop the gun and let his right hand come to the aid of his left. Nor did he dare to grope for the switch with his right hand for fear of that sleeve's also slipping and snarling him up. It was, he thought, remarkably fortunate that Haseltine never went in for this sort of thing while dressed as a doctor of philosophy!

"Stop!" he said again, "or I'll shoot!"

He didn't want to, but he told himself that after all, no one could be hurt very badly with a little twenty-two. Haseltine personally scorned anything smaller than a forty-five, and his expressed preference was for a tommy gun.

Congratulating himself on having remembered to undo the safety catch, Leonidas squeezed the trigger.

Nothing happened.

He squeezed it again.

Then he remembered that it was a woman's gun. Of course, it wouldn't have been loaded!

Almost as one continuous noise, he heard Terry's scream, another thud, and the sound of the front door squeaking open.

"I'm all right!" Terry said breathlessly as he reached the hallway. "Just knocked down—hurry, Bill, go after him!"

As he dashed down the front walk, Leonidas heard someone

racing along the gravel sidewalk toward Elm Street, and as fast as his legs could carry him, he followed.

He had written this sort of chase, too. Many, many times before. Haseltine, always outdistanced at the start, always by some succession of minor miracles managed to corner his quarry.

It never failed! Never!

He felt very foolish when he tripped over the hem of his gown and fell headlong on the corner of Walnut and Elm.

A large dog, which he dimly recognized as belonging to the Abercrombie boy, playfully bounced up to him, sniffed, growled, and refused to allow him to rise from the gravel.

"Nice doggie!" Leonidas said. "You're impeding justice!"

The dog continued to growl.

"It's Witherall," Leonidas said. "In other days, I have given you bones. Cat, Winston! Go get the cat!"

Winston ignored the suggestion.

"Play dead, Winston!" Leonidas said in desperation. "Play dead!"

With pride, Winston promptly played dead, and even permitted Leonidas to give him a congratulatory pat.

"Good Winston! Some day I must remember to have the dog of a saxophone playing boy do that to some worthy villain!"

He found Terry waiting for him halfway up the block.

"I started after you," she said, "but my heels threw me. I had to give up when I lost one pump—did you manage to get a glimpse of him?"

"For all I know," Leonidas said wearily, "he may wear an iron mask. On the other hand, I can describe with great accuracy the fangs of Winston Abercrombie, who will never get another bone from me, if I ever achieve another bone to give him."

"Couldn't you tell *any*thing about him?"

"He is on the large side," Leonidas said. "Quick, able, well versed in wrist grabbing, and not a one to stop at a mere command. Er—I rather wish you'd thought to warn me that your twenty-two was not loaded. I think perhaps I might have proceeded along different lines. Possibly with the iron tongs from the fireplace, or something equally substantial and lethal."

"*I* didn't know it wasn't loaded!" Terry said blankly. "It's Fran—what are you chuckling at, Bill?"

"Ordinarily," Leonidas told her, "the beautiful blonde with violet eyes claims she didn't know the gun *was* loaded."

"Well, it isn't mine, anyway, it's Franny's!" Terry returned. "I forget where she got it. Some photographer's prop, I think. I sort of decided it might be wise to bring it along in my bag tonight."

"I'm sorry," Leonidas said, "that it didn't—er—come in handier."

"*I'm* sorry," Terry returned, "that you didn't *see* that man. I'm terribly disappointed. Really, Bill, you should have snapped on a light!"

"Next time," Leonidas said generously, "I'll make you special assistant in charge of switches. A dress like yours, without sleeves, is obviously the only proper garb for such a job. I got tangled, in short, by my gown."

"Why *are* you wearing that thing, anyway?" Terry inquired. "I've been wondering."

"A long, long time ago," Leonidas said, "some three hours ago, in my prefreeze days, I tried it on—let us cut through this little path here that leads to my driveway, Terry. I'm sure that if Mrs. Finger should happen to peer out her window and notice us passing under the street light, we would only serve to recall to her something else she may have left in Mrs. Mullet's care. Her pet wallaby, say, or a packet of fried clams. Yes, I tried this gown on, and no opportunity of removing it has since arisen. By accident, in short, and not from choice—wait, Terry!"

As they were on the point of emerging from the path to his graveled drive, Leonidas paused and took hold of the girl's arm.

"What's—"

"Sssh!" Leonidas whispered, and pointed.

Outside his study window, a man stood on tiptoe. His hands were gripping the sill, and he was practically chinning himself in his efforts to peek through the slats of the Venetian blinds.

He was struggling so vigorously that Terry and Leonidas could hear his puffings and pantings.

"Who *is* he?" Terry breathed the words. "Who—ooh, look!"

A woman marched around the corner of the house.

"I don't understand it, Foster!" Leonidas recognized the slightly querulous tones of his former neighbor, Mrs. Haverstraw. "I simply do *not* understand it! He doesn't answer either bell. And he *must* be home if his study light is on!"

Leonidas sighed. Somehow it never would occur to Maude Haverstraw that someone might conceivably go away and leave a light burning in an empty house. The turning out of lights was her particular hobby, and during dim-out days, she had all but reduced the Oak Hill sector's warden to a frazzled pulp. Leonidas was in a position to know. He had been the warden.

"Who—" Terry began.

"Whisper!" Leonidas warned her softly. "It's the Haverstraws, and they've been known to spend an hour saying good night on the doorstep, when they originally dropped in three hours before to stay for an announced five minutes. We simply cannot have them descend upon us at this point! I wonder what in the world they want of me!"

"Must have gone to mail a letter." Foster Haverstraw finally let go the window sill. "Don't think he's in there, Maude. Think he's out."

"He never goes out to mail a letter!" his wife returned. "I don't think I *ever* knew him to go out and mail a letter. He always leaves his letters for the postman to take. Always."

"Think so just the same, Maude. Think he's dropped out to mail a letter. Just time for the last collection from the Oak Hill box. Seven o'clock. Be right back. Give him five minutes."

"Foster, you don't think anything's *happened* to him, do you?"

"Course not. Gone out to mail a letter."

"He *might* have fallen downstairs, Foster. He might be lying there this minute with a broken hip!"

"Bah!"

"Or a fractured skull. Or—"

Terry began to giggle as Mrs. Haverstraw extended the list of dire injuries to which Leonidas might have fallen a victim, but Leonidas himself took the situation less lightly. He knew that the presence of a strange child playing on the street had often sent Maude Haverstraw flying to the telephone to ask the police if a lost child had been reported. All unfamiliar animals were to her some little kiddie's lost pets, and her custom of taking them at once to the office of the Dalton *Times* had more than once been editorially regretted by the harassed staff. An extra puff of smoke from some innocent chimney, and Maude had the Fire Department out, just in case. If she now decided that he had a broken hip, Leonidas knew she was entirely capable of calling the police to investigate.

"Gone to mail a letter, *I* say. Give him five-ten minutes. Nice night. Maybe strolled around the block. We sit down and wait for the feller."

Leonidas took Terry's arm, and steered her to the flat puddingstone rock at the back of his garden.

"Incredible people!" Terry said.

"Speak low!" Leonidas warned. "They might take it into their respective heads to check up on my pumpkins, in which they took an almost morbid interest. I did all the wrong things, but mine pumpkined and theirs didn't, or words to that effect."

"But who are they?"

Leonidas told her. "We can only wait for them to depart," he concluded. "I assume you closed the front door?"

"Luckily. I assume you have a key?"

Terry shivered, and Leonidas took off his gown and put it about her shoulders.

"Thanks," she said. "Useless little interlude, wasn't it? I mean, that chase and all. But anyway, we have his shoe."

"His *shoe?*"

"He lost it in your hall. I think, Bill, that he'd been creeping around your house in his stocking feet, and that's why we never knew he was there. Anyway, that shoe will be something, won't it?"

"Where is it now, still in the hall?"

"I had it in my hand when I started to run after you," Terry said, "but I dropped it. It's on your lawn. A brown oxford with a rubber heel. It *is* something, isn't it? I mean, something we can show to the police."

"M'yes, I suppose we could," Leonidas said, "but I rather feel that to drive home the saga of Matt and Shorty, and Ernest Finger, we require something more—er—shall I say forceful, perhaps? Something more forceful than the fact that someone who rifled my desk wore brown oxfords at the time."

"But it's a clue, Bill!"

"If I rifled your desk," Leonidas said, "and was unwise enough to leave a shoe behind in the process, I think I should at once drop its mate into the Dalton River. M'yes, I rather think that by now, the companion to the shoe you found is doubtless bounding downstream toward Dalton Lower Falls."

"Bill," Terry said, "what'll we *do?* Who *was* that man? Don't you suppose he was the murderer? Of course, he must be!"

"That argument," Leonidas told her, "is generally known as

'post hoc, ergo propter hoc.' Because you ran over a Coca-Cola bottle last July, you therefore have a flat tire today. Because you ate dubious lobster Newburg last Thursday, you therefore have an odd feeling in your head this evening. Er—you see my point."

"I know all about 'post hoc,' and so on. I studied logic once. But," Terry persisted with the firmness of a woman convinced, "if that man didn't have something to do with killing Ernest, then what was he doing rifling your desk?"

Leonidas shook his head. "Why anyone should care to rifle my desk, I cannot imagine. It contains nothing of value to anyone but myself—and possibly my publishers. And to date, it has never occurred to them to send someone to my house to filch an unfinished manuscript! Why all this has been visited upon me, heaven alone knows."

"Couldn't this desk rifler have been Matt, or Shorty? Bill, it must have been! If you ask me, this is all a plot against you!"

"It seems so," Leonidas agreed. "But why should a simple ex-professor, a quiet, law-abiding citizen of quiet, suburban Dalton, have plots devised against him?"

"Enemies," Terry said promptly. "Haven't you any enemies?"

"Not an enemy in the world," Leonidas assured her. "I have no quarrels with anyone, no one has quarrels with me. No one —hm!"

"Thought of one?"

"Hm," Leonidas said reflectively. "Dear me, I never quite considered that angle before. But I'm sure it has nothing whatever to do with this! Nothing at all!"

"If you were to ask me," Terry said, "I'd say *any* angle is a good angle at this point!"

"Well," Leonidas said tentatively, "since the war, I've had thrust upon me any number of chairmanships and directorates —largely because of my beard and my pince-nez, of course. It is generally felt that my presence lends dignity. I suppose, in a manner of speaking, that I *have* stepped on a number of toes."

"You mean that people are jealous of you?"

"M'yes, possibly they are," Leonidas said. "But you see, knowing that my tenure of offices, so to speak, was solely for the duration of the war, and having no personal ambition or axes to grind, I've had no compunctions about getting things done— m'yes, I wonder if perhaps I haven't made an enemy or two in the process!"

"Let's be practical," Terry said. "Whose toes have you stepped on recently?"

"I'm afraid," Leonidas said, "that as chairman of the Good Government League of Dalton, I was instrumental in forcing the mayor to resign last month. He was really a very grasping man. I've—er—subjected the Finance Commission and the School Board to a rather thorough shaking up, too."

"No enemies," Terry said. "I see. Any more?"

"Well, I encouraged an investigation of the bank, in my capacity as a director," Leonidas said, "and the president retired —for reasons of health, of course. I delved into the affairs of the Dalton Home for the Aged—really, an incredible amount of graft was going on there. And I was forced to be quite unpleasant to the contractor responsible for the new wing of the Dalton Hospital. Then there was that matter of the Dalton Golf Club Debentures. And all that sort of thing."

"In short," Terry said with irony, "everyone in Dalton loves you dearly, like a brother. Honestly, Bill, you couldn't have been naïve enough to think there'd be no repercussions after a wholesale cleaning up like that?"

"I was visited by several rough-looking characters last month, after the Water Works investigation," Leonidas said, and chuckled.

"What happened?"

"I took thirty-one dollars from them at gin rummy, during the course of the evening, and they ate up two pans of brownies which Mrs. Mullet had made me. Now," he said, "I'll go and see if Foster and Maude have given up."

A moment later, he returned to the puddingstone rock.

"What luck?" Terry asked.

"Maude is in a nervous twitter about my broken hip, but thus far," Leonidas said, "Foster has managed to persuade her against calling the police in to investigate."

"She really wouldn't!"

"Once," Leonidas said reminiscently, "she had their entire chimney ripped out, brick by brick, because of a tap."

"A what?"

"Specifically, she referred to it as a teeny tap. To such a woman, nothing is wholly impossible, and I shall feel better after she departs. I think they'll go shortly, because Foster claims he has a sniffly feeling and thinks he should spray his nose. Now, Terry, back in the study I started to ask how well you knew Ernest Finger. I don't like to—er—pry into your affairs, but we can do nothing till I find out more about the man. D'you mind?"

Terry was silent for several minutes.

"I knew you'd ask me about him sooner or later," she said. "You must have gathered that I had more than a—a passing interest in him. I've been making up opening sentences in my mind, too. But the only way I know how to start is by saying that everyone makes mistakes, and that's why pencils have erasers, and stuff like that."

"I—er—gather that he was an error of yours?"

"Bill, don't you really know anything about him? Don't you even know he was the pride and joy of the Pomfret Inn?"

"The Pomfret Inn—you mean that unsavory roadhouse on the turnpike?" Leonidas asked in amazement.

"That dive. He looks different without his mustache, and of course he wasn't known professionally as Finger. He was Carlos Santos, the Good-Neighbor tenor—he used to be on Boston radio stations. That's how I first met him." She was silent again. "Well, there's no sense going into a lot of details and truck. I knew Ernest well. And he had some letters of mine that I've been trying to get back for over a year."

"Er—blackmail?"

"No, it's hard to explain, Bill. He didn't blackmail me, but he sort of held them over my head. It got to terrify me. I have a pretty good job. I'm at Miss Lowell's School for Girls. Being in the business yourself, you probably know Miss Lowell."

"Hers," Leonidas said, "is unquestionably the best girls' school in the country. Miss Lowell is the most thoroughly competent woman I ever met, and one of the most intelligent. And if one slight hint of your letters ever reached her ears, the old battleax would tarnish your reputation for life."

"I think," Terry's voice wasn't entirely steady, "you're the most understanding man I ever met. I've gone through solid torture about those letters. Then last week Ernest phoned me and said he'd become respectable and taken on a decent job, and was doing all the honest and upright things I'd once urged on him. He was really brilliant, you know, Bill."

"He didn't impress me as being stupid," Leonidas said.

"He didn't have to croon in joints like the Pomfret Inn, or dabble with—that's a thought! Did you ever clean up the Pomfret numbers racket, or the Pomfret Dog Track?"

"Pomfret is out of my bailiwick," Leonidas said. "You mean that Finger—er—dabbled with those things?"

"Yes, and he had brains enough to—oh, he could have made a success of anything he wanted to do! Anyway, I saw him after he phoned, and—well, it's hard to explain the feeling I got. Before, I'd only worried as to what he *might* do with those letters, but after seeing him, I *knew* he was going to use them in some way. So I decided to take the bull by the horns and try to buy them back. That's why I was perfectly willing to pick up an extra forty dollars from this silly job of Franny's!"

"But after seeing him there in the deep freeze," Leonidas said, "you stayed. Why? Why didn't you cut and run? Why—"

"Why didn't I rush at once to his apartment and get the letters? I think I'd have been tempted to," Terry said, "if *those* letters were all."

"I'm afraid I don't understand," Leonidas said. "You mean there are more?"

Terry drew a long breath. "I'd decided to try and buy my letters back, as I said. But this afternoon, just before I set out to come here, I had a brain wave. I wrote him a fine, violent letter saying that if he didn't give me my letters back, I'd go straight to the head of Meredith's, and tell him what he was innocently harboring for a French teacher. An ex-crooner, the Sinatra of Pomfret, who was also a small-time crook and confidence man. And so on, and so forth, and such. I wonder, Bill, how old you have to be before you tear up letters like that after you've written them?"

"I've no doubt that Methuselah," Leonidas said, "probably asked people that identical question in the same plaintive voice. You—er—threatened him further?"

"Murder was the least I promised. The minute I slipped the thing into the letter box, I came to," Terry said with a sigh. "I tried to get it back. I tried so hard I got my hand stuck, and stood there wriggling and tugging, and thinking about men who put their hands in lions' mouths. A postman finally uncaught me."

"Didn't you ask him—"

"Didn't I *ask* him for the letter? I put on an act," Terry said bitterly, "that would have melted a General Sherman tank into a little blob of steel. And the unfeeling brute merely advised me to write my boy friend another, and take it all back. He quoted a lot of rules at me, and he thought it was funny—why do people think the world is simple if you happen to have blond hair?"

"Helen of Troy asked that one," Leonidas said, "with equal sincerity, I'm sure. M'yes. I understand how retrieving your other indiscreet letters would hardly matter in the face of this threatening epistle which will arrive at Finger's apartment to-morrow morning—"

"Just in time for the cops to read! Bill, isn't there any way we can *stop* that letter from arriving?"

"I'm afraid not. You know how it is. Neither rain, nor hail, nor gloom of night," Leonidas told her sympathetically, "can presumably stay our postal couriers from the swift completion of their appointed rounds. Er—I remind myself of that every morning as I wait and wait for our Mr. Seeley to trudge up Oak Hill. No, we can't stop your letter, Terry. We are no James Brothers."

"I don't mean to hold up a post office, or rob the mails, or anything like that!" Terry said. "But isn't there something— well, something *smaller* we could do that would prevent its being delivered?"

"Tampering with the mails," Leonidas said, "is generally conceded to be an unwise act. Terry, I still don't understand why you attached yourself to me, under the circumstances!"

"When I first saw you, before I knew Ernest was dead, it occurred to me in a flash that you were just the sort of man I'd been wishing I knew. How I've yearned for an uncle or an older brother, or some protecting male with brains who could take on Ernest verbally, and get those letters back for me. You had all his weapons, and a lot more besides. I said to myself that I was going to tell you everything, and ask your advice." She paused. "And if you want to know, I still think you can get 'em all back! Bill, what relation was Ernest to those Fingers next door?"

Leonidas sighed. "Who knows?"

"He *must* be some relation! Finger isn't a common name!"

"While Fingers don't grow on trees," Leonidas said, "I confess that I have no inkling of how one might proceed to discover what relationship exists, if any."

"He must be related!"

"M'yes, but as you suggested a while ago, let us be practical. How would one go about quizzing the vigorous Mrs. Finger on the topic?"

"Well, I suppose you'd just have to ask her, that's all!"

"My dear Mrs. Finger," Leonidas said briskly, "I wonder if you chance to have a relation named Ernest Bostwick Finger. Indeed! By a strange coincidence, he's over in that deep freeze you were admiring so lavishly in my kitchen. Er—he's been there some time, and while he's not in my way, I wonder if you could possibly arrange to take him off my hands!"

"Bill, you make my hair stand on end!"

"That's one possible approach," Leonidas said. "I have also considered the brusque, or realistic approach. I lead her to the deep freeze, open it, point, and say, 'Is this any Finger of yours?' I have even gone so far as to consider games."

"Games?"

"Mrs. Finger," Leonidas said blandly, "do you ever play word games—word association, for example? Such wholesome fun, I always say. Take a word—why, take your own name! What d'you associate with Finger? Let's see. Finger ring. Finger-in-the-pie. Forefinger. Finger prints. Finger bowl. Lady finger—aha! Man Finger! Ernest Finger—do you have any association with that name? You *do?* Tell me all about it, Mrs. Finger! D'you happen to know anyone who might have stabbed him?"

"I thought he was shot!" Terry said blankly.

"Stabbed."

"What *with?*"

"With some instrument possessing a sharp blade," Leonidas said. "While an expert like the excellent Lieutenant Haseltine—"

"You mean Haseltine of that *'Has*-eltine to the *res*-cue' thing on the radio?" Terry interrupted. "I adore Haseltine!"

"M'yes. While the lynx-eyed lieutenant would at once know that the murder weapon was a carving knife," Leonidas said, "and doubtless be able to describe in considerable detail the markings of its bone handle, I frankly could not guess what specific cutting instrument was used to stab him. Let us refer to it merely as a very sharp knife."

"Why are you so insistent on its having been a very *sharp* knife?" Terry asked. "Not that I think it was dull, but you sort of endow it with a finely honed quality, if you know what I mean."

"Because his clothing was so neatly sliced," Leonidas said, "and because there was so very little blood, I infer that the knife was very sharp, that it was wielded very deftly, and—er—very much to the point. I think he died very quickly. I would also hazard a guess that he was taken unawares. Both his clothing and his hair—"

"I noticed that, too," Terry interrupted. "Not mussed or anything."

"Exactly. Now," Leonidas said, "I must investigate the Haverstraw situation. Certainly by now, they should have managed to tear themselves away, if only to cope with Foster's snuffle. What in the wide world they want of me, I can't imagine!"

At long last, the coast was clear.

"Thank heaven!" Terry said. "I don't like to pan your rock, but it's not the softest thing I ever sat on. Bill, I keep wondering if there mustn't be some connection between your toe stepping in the civic betterment and cleanup division, and the landing on you of the deep freeze, and Ernest."

"I might possibly be tempted to agree with you," Leonidas said as they started walking back to the driveway, "if only someone other than Ernest were in it. Say the ex-mayor, or the ex-banker, or the ex-steward of the Dalton Home for the Aged. But Meredith's Academy was the only bond between Finger and myself, Terry. And a very nebulous bond it was, too."

"Did you have a rival candidate for Ernest's job?" Terry asked thoughtfully. "Maybe someone was getting back at the two of you in one fell swoop."

"A rival candidate?" Leonidas chuckled. "My dear child, he was the *only* candidate! I felt so desperately lucky to get him, I even forgave him that frightful green suit with the white stripes! I bought the agency man a genuine steak for lunch, in my gala mood! I—"

"What about the agency man? How did he come to recommend Ernest?" Terry interrupted.

"He was George Whatting, whom I've known for years, and he didn't recommend Ernest. He diffidently produced him, after trying to urge me to break Meredith tradition and hire a woman. George said the fellow specifically asked if there might be an opening at Meredith's, since he lived in the vicinity. Terry!"

"What's the matter?" she asked as he stopped.

"Terry, if Ernest Finger was the slightly unsavory character you paint him, I wonder—m'yes, I wonder if perhaps he wasn't another Shurcliff! M'yes, I think that's the answer! I think I know now why he wanted a teaching position at Meredith's! Rich small boys!"

"What d'you mean?"

"Many years ago, when I, myself, was teaching," Leonidas said, "an individual named Shurcliff, a mathematics teacher, made quite a killing at the Academy before old Marcus Meredith caught on. You see, Terry, rich small boys provide a very fertile field for the unscrupulous. Boundless opportunities arise in every direction. Blackmail, for example."

He heard Terry draw her breath in sharply.

"Shurcliff specialized in leading the lads slightly astray," Leonidas said, "and then in collecting—from them, and from their unworldly sisters, cousins, and aunts. Of course in those days, expulsion from Meredith's was tantamount to social ostracism. The sisters and cousins and aunts willingly parted with diamond chokers to save their young from the horrible fate of being expelled from Meredith's and having to go to some western college instead of Harvard."

Terry giggled.

"It admittedly has its amusing side," Leonidas said, "but the diamond chokers mounted up into a very sizable sum, and Marcus Meredith never felt that he'd more than scraped the surface of Shurcliff's victims. For obvious reasons, people were quite reticent. Nowadays, I presume that an incipient Shurcliff might proceed in a more subtle fashion—I wonder, Terry! M'yes, I wonder if I don't begin to see what part you and your letters might have played in Finger's plans!"

"Me, and my letters? I don't get it, Bill!" Terry said as they walked on toward the driveway. "You've bounded too far ahead of me!"

"If Ernest Finger had a beautiful blonde with violet eyes under, so to speak, his thumb," Leonidas said, "to assist him in fleecing the older, more monied, and more impressionable youths, his net proceeds from Meredith's might have been many, many times the modest salary he officially was to have received."

"Bill, what a—what an utterly loathsome thought!" Terry said.

"M'yes, possibly. But didn't you say that after he took on this new teaching job, you became terrified because you felt that he was at last actually going to make demands on you?"

"I said it, and I felt it. But—well—but you've made all this up out of whole cloth, Bill! You haven't any proof that Ernest had any such plans!"

"Still," Leonidas told her, "I think something of the sort was brewing in his mind. M'yes. I think we will first pick up that abandoned shoe, Terry. Then I will divest you of that gown, and we'll sally forth to Ernest Finger's apartment, and see if we can't unearth some tangible proof—wait, Terry, step back!"

Once again, just as they reached the edge of his driveway, Leonidas grabbed her arm.

He could hear the leaves crackling as someone walked through the short cut, the path they had originally taken from the corner.

The Haverstraws, perhaps?

With a quick gesture, Leonidas drew Terry back into the shadow of the maples, and covered her shimmering dress with the baggy black robe again.

A man appeared—not Foster Haverstraw, Leonidas noted with relief—and started somewhat hesitantly down the graveled driveway.

Leonidas suddenly found himself bending forward, peering vainly at the man's feet.

For years he had listened to the sound of people walking down that driveway from the short cut, and it was always the same sound, even though the timing might vary according to the individual's haste, or lack of it.

It was always the same. Scrunch-scrunch, scrunch-scrunch.
But this man's footsteps were different.
This man was going scrunch-pad, scrunch-pad, scrunch-pad!
He was wearing only one shoe!

IV

"BILL! Only one shoe!" Terry was whispering, but in Leonidas' ear her voice took on the proportions of a blaring loudspeaker. "Only *one!*"

"Hush!"

"Go after him, Bill! Who *is* he? It *is* our man, Bill! It *is!* See how he keeps stopping and peering at the house—"

"*Shush!*"

Terry shushed, but she followed him on tiptoe as he stealthily started up the strip of lawn at the side of the driveway.

"Bill!"

She pinched him, forcefully and excitely, as the man's face was illuminated for a brief moment by the street light, and Leonidas heroically bit his underlip to shush himself and keep from exclaiming out loud.

"Bill! Did you see who he—"

"Yes, yes, I saw! Be still, Terry! I want to see what he's up to!"

Leonidas couldn't imagine what Mrs. Finger's son Jay would be wandering around his house for, with one shoe off and one shoe on, unless he was hunting his missing shoe. It hardly seemed reasonable to assume that the young man would go out for a casual evening stroll in any such diddle-diddle-dumpling-my-son-John fashion!

"Bill, he—"

"I want to see if he's hunting his shoe!"

Leonidas achieved such fierceness in his whisper that Terry at last subsided.

Keeping well in the shadow of the trees, they followed Jay as he proceeded in the same half-surreptitious, half-hesitant manner past Leonidas' house.

Then the fellow returned, and started slowly up the front walk.

"He *is* hunting for that shoe! I bet he heard me drop it!" Terry murmured. "See him bend over?"

Jay straightened up suddenly, turned on his heel, and sprinted off down the street as if he were anchor man on a relay team.

Galloped, Leonidas decided critically as the fellow disappeared from sight, might be a more nearly apt word with which to describe his pounding exit.

"Bill, why didn't you—"

"No!" Leonidas said firmly.

"No what?"

"No, don't ask me why I didn't romp after him," Leonidas said, "or advise me to rush after him anyway, will you? I mean, I followed a man with one shoe on before, and it didn't work out at all well. The only creature who derived the slightest pleasure from that fruitless chase was Winston Abercrombie."

"But, Bill, he was our man! Why didn't you at least call out to him, and—"

"Was it a right or a left shoe which you found, Terry?" Leonidas interrupted.

"A right or a left? Good heavens, Bill, *I* don't know! I'd just been knocked off my feet, if you remember, and I wasn't in a particularly observant mood! Bill, those Fingers have something to do with this! D'you recall how she kept looking at that deep freeze, and her crack about how *much* it must hold, and all that sort of thing? I thought it was sort of—well, sort of signi*fi*cant, at the time. Now I think it's downright *sinister!* Bill, I bet she knows! I bet they both—"

"Er—before you bet further, Terry," Leonidas said, "suppose we stroll over to the front lawn and find the shoe you dropped. If it's a left shoe, to match Jay Finger's shoeless left foot, we may possibly find it wise to detour from our plans long enough to conduct a brief investigation into our new neighbors. Just where did you drop it?"

"Oh, somewhere over there." Terry pointed.

Leonidas put on his pince-nez.

"Er—where?"

"Well, I can't see it either, at the moment," Terry said, "but it's there. Probably leaves fell on it, or blew over it, or something. Or maybe it bounced over into those bushes. At that point, I didn't stop to observe if it made a three-point landing, or not! It's *here!* It must be here! I mean, Jay Finger bent over, but I'm positive he never picked anything up! If we just grub around a bit, Bill, we'll find it all right!"

Leonidas sighed. "Very well, let us grub!"

They were at the fine-tooth-combing stage ten minutes later, when a beachwagon drew up at the foot of Leonidas' front walk.

Leonidas, still unable to rid himself of the nervous feeling that anything descending on him might be a Haverstraw, was relieved to find that the man who emerged from the car bore not the faintest resemblance to Foster.

He was, in fact, a tall, pleasant-looking young man, hatless and well dressed in a casual sort of way.

He wore rimless glasses, Leonidas further noted as he approached, and under his right arm, he carried a briefcase.

Leonidas, on his knees in front of the rhododendron bush, eyed that bulging leather briefcase. Was the fellow a salesman, or a solicitor, or an insurance man, or some new fellow director or board member?

"Mr. Witherall?" the young man inquired in a somewhat dubious voice, as if he rather expected Leonidas to be someone else. "Mr. Witherall?"

Leonidas made a quick decision.

"Mr. Witherall's out," he said blandly. "I expect, however, to see him later on in the evening. Er—would there perhaps be some message you might care to have me convey to him?"

The young man hesitated, looked uncertainly from Leonidas' mortarboard and baggy robe to Terry's evening gown and corsage of orchids, and somewhat nervously shifted the briefcase to his left arm.

Leonidas found himself feeling a little regretful of his hasty action, but after all, he had no time available for anyone with such a teeming briefcase as that. Unless he was very much mistaken, this was the guileless young man who had been unearthed in Dalton Centre, and bullied into auditing without charge the proceeds of the Dalton Community Fund Drive. While his cause was good and just, Leonidas felt that his figures could perfectly well wait a day or two.

"Well," the young man said, "well, the fact is, I—well, I wanted very much to see Mr. Witherall. In person. It's really a matter of importance."

"I'm sure he'll be very sorry to have missed you," Leonidas returned. "Er—we, as you doubtless may have gathered, are on a scavenger hunt."

"Oh. Oh, I see." The explanation seemed to make the fellow feel better, Leonidas thought. "Oh, I see. Well, thanks. You might tell him that Bedford Scrim called. That is, you might tell him that Bedford Scrim called *again*."

He turned, went back to his beachwagon, and forthwith departed.

"That one," Terry said, "didn't get across, Bill. He didn't believe you for two cents!"

"Really? It was my impression," Leonidas returned, "that he had implicit faith in my veracity. Bedford Scrim! So that is the Bedford Scrim who has been calling on me at intervals all day long! Now I wonder if he *is* that auditor, after all!"

"If you hadn't been such a smarty-pants," Terry said, "you

might have found out! Bedford Scrim—that name sounds
familiar! Bedford Scrim. Bedford Scrim. Now where have I
heard that name before?"

"I believe it's a sort of curtain," Leonidas said with a chuckle.
"At least, when I was billed for my guest-room draperies, the
account was rendered to me as 'Four Pairs Bedford Scrim.' It
gives one a false sense of having known this particular Bedford
Scrim always. What a pity he wore two shoes!"

"What a pity? What d'you mean, what a pity! Why shouldn't
he wear two shoes?"

Leonidas told her of the ballad he had improvised that afternoon about Bedford Scrim.

"I still consider it one of the most perfect villain-names I
ever encountered," he added. " 'Hey nonny nim for Bedford
Scrim!' It rolls on the tongue. But I suppose we'll have to
amend it, now that we've seen the fellow. Er—m'yes, that
would do it! 'Let's give him plaudits, I think he audits.' Terry,
are you *quite* sure you dropped that infernal shoe out here?
Didn't you toss it into the umbrella stand, now that you think
it over?"

"I dropped it right out here!" Terry said positively. "Right
out here on your lawn! I can't think why we can't find it, can
you?"

"Either its rightful owner has already collected it, or the
Haverstraws have it, or Winston Abercrombie has made off
with it," Leonidas said. "Winston has rashes of removing things
from yards and doorsteps. For a long while he specialized in
picking up all the fresh shirts left by a laundry-truck driver
whom he resented. M'yes, I'd say it was a tossup between Winston and Maude Haverstraw. Maude believes that an uncluttered
lawn is the key to heaven, or words to that effect."

"I'm beginning to hope," Terry said, "that I never meet
Maude!"

"If you do," Leonidas remarked, "I piously trust that the burden of explaining you does not fall on my shoulders. Well, we'll have to hold that shoe in abeyance, I fear. Now, let us—"

"Jay Finger might have taken it, Bill!"

"Although he bent over, I'm almost certain that he didn't. Now, Terry, I'm going in and remove this idiotic cap and gown, and then we'll get out the car and pay a visit to Finger's apartment. Come along."

Terry followed him to the front doorstep.

After a moment of looking at him curiously, she gave him a little poke.

"Bill, what's the matter? Are you asleep?"

"Er—no."

"Why don't you open the do—Bill Shakespeare, haven't you any keys?"

"Any keys?" Leonidas said lightly. "My dear child, I have keys galore! I have boxes of keys. For this door alone, I possess at least twelve keys. Of course, I've had many more made at one time or another, but I believe only about a dozen are extant, as one might say, at the moment. M'yes, indeed, I have plenty of keys! Oodles, as Mrs. Finger might put it."

"Bill, have you or have you not on your person, right now, a key to this door?"

"Regretfully, in a nutshell," Leonidas told her, "er—no."

"Bill!"

"Don't suggest that we break in, Terry. To call any undue attention to us or to the house would not, I feel, be a discreet gesture now."

"Doesn't anyone have a spare key?" Terry demanded.

"Mrs. Mullet has one."

"Thank God! Where does she live?"

"Er—in Pomfret."

"And we've got to get indoors to get your car keys, I suppose—" she broke off and shivered as the siren of a police car sounded briefly. "Ugh, that frightens me!"

"Don't let it distress you," Leonidas said. "That car is half a mile away on the turnpike. They often blow that siren at speeders."

"Just the same it's a nasty sound, and it makes me shiver. I—I've tried my best not to think of the police, Bill," Terry added. "But I do, every now and then, and just the passing thought chills me to the bone. I get a clammy feeling all over."

"On the whole," Leonidas said, "thinking of the Haverstraws bothers me more. I have this recurrent vision, this periodic nightmare, of their returning here, after Foster has been sprayed."

"But at least the Haverstraws can't lead us off to a dank prison cell!"

"True," Leonidas said. "Quite true. But after ten unadulterated minutes with them, you would find yourself wishing that they could. After two minutes of questioning by Maude Haverstraw, you would yearn for the stolid simplicity of a bit of rubber hose. Faced with the alternative of Maude's opening that deep freeze, or the torture of the Iron Maiden, I would unhesitatingly choose the latter."

"I suppose it's the headlines that get me," Terry said. " 'Insert, in Circle. Identified by Police as Author of Threatening Letter to Murdered Man, Orchidaceous Blonde Terry—' "

"By the way, where *did* those orchids come from?" Leonidas interrupted.

Terry shrugged. "Franny left them with the note. I gathered that whoever hired her threw them in. Oh, those headlines, all full of blonde hair and orchids! I wonder, Bill, do lady prisoners pick oakum or make car license plates these days?"

"Neither. They shampoo."

"They *what?*"

"Shampoo. I'm in a position to know," Leonidas informed her. "I'm on the House of Correction visiting board. Four times a year, I'm led by the lady warden to a place where women are shampooing each other like fury, and told how the girls are taught a good useful trade. Hair, she points out, not only grows but gets—gets—"

The siren yelped again.

This time, it sounded as if it were standing on the doorstep with them.

Slowly, Leonidas put on his pince-nez, and turned around.

One of Dalton's familiar black-and-white prowl cars was swerving to a stop at the foot of his walk.

Simultaneously, the Haverstraws' equally familiar sedan swung around the corner. Leonidas knew the throaty cough of its battered muffler as well as he knew his own voice.

"Hey, Witherall!" Sergeant MacCobble jumped out and beckoned peremptorily. "Come along, Witherall! Hurry up!"

"Leonidas!" Maude Haverstraw stuck her head out of the sedan's window as Foster drew up to the curbing and parked beyond the police car. "Leonidas! Hoo-hoo! Hoo-hoo! Leonidas!"

Terry looked up at him.

"Wow!" she said, simply and with distinctness. "Wow!"

"Come along, Witherall!" the sergeant was advancing up the flagstone walk. "We come for you!"

"Leonidas!" Maude got out of the sedan. "Hoo-hoo, I *want* you! I—"

Leonidas caught his pince-nez as they slipped from his nose.

"Er—what about the young lady, sergeant?" he inquired. "D'you want her, too?"

"We're after you, Witherall! You're the one we want! Of course, if she wants to come—"

"Any choice, Terry?" Leonidas smiled and swung his pince-nez.

She drew a deep breath.

"Henna rinse, mister?" she said. "Or how's for a nice hot-oil shampoo?"

Without any further hesitation, Leonidas took her arm and followed Sergeant MacCobble down the walk to the prowl car.

"Leonidas!" Maude said querulously. "Leonidas, I want—"

She broke off abruptly as she came face to face with Terry, and despite a certain amount of obvious exertion on her part, she seemed quite unable to close her mouth.

Probably it was only a sudden trick of light, like an oak-tree branch blowing in front of the street-light globe, Leonidas thought, but her eyes momentarily jumped out of their sockets, described a series of figure eights and entrechats, and then bounced back to their normal position in her head.

"Good evening, Maude!" The baggy black gown achieved almost the dignity of a courtier's sweeping cape as Leonidas bowed to her.

"Orchids!" Maude said. "Orchids—Leonidas, I want you! I want—"

"Hurry up, Witherall!" MacCobble said impatiently. "Get a move on!"

"I'm so sorry, Maude," Leonidas said. "Er—I have, as you see, a previous engagement with the police, regretfully."

"When will you be back?" Maude's eyes were riveted on Terry.

"If only," Leonidas said truthfully, "if only I were in a position to tell you, with any degree of accuracy! But—"

"You and the lady get in back!" MacCobble ordered. "Just push that pair of handcuffs over to one side. We won't need 'em for you!"

The prowl car roared off down the hill with its siren screaming full tilt.

"Bill!"

Finding that her voice was drowned out by the motor roar and the yelp of the siren, Terry finally leaned over and tugged violently at the baggy sleeve of Leonidas' gown.

"How'd they find *out*, Bill?" she howled.

Leonidas shrugged, and made a little gesture to indicate his complete ignorance on the topic.

"Why *you*, Bill, and not *me?*"

He shook his head.

"Aren't you worried?" she shouted in his ear. "I said, worried! Worried! Aren't you?"

Leonidas pointed to the handcuffs, and smiled cheerfully.

"They didn't put those on!" he shouted back. "I feel it's a good omen! I said, good omen!"

"What'll we *do?*"

"Sit back," Leonidas advised her in conversational tones as the siren stopped for a moment, "and enjoy the nice ride. I personally have not driven at such a clip since gas rationing."

To the accompaniment of more screeches from the siren, they drew up in front of the ornately spired and cupolaed brownstone headquarters of the Dalton Police Department.

"I got to hand it to you, Witherall!" Sergeant MacCobble said with grudging admiration as they got out of the car. "Don't scare easy, do you? Never thought you'd take it as calm as this!"

"To a man of clear conscience," Leonidas returned, "a ride in your vehicle is a source of genuine pleasure, I assure you!"

"You're a one!" MacCobble said. "Never think it of you! Hey, Daley, here he is! Take him in, will you? I got to go back and pick up that Carlos Santos fellow."

Leonidas felt Terry's arm grow rigid under his hand, and Terry found herself wincing at the sudden intensity of his grip.

Daley, one of the few young officers left on the force, greeted Leonidas with a brusque nod.

"Didn't think you'd come without," he paused and looked at Terry, "without urging. Gee, did she come with you, Mr. Witherall?"

"Er—yes," Leonidas said. "Yes, she did. Er—just for the ride, as one might say."

"One of Carlos Santos' girls, huh?"

"No!" Leonidas said firmly. "She came with me!"

Daley grinned. "Aren't you the old sport, Mr. Witherall! Well, well, well! Say, you got a ticket?" he added as an afterthought.

"Er—I beg your pardon," Leonidas said, "did you ask if I had a *ticket?*"

"Yeah, but you don't really need one! Honest," Daley began to laugh, "honest, I hand it to you! Fancy dress, *and* a blonde, too! And Mack had a bet with me you'd skip town first! Well, I suppose we might as well go in, Mr. Witherall, though I don't suppose nothing'll get started till after Mack brings Santos back."

They followed him up the worn stone steps and into a musty smelling vestibule.

"Bill, d'you understand he means *Ernest* when he says Santos?" Terry whispered.

"M'yes. I know."

"But how did anyone ever find out? We were right there at your house! How did anyone get *in?* How did they find *out?*"

"Maude Haverstraw doubtless flew in on her broomstick," Leonidas said.

"This way, you folks!" Daley beckoned them through a doorway. "This way!"

"But the—" Leonidas paused. "Er—I thought that one went *that* way!"

"Oh, we're not putting *you* in there with the common crooks!" Daley shook with laughter. "*You* come this way, Mr. Witherall! Here!"

After leading them through a long, narrow corridor whose tired buff walls were hung with life-sized and somewhat funereal photographs of past police chiefs, he grabbed the handle of a paneled golden-oak door at the end, and flung it open wide.

"Here you are!" Daley said.

Leonidas put on his pince-nez.

He was standing on the threshold of a good-sized rectangular hall which at first seemed to his bewildered eyes to be a kaleidoscopic maelstrom of orange banners, crepe-paper streamers, red autumn leaves, and vivid yellow chrysanthemums.

There were rows and rows of long wooden trestle tables, too. Tables covered with acres of orange paper, set with knives and forks and plates and glasses, and strewn with still more crepe-paper streamers, red autumn leaves, and vivid yellow chrysanthemums.

There were people.

There were several hundred of them, all chattering noisily. They also were strewn with crepe-paper streamers, red autumn leaves, and vivid yellow chrysanthemums—no, they weren't. Leonidas shook his head. They were merely in costumes.

Over in one corner, an orchestra of five women was busily tuning up.

"What *is* this?" Terry said in his ear. "Trial by ordeal, maybe?"

Leonidas turned to Daley.

"There must," he said firmly, "be some—er—some mistake!"

"Guess you're pretty surprised, huh?" Daley said with satisfaction.

"Surprised is a mild word," Leonidas returned. "I am frankly carried away."

"I'll tell the boys that," Daley said. "That'll please 'em. They worked hard. Wouldn't think we could do all this on the money we had, would you? I tell you, the boys sure worked hard. Looks good, don't it? Never guess it was the old gym, would you?"

"It's incredible!" Leonidas said honestly. "An incredible piece of work." He peered through his pince-nez at the lettering on the largest banner that was dangling precariously over the center of the hall, and a sudden hearty warmth entered his voice as he continued. "M'yes, Daley, I am frankly impressed! A splendid piece of work! Marvelous! M'yes, indeed, unbelievable! And all, if I may say so, in such excellent taste!"

Terry cocked her head on one side and stared up at him.

"Bill, you feel all ri—"

"How well," Leonidas interrupted quickly, "how well those banners look, do they not, Terry?" He put his hands on her shoulders, turned her so that she faced the largest orange banner, and pointed to the slogan blazoned across its top in two-foot black capitals. "How well they—er—express our purpose! How very aptly put! 'Have Fun for the Benefit of Others!' Can you read the rest, Terry, from here?"

" 'The—The Police Widows and Orphans Benevolent and Protective Association!' " Terry sounded as if she had just choked on something. " 'First Annual Autumn Dinner, Dance and Get-together. Music by Sully's Minstrels. Songs by—by Carlos Santos. Door Prizes. Bingo. Surprises Galore.' Uh—uh, yes, it is well put, isn't it? Expresses things nicely. Sums us up in two words. Surprises Galore."

"I rather think I forgot to tell you," Leonidas said, "that I am chairman of the advisory board of this organization. It—er—slipped my mind."

"Best chairman we ever had!" Daley said. "Yessir, we had a lot of chairmen, and some of the biggest names in this town, but nobody ever thought us up anything like this here before!"

"Mr. Witherall thought this up?" Terry asked sweetly. "Mr. Witherall did?"

"I'm sure I didn't, really!" Leonidas protested.

"He sure did! I was at the meeting, a couple weeks ago," Daley said. "Mr. Witherall, he said we should ought to do things to let folks know we existed, see? He suggested we have like a nice get-together, with plenty surprises, and a lot of color, and costumes, and music, and all. But honest, we never thought you'd do it, Mr. Witherall!"

"Er—what?" Leonidas asked.

"Why, come, of course! I mean, you promised you would when Mack called, but we thought you'd duck us. We didn't know you'd be such an old sport as to come in costume yourself, and bring a—a girl friend with you! Of course you *said* you'd come if we'd come and get you in a prowl car, but—well, honest, we'd have had a real welcoming committee for you if—well," Daley's flounderings had the effect of turning his face brick-red, "well, I hand it to you, Mr. Witherall, you're a sport!"

"Thank you," Leonidas said. "But I can't believe you'd think me not a man of my word—what is it, Terry? What did you say?"

"I said it was my knees again. Reaction. There's a little gilt thing over there that looks like a chair, Bill. I think maybe if it was put under me, I could probably sit down." She turned a dazzling smile on Officer Daley. "Is it all right if we go in and sit down?"

"Sure! Gee, sure!" He led them over to two gilt chairs in a corner. "I got to see to a couple of things, but I'll be right back. You'll sit at the head table, of course—I hope you'll say a few words later on, Mr. Witherall, maybe? The boys sure would appreciate it!"

"Delighted to, dear fellow!" Leonidas said. "With pleasure! M'yes, indeed!"

There was a dreamy look in Terry's eyes as she watched Daley depart.

"I'll be down to get you in a prowl car, honey," she said softly. "Better be ready about a quarter to eight. Now honey, don't be late—Bill! Bill *Shake*speare!"

"I do feel contrite!" Leonidas told her with sincerity. "I must have promised them I'd come, and then forgotten completely about it—during the last two hectic weeks, I've promised all things to all men in order to be left alone in peace and quiet."

"You call this," Terry waved her hand at the chattering mob, "peace and quiet? Bill, what'll we *do?* And they keep talking about Ernest!"

"You saw the sign. He was going to sing for them," Leonidas said.

"And they don't know what's happened?"

"They can't, if they talk so gaily about dashing off and picking him up."

"Do you think," Terry said, "with Ernest in that deep freeze in your kitchen, do you really think under the circumstances that this is the ideal place for us?"

"I think it is an excellent place," Leonidas said, "in which to pick up information concerning the habits and customs of Carlos Santos. The police," he paused and sniffed, "always know such strangely interesting details about people. In this case, I think they may even prove to be instructive details, as well. M'yes, chicken. Creamed chicken on toast."

"What *are* you raving about, Bill? We can't stay here! We can't! And you glibly promising to say a few words to the boys!"

"Why not? I intend to elicit information," Leonidas said, "and there is creamed chicken on toast. I smell it. And you told me some time ago that you were simply ravenous, didn't you?"

"But what'll they do when they don't find Ernest?" Terry demanded. "What happens then?"

"I dare say," Leonidas looked speculatively around the hall, "they can pick up an Irish tenor or two who'll oblige with 'Mother Machree.' At all events, I'm quite sure they'll never think to hunt Ernest in my kitchen. I shouldn't, in their place— ah, there's the head of the traffic squad—now, I wonder! Is it possible that he might know—m'yes, I wonder if it could possibly happen—"

"I know what's going to happen!" Terry told him. "In about two shakes there's going to be a loud bang, and I'm suddenly back in your front hall, picking up a brown shoe. I've just been out on my feet, that's all. Just wandering. I am *not* sitting on a gilt undertaker's chair at the Annual Autumn Bingo, Chowder and Marching party of the Dalton cops, who want me only they don't seem to know it! I'm really lying flat on that Shiraz, clutching a gent's brown brogue to my bosom—are you listening, Bill?"

"M'yes. Anderson!" Leonidas called out to the head of the traffic squad. "Oh, Anderson—good evening, Anderson, what a splendid pirate you make! Anderson, I wonder if you could possibly tell me anything about trucks. Er—red trucks."

Anderson, averting his eyes from Leonidas' mortarboard, asked what Mr. Witherall wanted to know about red trucks.

"I rather wondered," Leonidas said smoothly, "if I could possibly locate the owner of a red truck which clipped my car the other day—nothing serious, just a little fender dent," he added. "It's not my intention to make any fuss, but I thought I might call the incident to the owner's attention."

"You get the number?"

"The plates were obscured," Leonidas said, "and the truck drove off rapidly without its driver or his companion pausing to observe the extent of the damage. Er—that was the part which prompts me to write to the owner. I dislike that sort of thing."

He knew that Anderson disliked it, too.

"Those trucks are getting fresh again," Anderson said in grieved tones. "Every now and then, they get kind of fresh, and we have to crack down on 'em. You notice anything about the truck, or the driver—like anything we could work on?"

"Why, yes," Leonidas said. "I had rather a clear view of the driver and his friend—quite a dirty pair. I thought I saw them today on Main Street. I'm sure, however, that you would never be able to identify them. They referred to each other as Matt and Shorty."

Anderson began to laugh.

"I felt quite sure," Leonidas went on, "that you would not know—"

"Who says I don't know Matt and Shorty?" Anderson interrupted. "Sure I know Matt and Shorty!"

This time, the pince-nez fell from Leonidas' nose before he had a chance to catch them.

"Er—really?"

"Sure, they drive for Ferguson's Express, only about half the time," Anderson paused and laughed again. "Half the time, they're wandering around trying to pick up a couple of bucks on the side. They're like to drive Ferguson crazy, but he can't get anyone else to work for him, and there really ain't two better guys in the business, only they just keep picking up odd jobs all the time. They're good guys, Mr. Witherall. If they nicked you, it was probably an accident, see? And if they drove off, it was on account of they didn't know they'd nicked you. I never have trouble with good old Matt and Shorty."

"If you say so," Leonidas said, "I'm sure they are—er—good fellows. Do they live in Dalton?"

"Over Lower Falls way. Only most of the time," Anderson said, "when they ain't driving for Ferguson, they're hanging around the corner outside of Charley's Palace Bar, down the square. Tell you what, Mr. Witherall, I'll speak to Ferguson, and have him tell the boys they should watch themselves."

"That's very kind of you indeed!" Leonidas said. "Thank you, Anderson, very much!"

He turned to see what Terry's reaction would be to Anderson's tidings that Matt and Shorty were real, after all, and found her surrounded by what appeared to be the majority of the men in the hall.

Standing on the outskirts of the little group, he felt suddenly as much alone as if he were on a desert island. Oblivious to the orchestra and the stirring march it had struck up, oblivious to the police, to the orange streamers, the autumn leaves, the chrysanthemums and all the rest, he swung his pince-nez and thought things over.

In the twinkling of an eye, this whole bizarre Finger business had lost its aura of a hopeless quest. It had begun to assume a certain definite shape.

Matt and Shorty were real. They weren't fakes, after all. They existed. They could be found.

From them could be extracted some clue to the beachwagon and the identity of its driver who had presented them with the deep freeze.

At last, there was a beginning.

He found himself looking reflectively at the back of Terry's blonde head. He liked the girl. He wanted to believe every word she'd told him.

But that blonde birthday-present story was just a bit thick!

"I wonder!" he said. "I wonder!"

Slipping out the corridor through which Daley had led them, he hunted up a telephone booth.

Five minutes later, he slipped back into the hall.

Miss Lowell's report on Terry had been highly flattering, in an acidulous sort of way. In spite of her good looks, Miss Lowell considered her quite intelligent.

Sergeant MacCobble, shaking his head dourly, pushed his way through the crowd to Leonidas.

"I told them a good Irish tenor was all they needed! Come on, let's get started!"

"Er—anything wrong with this Santos?"

"Daley, tell 'em to find their places!" MacCobble ignored Leonidas' question. "Tell those women I want two verses of 'The Star-spangled Banner,' see, and tell Father Riley it's his blessing then. Then get that damn fruit cup on!"

With the advent of the fruit cup, MacCobble relaxed enough to smile.

"Give me a St. Patrick's Day parade to handle, any day!" he said. "I told my sister this morning if I lived to the fruit cup, I'd be a happy man. I don't know what's wrong with Santos. Either he forgot, or else he decided to come by himself." He lowered his voice. "It's all one to me! I'm not caring!"

"Er—I gather you're not too fond of him?" Leonidas inquired.

"Is the lady—I didn't catch the name—is she one of his fans?"

"I've heard him," Terry said. "I wasn't much impressed by his singing."

"Neither am I, and I'm glad Pat Riley's willing to oblige us if the fellow doesn't ever turn up!" MacCobble said. "Me, I don't know why the women go for him. But they do. There's my own sister going to that dive in Pomfret, screeching like a banshee every time he's opening his mouth. Baaa! Baaaa! He bleats like a sick baa-lamb, to my taste!"

"But the women like him, do they?"

"Oh, Mr. Witherall," MacCobble said, "it's a professor like you wouldn't know what he's done to Dalton and Pomfret and Carnavon and Framfield! He's not good enough to get over in the city. But out here! Here it's sweeping the high-school crowd out of his way, and the bridge-club ladies fainting all over the curb! Why, even up in your own Oak Hill district, there's respectable women spending all their time chasing him, and their husbands like to go crazy mad! Even your own neighbors, next door!"

"Neighbors?" Leonidas said. *"My* neighbors?"

"Who else but Mrs. Haverstraw? She—you get a grapefruit seed in your throat, Mr. Witherall?" MacCobble asked solicitously as Leonidas choked.

"Not your very fine fruit cup, but a remnant of last week's cold, I fear, caused that—er—spasm," Leonidas said. "So sorry —truly, MacCobble, is Mrs. Haverstraw an admirer of Carlos Santos'?"

"Between you and me, that's why Mr. Haverstraw moved away to Hurlborough," MacCobble said confidentially. "It'll be too far for her to go racing after Santos all the time—how's for saying a few words, Mr. Witherall, while they clear off the tables?"

Duly introduced by the sergeant, Leonidas found himself looking at a sea of faces which regarded him with polite interest, and not much else.

Leonidas smiled. No audience was really hard to anyone who had learned to hold and retain the interest of Meredith Academy's sixth form.

Waiting until the chairs had stopped creaking, he casually draped a string of artificial autumn leaves over the crown of his mortarboard.

Then, when the giggles began to mount, he told the first two policemen stories that flashed into his mind.

By the time the creamed chicken had given way to the orange sherbet, Sergeant MacCobble was calling him Leonidas, and occasionally Lonny.

And Leonidas was finding out almost more than he'd hoped about the affairs of Carlos Santos, alias Ernest Bostwick Finger.

According to MacCobble, Santos never caused the Pomfret Police Department no trouble himself, it was only all the women he stirred up that was the bother. Maude Haverstraw, furthermore, was known to the police of all the neighboring towns as Dalton's most fervent Santos addict. The police knew all right, the sergeant added with feeling, because she damn well parked her car anywhere the spirit moved her, in order to get a glimpse of her hero. In front of hydrants, smack in the middle of the main-street trolley tracks, bang across the intersection next to the firehouse, it was all the same to Maude Haverstraw if that was where she wanted to park!

"Er—haven't you been able to—er—restrain her?" Leonidas inquired.

"Nobody ever tried to restrain Niagara, did they?" MacCobble retorted. "Say, she barges through police lines like they wasn't there, and if anybody tries stopping her, why she just says she's the President of the Dalton Centre Women's Thursday Club, and the head of the Women Voters, and the Republican Ward Chairman of Oak Hill, and she just breezes right along. Oh, we give her parking tickets, sure. By the dozen. But what's two bucks to the likes of Mrs. Haverstraw?"

"Perhaps some more forceful gesture on your part," Leonidas suggested, "would deter—"

"You ain't got the political mind, Leonidas," MacCobble told him paternally. "That's why you got so much done around this town, yes. Sure. But I'm telling you the truth, it don't ever pay to rile those lady voters. Two harsh words to Mrs. Haverstraw, I'm telling you it's sabotage, that's what!"

"Er—sabotage?"

"The phone begins ringing. Will the police please come do something about this ball game that's going to break windows, will the police please do something about these little boys lighting a fire it's going to burn up the town, will the police please investigate this funny-looking man that's lurking on the corner—and if we didn't answer every call, she'd get all those women passing resolutions about we was inefficient. She got us on the ropes. She got Santos on the ropes, too. He finally asked Oakes, the police captain over in Pomfret, if for God's sakes he couldn't keep her away—Daley, go tell them women to stop that diddly stuff and play something somebody can hum!"

"I gather that Captain Oakes met with no success?" Leonidas said, as the orchestra rather abruptly broke off in the middle of "Dark Eyes" to ask in a sprightly fashion if anyone there had seen Kelly?

"That's more like it!" MacCobble began to hum. "I like songs you can hum! No, Oakes couldn't do a thing about her, Leonidas. He even come over here and talked to Mr. Haverstraw. Haverstraw—well, you know how it is. He's a nice guy, but he's kind of helpless. He told Oakes he'd decided it was like a sort of disease, and she'd probably get over it, and in the meantime to send the parking fines to him and he'd take care of 'em, and give him a box of Corona Coronas a mile long. It's a wonder she didn't horn in on this tonight. I expected her—how's for you give us some more stories, Leonidas? Maybe a bit of a song, eh?"

Leonidas balked at a song, but his stories were a rousing success.

Terry shook her head when he sat down at last to the accompaniment of thunderous applause.

"Trouble with you, Bill, you're so good they'll never let us get out of here! Another half hour, and you'll be made an honorary cop. Big Chief Flat-heel!"

"My chief concern," Leonidas told her, "is the future, for the benefit of which I am attempting to hoard good will. We may need it. Er—before we have to fight them, we will have joined them, so to speak. I have mentally altered our plans somewhat, Terry, but don't worry. Very shortly we shall leave."

The mere suggestion of his imminent departure elicited a storm of protest from all quarters, and MacCobble looked particularly downcast.

"But I understand how it is with you," he acknowledged grudgingly. "You're a busy man. I suppose it's after being the bankers, or—oh, heavenly day, there's herself now!"

Leonidas looked in the direction MacCobble was pointing, and recognized Maude Haverstraw's fuchsia-feathered hat in the doorway at the far end of the hall.

"I don't know what'll be worse," MacCobble said sadly, "if she hasn't got a ticket and won't be after buying one, or if she finds out he hasn't come yet—you're not going already yourself?"

"We'll just slip out the corridor," Leonidas said. "I'm sorry we have to run. We've had a splendid dinner and a wonderful time, and if we can possibly make it, we'll drop back later. The whole affair has been a triumph, Sergeant. I'm proud of the—er—boys!"

As they hurried away, Terry announced that it had been ticket trouble.

"With Sister Haverstraw, I mean. But I think they're bully-

ing her into buying a brace. Well, Bill, she certainly can't know
anything about Ernest's fate if she came here to hear him sing!"

"Amazing!" Leonidas remarked. "My own neighbor, my
next-door neighbor, and I have so patently omitted to grasp her
other side, so to speak. On the other hand, Terry, I am inclined
to think I should."

"Should what?"

"Come here to listen to Ernest," Leonidas said thoughtfully,
"even if it happened that I knew he had been killed. It is a
gesture which would show the world so plainly that of course
you *could*n't know about him. Terry," he held open the door
of the musty smelling vestibule and then followed her down
the worn stone steps, "I think that instead of proceeding at
once to Ernest's apartment, we'll drop instead down to Charley's
Palace Bar—"

"Bill!" Terry clutched his arm. "Look, over by the lamppost!"

"Not Maude, I trust!" Leonidas fumbled for his pince-nez.
"Oh! Oh. M'yes. I see."

Bedford Scrim had detached himself from the lamppost
against which he'd been leaning, and was walking toward
them.

"I think—"

"Ah. Good evening!" Leonidas said warmly. "Good evening,
Mr. Scrim. I'm bearing in mind your little message to Mr.
Witherall!"

"But—"

"So nice to see you again! Lovely night, isn't it?" In a whisper to Terry, he added, "Walk a little faster, please!"

"But—" Bedford Scrim raised his voice.

"Good night!" Leonidas called out. "Hurry up, Terry!"

They practically scuttled around the corner.

"What now?" Terry demanded breathlessly. "I suppose you
know that man is *following* us?"

"Keep walking!" Leonidas said. "He can hardly be brash enough to chase us, after all—watch your heels and your skirts, Terry! We're going to cut through this alley at the right!"

He knew the alley well, because his favorite secondhand bookstore was on the other end of it.

With one hand on her elbow, he guided her expertly around packing cases and ash barrels and empty cardboard cartons.

"What a nasty place! Bill, I still think Scrim is following us!"

Leonidas knew he was.

"Persistent fellow," he said lightly.

"But why should he—"

"Down a step, and in here, quick!"

He opened the door of the bookstore, almost pushed Terry inside, and led her quickly to the crammed, ceiling-high stacks in the rear of the shop.

A wizened little man wearing a green eye shade glanced up casually from a desk in the corner.

"Evening, Mr. Witherall," he said casually, as if it were a nightly custom for Leonidas to appear there in his cap and gown, and accompanied by a blonde girl wearing an orchid corsage.

"Good evening," Leonidas said. "Er—Mr. Crowninshield, would you permit us to hide for a few moments among your books?"

"Oh, certainly. Certainly, Mr. Witherall. Anywhere at all. Anywhere. Biography would doubtless be the best place."

He turned back to his book while Leonidas hurriedly shoved Terry toward the biography section.

Almost at once the store's front door opened.

Mr. Crowninshield got up from his desk.

"Anything I can do for you, sir?"

"Well, I—er—have you seen a lady and a gentleman?" Bedford Scrim's voice asked hesitatingly. "A lady in evening clothes, and a man in a cap and gown?"

"I'm afraid not," Mr. Crowninshield said. "Unusual combination, on the whole," he added pensively.

"Haven't you seen them? You haven't?" Scrim sounded more than faintly thwarted, Leonidas thought. "Didn't they come in here?"

"This is a bookstore," Crowninshield said. "We don't very often get that combination in a bookstore. Very rarely."

"Oh. Well, thanks, anyway."

"Don't mention it," Crowninshield said.

Terry and Leonidas heard the door slam, and then the rustlings and creakings as Crowninshield returned to his desk and sat down.

"No!" Leonidas put out a restraining hand as Terry started to move from behind the stacks. "I think we'll wait a moment."

"What in the world is that man—Bill, d'you suppose he was actually waiting there outside the police station for *us?*"

"I'm sure no one could have followed that careening prowl car from my house to the station," Leonidas said, "but on the other hand, I dare say that ear-splitting siren could have guided anyone to our destination without much difficulty. Is he still outside there, Crowninshield?"

"Yes."

Ten minutes passed before Bedford Scrim departed, and Leonidas waited nearly another ten before he permitted Terry to emerge from the biographies.

"Very kind of you, Crowninshield," he said. "We're deeply appreciative."

"Oh, any time, Mr. Witherall!" Crowninshield said. "Always glad to see you." He bowed gravely to Terry. "Good night!"

Before they stepped up from the store's entrance to the street,

Leonidas paused, removed his mortarboard, and slung his baggy gown over his arm.

"I've had quite enough of them!" he said. "Now—"

"Bill, what an amazing little man!" Terry interrupted. "And what in the world did Bedford Scrim follow us like that for?"

"Crowninshield is a Sanscrit scholar, and he views the world very dispassionately, indeed," Leonidas said. "As for Bedford Scrim and his motive in pursuing us, I don't pretend to understand either."

"He knows you're Witherall, all right! I told you that back at your house, Bill!" Terry shivered suddenly. "No, I'm not cold," she said in answer to Leonidas' solicitous question. "It's just that there's something sort of sinister about being followed like that, isn't there? What d'you suppose he can want?"

Leonidas shrugged. "Whoever he is and whatever he wants, I haven't time for him now. We're going around the corner and across the square to Charley's Palace Bar. I believe it's only a step beyond the Minturn Club—"

"Charley's? Of *all* places, why?" Terry demanded.

"We're going to track down Matt and Shorty."

"What d'you *mean?*"

"I forgot," Leonidas said, "that you missed hearing Anderson's nugget of information about them." He summed up the situation for her, briefly. "So we are going—"

"Bill Shakespeare, you're not naïve enough to expect to find that pair there, just because of what Anderson said!"

"If we don't find them," Leonidas told her, "we will doubtless lay hand on someone who will be able to locate them more specifically for us—Terry!"

"I suppose," she said with irony as she rounded the corner a step behind him, "that the dear boys are standing right there waiting for you, like something on a Christmas tree?"

"They are!"

"Bill, never—"

"See, there's Matt, standing under the arc light!" Leonidas pointed to the corner diagonally across from them. "Hurry up, Terry!" he lengthened his stride. "Hurry! The red truck is parked there by the curb, and the motor's running—"

Oblivious to the traffic, Leonidas sprinted across Dalton Square.

He achieved the sidewalk safely, and had his mouth open to call out and address Matt by name when both his arms were grabbed, and he was swung violently around in the opposite direction.

"At last we've got you! Well, well, Witherall!"

Leonidas, struggling vainly to extricate himself from the grip of two sturdy men whom he had never seen before in his life, helplessly watched Matt jump into the red truck, and sadly watched the vehicle as it rolled away down the street.

V

FIVE minutes later, he stood before a chrysanthemum-laden mahogany table in the Minturn Club dining room, staring down at the white banquet cloth and at his hands, resting on either side of a gold-banded Lenox plate containing chicken à la king, and trying to figure out exactly how he had arrived there, anyway.

At least he knew where he was.

And he knew, in a vague way, what the banquet was all about.

Somehow it was involved with somebody's cheery notion that good will and fellowship should permeate the assorted directors of the various banks in Dalton County. Although, for his part, Leonidas thought, he entertained virtually no vestige of good will and even less of a feeling of fellowship for those two muscular oafs from the Wemberley South Co-operative Bank who had reached out and grabbed him as he raced past the Minturn Club's front door. Merely because they had been asked by some harassed chairman to take a peek about outside and see if they could catch a glimpse of old Witherall—the one with a beard, who looked like Shakespeare—such a request did not, in Leonidas' opinion, constitute a legitimate excuse for their hijacking him in any such strenuous fashion.

He sighed, fumbled for his pince-nez, and wondered how many other functions he had faithfully promised to attend, and then completely forgotten about, during his struggles to turn out three hundred and fifteen coherent pages of Gallant Lieutenant!

Although his face wore what he hoped was an expression of rapt attention, he was actually only half-listening to the adjective-ridden and abysmally ungrammatical speech of the toastmaster, who had clapped him on the back as if he'd just scored a winning touchdown when the two oafs from Wemberley had borne him, still protesting, into the dining room.

"You stand right here at head table!" he'd said heartily, "while I tell the boys all about you, Leonidas! You stand right here!"

So Leonidas continued to stand right there, while the toastmaster piled adjectives into combinations so bizarre and incredible that even a Meredith sixth-former wouldn't have dared to attempt them!

"I want all the boys here to know you!" The toastmaster, Leonidas remembered, had added with great enthusiasm. "I want all the boys to *know* you!"

As he rather wearily affixed his pince-nez, Leonidas looked around at the pink eggs of faces looming up behind the bowls of chrysanthemums, and thought how very little he, personally, wanted to know the boys. While they were doubtless all good men and true, the only boys he yearned to meet were Matt and Shorty!

His eyes lighted on the menu card, and he permitted himself the sardonic reflection that even a lot of bank directors couldn't let their imaginations soar beyond fruit cup—on an ice bed, to be sure, but still fruit cup—and creamed chicken—even if they added mushrooms and referred to it as Minturn Club chicken à la king—and orange sherbet. Of course, they ran slightly ahead of the Dalton police in the matter of Colossal Stuffed Olives (Imported), Selected Hearts of Celery, and Crisp Lettuce with French Dressing Minturn Club. And someone had taken the trouble to mark with an asterisk such items as contained a whiff of onion.

He suddenly caught sight of his own name on the lower half of the card.

"Leonidas Witherall."

Then came a line of double dots.

Then it said, "Speech."

So that was what all those adjectives were leading up to! He was in the process of being introduced formally to all the boys!

Leonidas began to listen to the toastmaster as if every word that dropped from his lips were solid gold.

"So I want you boys to meet this man, and I know he's got a real message for us, one we won't forget in a hurry, and that'll do us real good, one who—whom—who I am proud to have the honor and privilege of introducing, who has the whole-hearted respect and good will of this community which is mighty glad to have such a public-spirited citizen in their midst, and by the way, I'm sure, knowing him as I do, that he'll be glad to answer any questions later about all his various investigations and so forth, and I think it was pretty swell of him to find the time out of his busy life to come here and give us a little talk tonight in spite of all his other responsibilities, and believe me, he has a lot of them, and so here he is, fellow members, Mr. Leonidas Witherall of the well-known Oak Hill section of this town!"

There was only one way out, and Leonidas promptly took it.

Assuming his most scholarly air, he launched into a neat and masterly little speech which said absolutely nothing, praised practically everything, trusted implicitly in the future despite its obvious uncertainties, and gave a generally paternal assurance that better times were sure to be around the corner if every man present only put his shoulder to the wheel.

Then, on sudden inspiration, he told the policemen stories, and sat down.

The muscular oafs from Wemberley, with tears of laughter running down their cheeks, pounded him on the back and told him he was terrific, but terrific! And Leonidas thanked them politely, and wondered what had become of Terry.

If she had seen what happened to him, it would have availed her nothing to attempt to follow, since women were not allowed within the sacred precincts of the Minturn Club. That was the first rule on the books, and the walls had almost disintegrated when the demands of war had forced the house committee to hire girl waiters. Somehow the precedent had been established that only girls were eligible whose parents had never heard of corrective dentistry, and whose own eyesight was poor. Consequently all the Minturn girl waiters wore glasses and had teeth like old, uneven tombstones. While one noticed that they weren't men, as old Professor Skellings said, one never bothered to think of them as women, either.

The girl waiting on him at head table tonight was such a glowing exception to the rule that Leonidas found himself openly staring at her as she replenished his water glass.

She was a small, pert, red-headed child with snapping blue eyes, toothpaste-advertisement teeth, and a singularly infectious grin.

She turned it on Leonidas and said "Hiya!" as if she had known him well for years, and Leonidas grinned back.

If he couldn't manage to break away gracefully in the next five minutes, he decided, as he helped himself to a Colossal Stuffed Olive, he would present this child with a dollar and ask her to take a look around outside for Terry. But after all that build-up as a busy man of affairs, he ought to be able to cut and run without any difficulty!

"Guy three down's trying to talk to you, Mr. Witherall!" the pert child said. "To your right."

"Oh! Oh, thank you! Yes, Mason?" Leonidas leaned forward and turned his head toward the president of the Dalton bank.

"Asking you about Bedford Scrim," Mason said unexpectedly.

"Er—Scrim? Bedford Scrim?" Leonidas tried to look judicial as he played for time. "Scrim, eh?"

"I asked you about him a few weeks ago—someone had suggested his taking Berry's place as director, if Berry's called back to Washington again. You told me you were debating Scrim in your mind then, as I remember."

Probably, Leonidas thought guiltily, he had been debating scrim, the guest-room curtains, and not Bedford Scrim, the man.

"M'yes. M'yes, indeed. Scrim. Well, Mason, I hardly know what to say," Leonidas said thoughtfully. "I don't really know. Er—how do you feel about Scrim, yourself?"

"Well, I can't make up my mind if he's like his uncle or not," Mason returned.

Not having the remotest idea who the uncle of Bedford Scrim could be, or what he was like, Leonidas found that opinion of no practical value.

"Er—possibly not," he said. "Possibly not. And yet, on the other hand, who knows, Mason? Perhaps he is more like his uncle than one might suspect."

Mason nodded vigorously. "That's what I'm inclined to think, myself, but Berry and Carson swear he's honest and decent. They think he's absolutely all right. Though how he could have been personal secretary to that crook and not have known he was a crook—you must have run into the fellow during that investigation of yours, Witherall!"

"Although I admittedly have run into many people during the course of one investigation or another," Leonidas said with truth, "I never happened to—er—run into Bedford Scrim. I know young Scrim only in passing, as one might put it."

"Nothing came of those threats, I gather?" Mason asked.

"Er—what threats?" Leonidas asked.

"His uncle's threats to get you? No, I don't suppose he'd have dared. Well, you're very fair to Scrim, Witherall. Fairer than I'd be in your place, but of course if he never figured in the investigation, there may be some basis to what Berry and Carson claim about him. They're convinced he didn't know—"

Someone claimed Mason's attention farther down the table, and he left his sentence dangling in mid-air.

Leonidas' eyes narrowed.

He swung around suddenly and tapped one of the muscular Wemberley bank men on the shoulder.

"I wonder," he said, "if you happen to know Bedford Scrim?"

"Know him by sight. Not personally. Say, Witherall, that story about the cop in the air-raid shelter was terrific! I want you to tell me that so I'll have it just right. That's one of the kind you have to tell just right, or it flops—"

"Gladly," Leonidas said. "Er—about Scrim. Does he work here in Dalton at the moment, d'you know?"

"Sure, he's back at his old job, general manager at the mills. Never should've left. *I* always thought," he added confidentially, "that his uncle probably framed him some way so he felt he had to go. Honest John was a genius at that sort of thing. By the way, Witherall, I certainly hand it to you—you washed old Honest John right up on the shore, all right!"

The smile which Leonidas forced to his lips felt as if it were going to crack and fall down into the orange sherbet.

Only one man in Dalton was universally known as Honest John.

That was Honest John Scudder.

And Honest John Scudder was the ex-mayor of Dalton.

Leonidas' pince-nez began to twirl rapidly.

And Scrim, Bedford Scrim, had been his secretary, and was also his nephew!

And Honest John's threats, although they had never been

openly or publicly expressed, had none the less filtered back to Leonidas' ears. In Honest John's opinion, no fate was too gruesome for the chairman of the Good Government League which had been instrumental in forcing his resignation.

But like Mason, Leonidas had never thought that Honest John would dare to take any retaliatory steps. Although Honest John was probably as far from honest as any man could be, Honest John was no fool!

But Terry's ironic comment came floating back to his mind.

"Sure, Bill Shakespeare, no enemies! Everyone in Dalton probably loves you dearly, like a brother!"

Could all this business of the deep freeze and Ernest Finger be some outcropping of revenge?

After all, Scrim had followed them!

When you came right down to it, Scrim had been pursuing him all day!

"You're not going!" the Wemberley bank director said protestingly as Leonidas pushed back his chair. "You can't go! Not before you tell me again just what the cop in the air-raid shelter said to the girl!"

"I'm so sorry!" Leonidas said. "There's—er—there's some business I must attend to. A man at my house whom I must see. I should, of course, prefer to stay, but duty beckons, and—"

The Wemberley man shouted to the toastmaster that Witherall said he had to leave, the toastmaster shouted back to the Wemberley man, and suddenly everyone at the head table seemed to be shouting at once to everyone else.

In the midst of the confusion, the pert waitress touched Leonidas on the arm.

"Where's ma, Mr. Witherall?"

"Er—I beg your pardon?"

"I said," she raised her voice, "where's ma?"

That was precisely what Leonidas had understood her to say, and the question still puzzled him.

"Ma?" he said. "Er—*ma?*"

"Is ma still at your house? Is she still in your kitchen?"

Leonidas felt a sense of momentary relief that she at least had not inquired if pa were still in his kitchen!

"Er—your mother?"

"Sure, Mr. Witherall. I'm Sonia. I'm Mrs. Mullet's daughter."

"Sonia?"

"Well, maybe she calls me Gerty when she speaks of me, but I changed it to Sonia. Did ma work late up to your house?"

"Why, no. She left early, as a matter of fact," Leonidas said. "I—er—didn't know that you were her daughter."

"Ma didn't come—"

"Well, Witherall, we've rustled up a car to take you home!" the toastmaster bustled up and edged Sonia, alias Gerty, aside. "Come along, if you must go!"

"Why, thank you, but I don't require a car!" Leonidas had a sudden vision of Terry waiting outside for him, of explanations, raised eyebrows, and general complications. "Thank you, no!"

"Mason's chauffeur is going to run you home—it's the very least we can do for you, Witherall, after that dandy talk you gave us!" He took Leonidas by the elbow and steered him out of the dining room. "We think it's pretty fine of you to have troubled to come, with all you have to do, and if you weren't in a hurry, I'd have the boys give you a rising vote of thanks— you were terrific! Simply terrific! Frankly, I want to talk to you some time about giving a little speech at the state banquet —did you have a coat?" he paused briefly in the hall. "Oh, a cape!" he said, as the checkroom girl thrust the cap and gown at Leonidas. "Well, I want you to think over the state-banquet business, if you will—Mason's car is right out here." Leonidas found himself being inserted into the cushioned depths of a long black limousine. "There—there you are! Forty Birch Hill, Edward! I said," he fairly screamed the words at the chauffeur, *"Forty Birch Hill Road!* You got that?"

Leonidas, feeling completely breathless although he hadn't had a chance to open his mouth, leaned forward as the car started away from the curb, and spoke to the chauffeur.

"Just pull up at the next corner, please!"

The limousine rolled by the next corner, and Leonidas leaned forward again.

"Stop at the *next* corner, please!" he raised his voice, and spoke with great distinctness.

At the end of the fourth block, he stood up in a half-crouching position, holding onto the lap-robe cord to keep his balance, and howled in the man's ear.

"STOP!"

"Yessir," the chauffeur said calmly. "Yessir, I got it. Don't you worry none. Forty Birch Hill Road."

Nothing, Leonidas found as he finally subsided in a fit of coughing, could be done about the situation. Not unless he wanted to wrench open the door and hurl himself bodily out of the car. Even that would be impossible, he reflected, since no door handles were visible in the interior of Mason's luxurious vehicle. He couldn't even see a button to push.

So, as if he were a priceless piece of Ming china, he was sedately and smoothly returned home to Forty Birch Hill Road.

"Right place, isn't it, sir?" the man asked with quiet pride as he held the car door open.

"Thank you!" Leonidas said hoarsely, and strode up the front walk.

Only a very foolhardy soul, he thought, only someone like Lieutenant Haseltine, would recklessly squander his strength in any futile effort to bandy words with Mason's chauffeur!

But everything had probably turned out for the best, he decided. He really needed his own car to drive in later over to Pomfret, where in some fashion he must wangle his way into Ernest Finger's apartment. Now, after ridding himself of his cap and gown, he would drive back to Dalton Square, locate poor Terry, and make another attempt to lay his hands on Matt and Shorty.

"I wonder," he murmured, "could there possibly be some connection between Bedford Scrim and Ernest Finger? Now I won—"

He stopped short on his front doorstep.

He still had no key!

And those accursed, unmovable metal screens were on all the lower windows except those two over the kitchen sink.

Beyond any peradventure of a doubt, if he tried to break into his own kitchen, some Finger or other from next door—say the poetically inclined Cupcake, peering wistfully at the moon from her bedroom window—would spot him and summon the police.

And for all the good will he had generated, Leonidas hesitated to draw on the stock.

But it couldn't be helped. He had to get the car keys!

Slinging his gown over his shoulder, he started around toward the back door.

Just as he succeeded in boosting himself up to the window sill, he heard someone cough behind him.

Wearily, he turned his head.

Then he blinked.

It wasn't a Finger.

Maude and Foster Haverstraw stood there, seemingly having materialized out of thin air.

Leonidas scrambled down from the sill.

"Good evening!" he said, feeling that it wasn't a particularly brilliant remark, but being totally unable to think of anything else. "Er—good evening!"

"I didn't know you had a niece, Leonidas!" Maude went straight to the point, in her usual direct manner. "Mrs. Finger said that blonde girl was your niece! You never *told* me you had a brother!"

"I never—er," Leonidas began to recover, "mention my brother's name. Following a difference of opinion some years back, his name has never crossed my lips. Since the entire topic is exceedingly painful to me, I am sure you will forgive me if I do not—er—expatiate upon it. His daughter, however, is a charming girl. Er—it was my impression—"

While he wondered how he could tactfully say he thought she was safely ensconced at the Police Widows Annual Autumn party, without involving himself in a lot of lengthy explanations as to how he knew she'd been there and what he had been doing there himself, Foster cleared his throat, and spoke up.

"Locked out, hey?"

"Er—no, Foster," Leonidas said quickly. "No, no, not at all! Just checking up on this window catch here, that's all. It—"

"Bet you *are* locked out!" Foster said with a satisfied chuckle.

"Of course he is!" Maude's high-pitched laugh tinkled out, Leonidas thought dismally, like the falling of broken glass. "Oh, you *men!* Always so ashamed to admit you forgot your keys! Come along, Leonidas. *I* will let you in!"

"Er—"

"I still have that spare key you left at our house once when you were expecting a package," Maude started for the front door. "And if you hadn't returned from the police party, Foster and I had about decided to use it, anyway, and go right in."

"Er—indeed!" So she knew where he'd been!

"They said," Maude went on, "you were simply wonderful

at that police party. We didn't bother to stay when we found out Ca—"

"Got the key?" Foster interrupted brusquely.

"Right here." Instead of giving it to Leonidas, Maude put the key in the lock, turned it deftly, and walked in.

With a feeling of definite uneasiness, Leonidas noticed that she quite automatically gave the knob the proper little hitch that enabled the key to turn without sticking.

This was, although he hated to think so and faced the very thought with repugnance, this was very obviously not the first time she had opened his front door!

"Charming people, the Fingers," Maude said as he and Foster followed her into the hall. "You're going to love them. So different! They have another son—Foster, didn't you think that was queer?"

"Why shouldn't she have another son? No law against it!"

"I mean, the way she and Jay talked about him. They didn't mention his name, or *say* anything about him. It was almost as if they didn't *wish* to, I thought. As if they had something to *hide!*"

"Er—did they—" But before Leonidas could ask how old this other Finger son was, Foster sniffed and said he hadn't noticed anything queer.

"Place was such a damned mess, you couldn't notice anything but clutter! Never saw such clutter!"

"Well, she's the untidy type, but of course she's literary—did you know she wrote, Leonidas?"

"No. Er—" he stepped in front of Maude as she and Foster started to make a beeline for the kitchen. "Can I get you a drink of water, perhaps?"

"Just after the rakes," Foster said as they brushed past him. "It's all right. We know where the light switch is—"

Gritting his teeth, Leonidas reached out for the Delft vase

on the hall table, and slammed it with all his strength against the newel post.

"Oh!"

Maude and Foster stopped, and turned around.

At least, Leonidas thought grimly, his sacrifice hadn't been entirely in vain!

At least, for the moment, they had been prevented from entering his kitchen.

And once in that kitchen, no power on earth could keep Maude away from that deep freeze.

"Oh!" Maude said again. "Your Delft vase! Oh, what a pity—how could that have *happened!* It's simply shattered!"

"It caught," Leonidas said sadly, "in my sleeve—I wonder if you'd help me pick up the pieces?"

"Better just sweep 'em," Foster said.

"That vase," Leonidas said firmly, "is one of my most cherished possessions, and it is my intention to gather up the pieces with great care, and cause them to be put together again. Er—will you be good enough to retrieve that piece beside your foot, Foster, before you step on it? Of course, I can *quite* understand," he added in a hurt voice, "how such an accident to any of my possessions would have no particular meaning to anyone else, but this happens to matter to me. Rather poignantly. It—er—was my dear mother's vase."

Actually he had picked it up in a junk shop, but Leonidas was pleased to note that the mother touch appeared to move Foster considerably.

"Come on, Maude, help him! Too bad, Witherall. Great pity. Nasty shame. Pitch in, Maude, come, come!"

"Just which rakes," Leonidas waited until they were both down on their hands and knees, and then he carefully got between them and the kitchen door, "which rakes were you after, Foster?"

"We didn't dare trust our *best* tools to the moving men—why, didn't Mrs. Mullet *tell* you?" Maude demanded. "Didn't she tell you we left our best tools in your cellar yesterday?"

"Er—no." At least, if Mrs. Mullet had apprised him of the fact, he'd ignored the information, Leonidas thought, and violently began to regret that his cellar door led from his kitchen. "No, she didn't. I'll just run down and get them for you—"

Foster bobbed up to his feet at once.

"Can't possibly carry them all by yourself!" he said anxiously. "Sure you can't. Might drop 'em. Irreplaceable, you know. *I'll* go—"

"We'll *all* go!" Maude said with finality as she, too, arose.

"By all means, let us all go," Leonidas said desperately. "Many hands make light work, and all that sort of thing. First, however," he smiled sadly, "let us pick up dear mother's cherished Delft vase!"

While he could keep Foster away from the deep freeze, he decided that short of mayhem he knew no way to steer Maude from the thing. She simply could not be permitted to enter the kitchen, and that was all there was to it! He had to devise some scheme!

When the last blue fragment had been picked up from the hall floor, he turned to her with a deference that would instantly have aroused her suspicions, had she been a more subtle individual.

"I *do* dislike asking you a favor, Maude, but I wonder if, now that you're here, you could possibly advise me on a problem of mine?"

Maude bit. She said she'd be only too glad to advise him on anything, if she could.

"It's the guest-room curtains," Leonidas said. "Now you have a *way* with curtains, Maude. I don't know what it is, but you *do* something to curtains. Would you—er—could I prevail on you to look at my guest room? To—er—*study* it, if I may use the phrase, and to tell me honestly just what, in your candied—I mean, candid—opinion, I ought to do about them?"

He feared for a moment that he had overdone it, but Maude smiled a bright smile that showed all her teeth and somehow fleetingly reminded him of Winston Abercrombie in his playful mood.

"I'd be glad to, Leonidas!" she said. "Of course, *I've* always felt that I had the curtain touch, myself, but I didn't think that a *man* would notice!"

"You have the curtain touch, dear lady!" Leonidas said. "Even a mere man can recognize that touch of genius. Now, I don't recall if you've ever been in my guest room, but if you'd go and really study those windows for me? Ah, but that is kind of you!"

He drew a long breath of relief as she mounted the stairs.

"Now, Foster," he said briskly, "suppose we get those tools of yours out of the cellar, shall we? You really shouldn't have left them down there, you know. They might have got damp, and rust—"

Still gabbling rapidly, he steered Foster through the kitchen in much the same manner that the toastmaster had steered him out of the Minturn Club.

Foster never even noticed the deep freeze!

"Now do be very careful going down here, please, Foster!" he continued as he snapped on the cellar light. "There's that very awkward turn, and then there's a deceptively short rise on the last step. I'm always warning Mrs. Mullet of the danger of tripping on it, but I feel sure that one day the good woman will nonetheless—will nonetheless—er—"

The rest of his sentence trailed off into nothingness as Leonidas came to an abrupt stop at the foot of the cellar stairs.

There, over by the oil burner, was the good woman, herself! Sitting in an old rocking chair.

Bound!

Gagged!

And blindfolded!

Leonidas gulped.

This was pretty much the end. Foster would yell for Maude. Maude would come, on the double. Police. Deep freeze. Ernest Finger.

Boom! Leonidas thought unhappily.

He turned to look at Foster and get it over with.

But Foster was busy in the corner with his precious garden tools.

Foster hadn't even seen Mrs. Mullet!

Could he—Leonidas almost didn't dare to let the fanciful notion flit across his mind—could he possibly keep Foster from seeing her?

He could but try!

"No rust, Foster, I hope?" To his own ears, his voice sounded as if he were inside an empty beer barrel, whispering through the bung.

But Foster didn't seem to notice anything wrong.

"No rust at all. They're fine. All right. You almost had me worried for a minute with your talk about dampness, but they're fine."

"Splendid!" Leonidas said. "Capital!"

From the shelves beyond the oil burner, he twitched down an old quilt which Mrs. Mullet sometimes used as a dust cover. With a quick gesture, he draped it over Mrs. Mullet, chair and all.

In his heart, he devoutly hoped Mrs. Mullet would understand, ultimately, that he couldn't possibly rescue her now!

"I think I'd best carry *this* myself." Foster was handling what looked to Leonidas like an ordinary hoe, but he touched it as if he were caressing crown jewels. "You take that rake—" he paused. "That quilt over there!"

"Er—what about it?"

"Just the thing! We'll lay the best rakes on it, and bundle 'em up!"

"I wouldn't chance it, Foster! Not that rotten old quilt!" Leonidas' horror was strictly genuine, and from the depths of his being. "If that rotten old quilt should come apart halfway up the stairs—well, Foster, as you yourself said, these tools are irreplaceable! *I* feel that they should be carried. By hand."

"Quilt doesn't look rotten," Foster returned critically. "Looks all right."

"Foster, I have no insurance that covers injury to valuable tools through careless handling!" Leonidas shook his head gravely. "Let us not take reckless chances! Let us be practical! I'm very sure that Maude would not wish you to damage these excellent implements!"

"Well, s'pose you're right. Have to lug 'em in our arms. Probably best thing."

Before Foster and the tools had been maneuvered out of the cellar past Mrs. Mullet, up the cellar stairs with their awkward, right-angle turn, and through the kitchen and past the deep freeze, Leonidas' forehead was wet with perspiration.

"Know what?" Foster inquired, as the last tool was carefully propped against the newel post. "Think you ought to take a whack at some conditioning classes at the club. Shouldn't be dripping like that just from lugging a few hoes! Look at me!"

"I've had," Leonidas said, "rather a trying day. Quite nerveracking, on the whole."

"Too sedentary, that's the trouble with you, Leonidas. Don't have anything to stir you up. Need more excitement," Foster said. "Ought to get around, get mixed up in things more. Too much sitting around in directors' chairs and such. Not enough action. Well, let's take a look at these curtains of yours. Like curtains myself. Not bad at 'em. Didn't think you'd be a one to care two hoots about 'em, though. Where are they?"

Twenty minutes later, while Maude and Foster bickered about decorative schemes, Leonidas came to the bitter realization that he had very definitely overdone the curtain angle.

By the time they finally compromised on chintz, just like the chintz in their own guest room, Leonidas felt as if he had been put through a mangle.

By the time the last precious rake had been carefully stowed away in their car, he was beyond any feeling whatsoever.

He was too exhausted, as he closed the door after watching them depart, even to sigh with relief.

It was even a physical effort to count the strokes of the living-room clock, and even after he'd counted, he didn't believe it was only eleven.

"Not," he murmured, "unless it's eleven tomorrow morning!"

He couldn't set out now with any hope of finding Terry waiting for him outside the front door of the Minturn Club. Wherever she had gone, wherever she was now, she'd simply have to keep right on staying there. There was nothing he could do about it.

As for Matt and Shorty, he couldn't now honestly entertain any optimistic thoughts about locating them, either.

And even if he knew the whereabouts of all three, and could fly to them with the wings of an eagle, he still had to see to Mrs. Mullet first.

And in his candied opinion, it was going to be a very tough interview!

He squared his shoulders and started for the cellar.

But before he reached the kitchen, the front-door chimes rang out.

"If Foster and Maude have forgotten a dibble," Leonidas told himself in an ominous voice, "I shall thrust it through their skulls!"

He opened the door.

Sonia Mullet stood outside, dressed in slacks and a tightly fitting white sweater. A sequin-studded fascinator was draped over her red curls.

Beside her was one of the largest youths Leonidas had ever seen, the sort of fellow whom the coaches at Meredith's were always wistfully describing to him as all they needed for a winning team, any winning team at all. He wore the uniform of a marine private, and after noting the suspicious expression on his perfectly square face, Leonidas had to stifle his inclination to say hurriedly that he was, after all, a friend.

"Hiya, Mr. Witherall!" Sonia said. "This's Chuck. Say hello, Chuck."

"Hello," Chuck said dutifully.

"How do you do?" Leonidas returned.

"Say, Mr. Witherall, I'm worried about ma. She hasn't come home yet."

"Er—she hasn't?" Leonidas began to find something slightly disconcerting in Chuck's steady, suspicious stare.

"No, say, isn't she here?"

Could he, Leonidas asked himself rapidly, could he say he was terribly, terribly sorry, but her mother was at the moment bound and gagged and blindfolded, sitting in a rocking chair by the oil burner in his cellar, with an old patchwork quilt thrown over her?

He ought to.

He would.

That is, he would have, he amended, if Chuck were a whit less suspicious, and a few inches—say six inches—smaller all around.

"I'm so sorry," he said courteously. "I told her to leave early this afternoon. Around four, I believe it was. Er—have you thought that she may be visiting some friend or relative?"

"That's what we decided," Chuck said, "only we've called everywheres, and nobody's seen her—did she happen to tell you she was going anywheres special?"

Leonidas shook his head. "I was rather busy when she left," he said. "Have you exhausted all possible resources? I mean, have you called everyone you can think of? I'm very sure," he added, "that no harm has befallen her, or you would have known it before now."

"That's what Chuck said—" Sonia began.

"*I* said double feature!" Chuck interrupted.

"Er—I beg your pardon?"

"Chuck thinks she's gone to the movies," Sonia said. "It's a Haseltine to the Strand, and she's a sucker for Haseltine. Maybe she sat through it twice. Well, we'll go wait for the last show to get out, I guess. So long, Mr. Witherall—say!"

"Yes?"

"Say, *I* know who you look like ma always wondered about! *Shakespeare!* Look, Chuck! Shakespeare!"

"I know," Chuck said. "I thought so right off. I thought Shakespeare to myself. I know Shakespeare. Good night!"

He threw Leonidas a snappy salute, and the pair departed.

"I wonder," Leonidas murmured as he closed the door, "if perhaps I might not have told them after all! Ah, well, it's too late now. And one never knows about those large youths—"

First, he thought as he set out again for the cellar, first the promise of a taxi home. Mrs. Mullet adored taxis. Then profound apologies that such a thing had happened in his house. Promises to call the police, to search out and track down the villain responsible for this dastardly deed.

Of course, he mentally footnoted, the villain had been the

fellow who later rifled his desk. It must have been. After all,
he couldn't have been subjected to a swarm of riflers! There
must only have been one!

If he could manage to talk Mrs. Mullet down, Leonidas decided, he could get away with it. He'd simply give her no chance
to ask why he hadn't freed her when he came to the cellar
with Foster. That episode would be ignored.

After seven hours down there—of course, what he had
thought was her angry chatter and the sound of her departure
had been instead the noise of her being set upon and tied up.
After seven hours of limbo, duress and confinement, she would
doubtless be too tired to care very much about the deep freeze,
or what it might contain. She could be led past it.

He tiptoed down the cellar stairs, walked over to the rocker,
and twitched off the quilt.

Then he removed the gag—one of his own monogrammed
handkerchiefs, he noted, filched from the hamper of clean
laundry standing over by the set tubs.

He frankly expected a torrent of words, and almost automatically took a step back to brace himself for them. In a Haseltine
epic, people whose gags were removed alternately poured forth
a torrent of words—usually highly informative—or else they
choked pitifully, and asked in a parched voice for water.

Mrs. Mullet did neither.

She simply did not react at all.

With fingers that trembled, Leonidas untied her blindfold—
another of his own handkerchiefs.

Mrs. Mullet's eyes were tightly shut.

Thoroughly alarmed, Leonidas leaned close to her, and listened.

She was breathing. She was at least alive!

Was she drugged?

It took him several minutes to realize that Mrs. Mullet was sound asleep.

He took off the clothesline that had been used to bind her wrists and ankles, waited a moment, and then coughed.

"Ahem!" he said.

Mrs. Mullet didn't stir.

He reached out and prodded her gently.

Nothing happened.

At last, he took her by the shoulders, and shook her firmly.

Mrs. Mullet opened her eyes, yawned luxuriously, and looked up at him.

"In my candied opinion, Mr. Witherall," she told him between yawns, "you certainly took your time getting here!"

"Mrs. Mullet, I have no words with which to sum up this calamity! What happened? Are you quite all right?" Leonidas' anxiety was heartfelt.

Mrs. Mullet patted a few wisps of straggling gray hair into place, then stretched her arms above her head, rocked back and forth, and smiled.

"It's the first good sleep I've had in years!" she said. "I suffer terrible from imsomnia, you know. No, Mr. Witherall, I got that much to say. I never slept any sounder. And I know who he was, too!"

"You—you know? *Who*, Mrs. Mullet?" Leonidas demanded. "Who *was* it?"

"You know after you locked the study door on me when I was trying to tell you about the Fingers and you wouldn't listen—say, what time is it now?" she shook her head when he told her. "I bet my Gerty's out of her head from worrying where I am! Well, I went out into the kitchen, and in my candied opinion, this fellow must of been waiting behind the door, thinking I'd never see him at all. But when I started to hang my apron up in the closet next to the door, my starting over that way must have made him nervous, I guess. I guess he wasn't taking any chances, so he up and got me. I remember thinking then," she added reminiscently, "if you'll forgive me being so outspoken, Mr. Witherall, I thought to myself that was the hell of a way to treat a lady!"

Leonidas agreed. "But who *was* he? Who was this fellow who hit you?"

"He didn't hit me. He flipped something around my throat from behind, like. First I knew, I felt something brush my throat, like. Next thing, I thought I was choking to death."

"Hm. A garrote," Leonidas said thoughtfully.

"I don't know what you call it, but it's a sneaky way to get hold of anybody! You never knew Mullet, did you?—no, course you never. He died before you even moved to Dalton. Well, all I got to say is Mullet was a great man with his fists, and I picked up a bit from him, and if this fellow'd only come at me like a man and tried to slug me, Mr. Witherall, I'd have given a good account of myself, let me tell you!"

"While I regret the thought of your being—er—slugged," Leonidas said sincerely, "I almost wish he had tried to—er—take a poke at you in a manly fashion. Tell me, Mrs. Mullet, who *was* this fellow?"

"Oh, I never *saw* him!" Mrs. Mullet said. "I never got a gander at him, as you might say. But I *know* him, all right!"

"I see." Leonidas couldn't keep his disappointment from echoing in his voice. "You merely mean that you would know him again, and not that you actually know him now. M'yes, I see."

"*I* mean I know him, right now, and I'd know him again, and I'd know him if I met him in a crowd, or just walking down the street. Or at night, even. I don't know how to explain it to you, Mr. Witherall, but after somebody's carried you down a flight of steps and tied you up and all, you get to know a lot about him!"

At least, Leonidas reflected as he impartially surveyed Mrs. Mullet's ample figure, at least you could conclude that the fellow was on the hefty side!

"He's strong," Mrs. Mullet said. "He's right in the pink. Never puffed, even—"

Leonidas suddenly thought of Foster Haverstraw. Foster was in the pink. Always. Foster ran around the livelong day with laden wheelbarrows, singing to show the world that he was in the pink and not the least bit winded.

"He hadn't any shoes on," Mrs. Mullet continued, "and he wore white socks. I must've gone out like a light, at first, but I was sort of coming to again by the time he carried me down here. Only I couldn't call out because my throat hurt so—and I don't think it'd have mattered much if I'd yelled, Mr. Wither-all. You wasn't in a listening frame of mind. Anyway, before he got through binding me up, I came to enough to think, like. I mean I could think in my mind, but I couldn't do anything about it. I was floating, like."

"M'yes. Semi-comatose," Leonidas said.

"You *do* put things lovely, Mr. Witherall!" Mrs. Mullet said. "Anyway, he didn't blindfold me too good. I could see his feet. His socks. He was wearing white woolen socks, hand-knit, with a cable stitch. I know that stitch. I taught it to Mrs. Haver-straw."

"Indeed!" Leonidas said. "Indeed!"

He remembered that Jay Finger had been wearing white socks, too. He had a very clear mental picture of that stockinged foot as it padded along on his graveled driveway.

"Er—those Fingers, Mrs. Mullet," he went on. "Er—did you—"

"Oh, them Fingers! They been in my hair all day, Mr. Witherall! You wouldn't believe it, the way they kept running over. Mrs. Haverstraw, she'd talk my ear off me and pump me with questions about you till I was fit to be tied, but all you had to say was like 'Uh-huh,' or 'Is that so!' and she done all the talking. This Mrs. Finger, *she* wants you should answer! And that little girl. That Cupcake—she's a holy terror! She uses bigger words than you do! Mr. Witherall," Mrs. Mullet said suddenly, "what's this all about, anyways?"

Leonidas told her frankly that he didn't know.

"But I'm sure it's been a most trying ordeal for you, Mrs. Mullet, and I cannot tell you how I regret its having taken place in my house. Er—did you go to sleep directly after you were left here?"

"I guess I must of, after a little while. You see, I went to a whist party last night, and then I had my imsomnia something terrible, and then those Fingers bothering me all day, and my work, and all the interruptions—I tell you, I was tired! But I'm fresh as a daisy now. Say, did they get the goldfish and the mussels and the butter? I was afraid you wouldn't understand."

"I didn't," Leonidas said, "but the Fingers got them—"

"Runner-overs, that's what *they* are!" Mrs. Mullet shook her head. "That's their kind. They won't be borrowing us out of house and home like the Haverstraws, but they'll be running in, running out, all the time! What was he after, Mr. Witherall, this fellow that tied me up?"

"Oh, I'm sure it was nothing of mine!" Leonidas said lightly. "He went through my desk, but I feel it was all a mistake on his part. I've come to the conclusion that he must have been in the wrong house. Now, Mrs. Mullet, if you are able to stand up, we—"

"In my candied opinion, he was certainly going *at* things pretty hard for somebody in the wrong house!" Mrs. Mullet interrupted. "*I* don't think he was in any wrong house at all! I think that fellow knew where he was, and what he was doing, and what he wanted! What did he *do* to your desk, anyway?"

"Oh, he just rifled it," Leonidas said with nonchalance. "Mussed it up a bit. Now, if you can stand, I'll assist you upstairs, and we'll summon a taxi and have you whisked home in no time. Er—on the house, of course. My treat."

"A *taxi?*"

"Certainly! You don't think I'd expect you to take the *bus,* Mrs. Mullet, after what *you've* been through?" Leonidas clucked his tongue. "Tch, tch, no! No, dear lady, you shall have a taxi! I'll call the police myself, later—no need of your exhausting yourself further by being exposed to their questions tonight. Besides, there is so very little for you to tell them. That can all be taken care of tomorrow. Now—ah, fine! You *can* stand up! Splendid! Capital! Now we'll get a taxi for you!"

"I don't want one," Mrs. Mullet said. "I don't *want* a taxi!"

"But," Leonidas felt a little dashed by the force of her protest, "but I thought that you were very fond of taxis!"

"Sure, I like 'em fine, but I'm not going home!"

"Er—not going?"

"This is the first time in my life I ever got mixed up," Mrs. Mullet told him firmly, "with adventure, and I'm going to find out what it's all about! Why, I remember thinking to myself as that fellow tied me up, why it was just like Haseltine! But I don't suppose you'd know anything about Haseltine, Mr. Witherall!"

"I do, but—"

"You do, honest? Oh, if you only wrote something like that, now, instead of that dry stuff—sure, I know you told me I wasn't never to look at the papers on your desk, but I did once, and I must say it was awful dry and stupid! All about words!"

"*Words?*" Leonidas frowned, and then he began to smile.

Mrs. Mullet must have happened on his old monograph on the Eleventh Century Vowel Shift, which he had unearthed from the attic to show Professor Skellings. "M'yes, it's hardly light reading!"

"Well, I suppose if that's what you write, it's what you write, and it can't be helped," Mrs. Mullet said. "But I don't want to go home, Mr. Witherall! I want to find out what that fellow was after, and what's going on!"

Leonidas looked at her thoughtfully for a moment as he swung his pince-nez. He had not only underestimated Maude Haverstraw, he decided. He had also woefully underestimated Mrs. Mullet.

"I'll be honest with you," he said at last. "I want to find out, too. In a small way, while being hampered to an incredible degree by fate, I am attempting to unravel the situation. Will you, therefore, take a taxi home, and—er—momentarily dismiss all this from your mind? I hasten to add that I owe you time and a half for overtime, plus a bonus for—er—heroic action over and beyond the call of ordinary duty."

"You're in trouble, aren't you?" Mrs. Mullet said shrewdly.

If he denied it, she would only argue the point. If he concurred, she would never go!

"Er—not at the moment, Mrs. Mullet. But I'm going to be, if I'm unable to unravel certain problems! Won't you take that taxi and go home?"

"You're in trouble, and you hadn't ought to be left alone!"

Leonidas sighed.

"Mrs. Mullet, come up to my study. I think I can show you something which will perhaps make you understand!"

As a Haseltine fan, she might do for Haseltine's creator what she obviously wasn't going to do for her boss, Leonidas thought as they mounted the cellar stairs. She would have to have it proved to her that he was Morgatroyd Jones.

On one hand, he rather hated to let her know, but on the other hand, he feared that abandonment to which the intoxication of the Haseltine mood sometimes led. Now that the spirit of adventure had apparently entered into her soul, there was no telling to what dizzy heights Mrs. Mullet might try to soar. As Leonidas Witherall, he might handle her with deference and with gloves, and get nowhere. But as Morgatroyd Jones, he could convince her that her highest duty lay in passive submission to facts. Morgatroyd, in short, could not only whisk her home in a taxi. Morgatroyd could keep her from talking.

He saw that she noticed the deep freeze, but he hurried her into the study before she had a chance to comment on its presence.

"Oh, look at that ink, all over the clean blotter!" she said unhappily. "And on the rug—glory be, it almost spoiled your book!"

Leonidas took the title page of Haseltine from the box of manuscript, and held it out to her.

"If you'd look at this, please?"

"Mr. Witherall!" Her face, when she looked up at him, was wreathed in smiles. "Why, Mr. With-erall! Mis-ter *With*-erall!"

"M'yes. Now that you know I am the author of Haseltine," Leonidas said, "will you believe me that I know what I'm saying when I tell you I have considerable unraveling to do? Will you go home, so that I may work out my problem? So that Sonia—er—I mean, Gerty, won't have to trudge here again, worrying her heart out about the whereabouts of her mother?"

He put so much feeling into his voice that the pert Sonia-Gerty took on the outward aspects of the poor little match girl plowing through snowdrifts without any shoes on her frozen feet.

"So Gerty's been here after me, has she? Well, well!" Mrs.

Mullet seemed pleased. "Gerty's a good girl, Mr. Witherall!"

"A charming girl," Leonidas said. "A credit—"

"Who was with her, Jimmy or Ed?"

"A large boy named Chuck. Now, Mrs. Mullet, will you—"

"Oh, that Chuck!" Mrs. Mullet said. "Is he home again? Gee, Mr. Witherall, if only *he'd* been here this afternoon, there wouldn't have been nothing left of that fellow but his white woolen socks! Chuck would've shown him, all right!"

"I'm sure Chuck would have," Leonidas said. "Now, truly, you can best help me by leaving—"

"Did Lady Alicia ever?"

"Er—I beg your pardon?" Leonidas said. "Did she ever what?"

"Leave Haseltine?"

"Often," Leonidas said promptly. "I know. Er—she has left him on my own little typewriter!"

"But never when he was in trouble, no, sir! Why, you can't tell what that fellow was after, Mr. Witherall, or if he might come back—you hadn't ought to be here all alone! You need someone like Lady Alicia to warn you, and help you, like. Like telling you about little noises, and hands at the window, and all. No, sir, the Lady Alicia don't run away just because there's a little trouble brewing!"

Leonidas drew a long breath. He had not anticipated that Mrs. Mullet might identify herself with the beautiful Lady Alicia!

"Mrs. Mullet, did you notice that deep freeze in the kitchen?"

"Yes, and I hear little sounds like—"

"Mrs. Mullet, in that deep freeze," he lowered his voice impressively, "is the body of a man who has been murdered and left here! He—"

Leonidas stopped.

He, also, heard little sounds.

Grabbing the fire tongs from the hearth, he rushed for the kitchen, with Mrs. Mullet pattering along behind him.

Again, the curtain was blowing at the casement window over the sink.

Again, the back door was wide open.

And through it was disappearing the end of the deep freeze.

VI

DURING the fraction of a split second it took him to reach the door, Leonidas' mind assumed the general aspect of a whirlpool.

In that infinitesimal space of time, he rejected his overpowering impulse to pause, put on his pince-nez, and stare blankly at this ghastly phenomenon of the retreating deep freeze. He knew there was no need for the pince-nez gesture. The emptiness of the kitchen floor proved that the freeze was not there, that it was therefore quite possible for it to be wending its way elsewhere.

He rejected his desire to scream out loudly that this couldn't be true, and that it couldn't be happening to him. He knew that it was.

He rejected his capricious yearning to sit down and work out on paper, even as he occasionally worked out series of motivations in Haseltine, the reasons anyone might have for removing that infernal freeze from his kitchen at this particular point. Reasons? He would willingly settle for just *one* reason, if anyone could pull it out of a tall silk hat without being trampled to death in the onrush of rabbits!

Finally, he rejected his wish to know who was responsible for this. More than he wanted to know, he wanted not to know. The possibilities were too appalling to contemplate.

As he reached the door at the end of the split second, he snapped on the switch of the light outside, over the back door.

Somehow he had vaguely expected to see the deep freeze disappearing in the distance, like an express train disappearing down a long strip of straight track in a moving picture.

Instead, it was sitting on its wheeled platform only a few yards beyond him, on his back walk.

Matt stood on one side of it.

Shorty stood on the other.

Both were grinning at him foolishly.

Leonidas leaned against the doorjamb, knowing that even if there had been no doorjamb handy, he probably would have leaned anyway until he crashed to the floor. Something was amiss with his sense of balance.

"Matt!" he said. "Shorty!"

He was mentally adding their glazed expressions to their foolish grins when Mrs. Mullet wedged her way into the doorway beside him.

"Tch, tch!" she clucked her tongue. "Higher than kites, *as* usual! What do you two think you're doing, I'd like to know?"

"Now, Annie!" Shorty said. "Now, Annie!"

"Matt," Leonidas said, "come here!"

With all the dignity of an admiral reviewing his fleet, Matt started toward him.

After two steps, he stopped, swayed slightly, and then inclined his head in a gracious nod.

"Chum," he said very distinctly, as if he were trying to bite the word in two, "chum, we hadn't ought to of done it to you!"

Moving with similar stiff-legged dignity, Shorty joined Matt.

"That's right!" he said. "That's right. Meant to come take it away earlier, din't we, Matt?"

"That's right," Matt said. "Taking it now, chum. Taking it right *now*."

They turned back to the platform and started to move the freeze down the walk.

Leonidas almost leapt in front of them.

"Now, boys," he said, "let's sit down and talk this over a bit, shall we?"

Matt shook his head.

"Nope," he said. "Hadn't ought to of left it, and we knew it, chum. Bothered us very much. We got to thinking of it after we left, chum. Didn't think it was right we should leave this on a nice guy like you with a beard like my old man—ain't it the truth, Annie, he's got a beard like my old man?"

Mrs. Mullet conceded the point as she planted herself in the path of the freeze.

"That he did, rest his soul, and now you take this thing back to Mr. Witherall's kitchen, d'you hear?"

"My old man," Matt's voice gained in volume, "was the finest old man a man ever had, see, and I'll lick the first guy says he wasn't!"

"Your father," Leonidas said, "was a fine man, a *fine* man! Now, wheel the freeze—"

"Hah!" Matt said with triumph. "You admit it! But look here, chum, *you* didn't know him!"

"Your father loved Mr. Witherall like his own brother!" Mrs. Mullet said. "Your father would want you boys to bring his freeze right back into his kitchen, too, Matt Shay!"

Matt shook his head. "My old man wouldn't want me to leave that where nobody wanted it. We ain't going to do it to him. Come on, Shorty!"

"It *might* be mine after all," Leonidas said quickly. "You never told me where you got it!"

"We got it off a guy on a beachwagon, and we told you so, chum. Guy gave us ten bucks. Told us to take it from there to Forty—"

"From *where* to Forty?" Leonidas interrupted.

"From the turnpike on the corner of Linden, that's where!"

"You mean," Leonidas said slowly, "right by Meredith's Academy, the boys' school?"

"That's the place, chum. Take it to Forty, he tells us, and writes it down·on a slip."

"Who was he, Matt?" Leonidas tried to sound casual. "Who was this guy?"

Matt shrugged so elaborately he nearly fell. "Who knows, chum? Been working on a flat tire. Face all dirty. Hands all dirty. Who knows who he was? Told us to take it to Forty. Hear that, Shorty?"

Both of them suddenly began to laugh uproariously.

"What's so funny about it you have to hang onto yourselves to stay on your feet?" Mrs. Mullet demanded.

"He meant *One*-forty, Annie, see?" Matt explained. "So now we're going to take it to *One*-forty."

"Oh, *no!*" Leonidas said. "Not *there!*"

"Oh, *yes!*" Matt returned. "*One*-forty! Been bothering us. Bothered us all night. Here's this guy with a beard like my old man, the best old man any man—"

"You told him that," Shorty said.

"Did I tell him we cried?"

"No. Tell him."

"Bothered us so, chum, we cried," Matt said with poignant simplicity. "All on account of we oughtn't've left it here. You didn't want it. Wrong house. Left it anyway. Now we're going to take it to One-forty, One-forty, One-forty—"

"But they don't *want* it at One-forty!" Leonidas had to raise his voice to make himself heard over Matt's happy crooning. "Bring it back to my kitchen. *I* want it! Bring it back!"

"Come on with you, Matt Shay!" Mrs. Mullet chimed in. "Bring it back to us, there's a good lad!"

Matt gave her a playful push that sent her reeling.

"Go 'way, Annie Mullet!" he said. "Go 'way! Maybe they don't want it at One-forty, but they're going to *get* it, they're going to *get* it, they're going to *get* it, and *you,* you nice old man with a beard, you won't have to keep it any *longer!*"

"Matt!" Leonidas said desperately. "Matt, fifty bucks to put it back in my kitchen! Fifty apiece!"

"Any friend of my old man's with a beard is a friend of mine, chum, and I wouldn't be taking a pinny off him! Won't cost you a pinny, chum! Not a pinny!"

"Penny," Shorty corrected him. "Penny. Not pinny."

"Not a pinny-penny. All for free!" Matt slapped Leonidas merrily on the back, then solicitously picked him up from the lawn, dusted him off, and straightened his tie. "The trouble with you, chum," he added confidentially, "you had a few too many, that's what! You go right to bed, chum. Nobody'll notice. Come on, Shorty. We got to get started. Out of the way, chum! Out of the way, Annie! Don't want to hurt you. Get hurt if you stay in the way. One-forty, One-forty, One-forty—"

"Any suggestions?" Leonidas inquired of Mrs. Mullet in a resigned voice as Matt and Shorty ranged themselves on either side of the wheeled platform. "Er—short of a lethal bolt from the blue, could they possibly be stopped, d'you think?"

She shook her head. "I know them two, Mr. Witherall. If they make up their minds, you can't do a thing. Not even Chuck could do a thing. Not even *two* Chucks could—"

"Let her *roll!*" Matt said.

They whooped in unison, and let her roll.

With the same brisk efficiency which had so impressed Leonidas when he saw them first, earlier in the afternoon, they rolled the deep freeze down his driveway.

As they had aimed it previously at his own back door, so they were now aiming it, with unbelievable precision, at the back door of One-forty. Leonidas couldn't imagine what might be guiding them. Doubtless the pair was endowed with second sight.

Feeling more helpless, more foiled, more thwarted, more

frustrated than he'd ever felt in all his life, he watched them trundle the deep freeze along the gravel of the outside garden path.

With unlimited time at his disposal and his typewriter in front of him, he could solve this, Leonidas thought bitterly. If Haseltine were ever caught in such an idiotic impasse, the gallant lieutenant would find a way out!

But the gallant lieutenant never had foist on him two amiably stubborn drunks whose strength was as the strength of ten. These were no villainous wretches who could be liquidated by a few bursts from a tommy gun. Haseltine, furthermore, went into action in broad open spaces, on sweeping prairies, eerie moors, golden-sanded beaches. Haseltine had elbowroom. Haseltine wasn't handicapped by the restrictions of smug, suburban Oak Hill, where any attempt at outflanking Matt and Shorty would create a row that would have every smug, suburban householder within earshot burning the telephone wires for the police.

Mrs. Mullet had been right. Two Chucks, even a dozen Chucks, couldn't stop them. Even if they could, the ensuing brawl would simply precipitate that evil moment when the Dalton police would lift up the freeze's heavy lid, and peer inside at the haddock fillets, the leg of lamb, and Ernest Finger.

Leonidas winced as Matt and Shorty rolled on unfalteringly through the gateway of his garden, and onto the moonlit grounds of One-forty.

" 'The Moving Finger,' " he said. "M'yes. 'The Moving Finger writes, and having writ, moves on. Nor all your piety nor wit can lure it back to cancel half a line, nor all your tears wash out a word of it.' M'yes. M'yes, indeed, how true!"

"My, my, that sounded fine!" Mrs. Mullet said appreciatively. "Poetry, wasn't it? Something *you* wrote, Mr. Witherall?"

"Er—no. A man named Omar Khayyám is responsible," Leonidas told her. "Although he didn't have that particular moving Finger in mind, he put it rather well."

"Whose?" Mrs. Mullet inquired.

"Er—whose what?"

"You said, back there in the study, there was a body in it. Whose? Anybody," she added off-handedly, "anybody *I* know's?"

"It's a man named Ernest Bostwick Finger." Leonidas was too depressed at the fateful exit of the deep freeze to feel or evince much surprise at her casual acceptance of the freeze's contents. "Fate is cruel, Mrs. Mullet. To think that now, at this late postzero hour, with all—er—with who knows what about to pop, I should learn that the deep freeze was picked up virtually on Meredith's front doorstep, that the driver of the beachwagon who palmed it off on Matt and Shorty was camouflaged with dirt and grease—ah, me, to coin a phrase!"

"Where are you going?" Mrs. Mullet inquired as Leonidas sighed, turned on his heel, and walked slowly back to the kitchen.

"Where? How empty," he remarked absently, "how strangely empty this room seems without that freeze! I was getting used to it, m'yes, I was beginning to look on that thing as my very own. Where am I going?" he swung his pince-nez thoughtfully. "I don't know, Mrs. Mullet, I really don't know. My inclination is to set out rapidly on a long, long journey."

"You're going to take a *trip?*"

"D'you realize," Leonidas spoke with the calm of utter despair, "what will happen within the next four or five minutes? Matt and Shorty will batter their way into One-forty with that freeze. Mrs. Finger, who asserted in my hearing that she wanted beyond all else to lay her hot little hands on a deep freeze, will take it. With gusto. Since she all but crawled into it while she was here, I think we may safely assume she'll have that lid up in something less than jig time. Then she will discover—er—that other Finger."

"One of hers?" Mrs. Mullet asked interestedly.

Leonidas shrugged. "I keep hoping not, but for all I know, it may be her other son whom the Haverstraws found out about. Mrs. Finger knows that freeze was over here. She knows—Mrs. Mullet, where did that tag come from?"

He pointed to an oblong of pale blue pasteboard on the ledge by the kitchen sink.

"Oh, that? I picked it up off the floor just now, before I went out on the step with you," she said. "It was right in the middle of the floor."

Leonidas subjected the tag to a close scrutiny even though he knew perfectly well that it was one of Meredith's official tags.

"Wonder if it was maybe underneath the freeze, huh?" Mrs. Mullet echoed his thoughts. "Maybe it was tied onto something, and fell off when Matt and Shorty moved the freeze out. Or stuck in it, or something."

"If that deep freeze came from Meredith's," Leonidas said slowly, "if that is one of our own deep freezes from the kitchens there, if—"

He stood for a moment and stared down at the tag in his hand.

"Why not?" he murmured at last. "M'yes, why not? Mrs. Mullet!" he turned to her and spoke with crisp decision. "Get your hat and coat, and run home. As if, to quote Haseltine, for your very life!"

"Why?"

"Why? I told you," Leonidas said with more than a trace of impatience, "what was going to happen! Mrs. Finger will find that body, summon the police—boom! You run along home before cordons of Dalton's finest begin to surround this house!"

"What are *you* going to do?"

"I," Leonidas said briskly, "am going to become a renegade, or hunted thing. Years from now you will doubtless hear of me, a tattered beachcomber on some Pacific isle, a bearded derelict squatting outside a sun-baked mud hut on the fringe of the Caribbean—do hurry up, Mrs. Mullet! Get out while the getting is good!"

She followed him into the hall and watched him remove from the closet his light topcoat, and his best black Homburg hat.

"Not going by car?" she asked, as he chose a silver-knobbed Malacca stick from the cane rack.

"No. I have neither the gasoline to go far nor tires good enough to go fast," Leonidas told her. "Besides, I fear that a car might prove a cumbersome burden in the sort of action which I foresee lies ahead. While a man can easily dart behind a tree, or shinny over a fence, a man with a car has no such simple—" he broke off. "Dear Mrs. Mullet, will you *please*—"

"So you're going to walk, are you?" she interrupted.

"Yes. Now, *will* you please—"

"Don't mind if I do," Mrs. Mullet said. "A nice walk'll be good for me after all that sitting. Just what I need."

Leonidas knew that she had deliberately chosen to misunderstand what he had been about to say, and that she had shrewdly calculated that he had no time to protest. He hadn't, either.

"Hurry!" he said briefly.

After all, if he was planning to dodge the Dalton police until such a time as he tracked down Finger's murderer, he certainly ought to be able to dodge Mrs. Mullet, once they were away from the house!

Two minutes later, she was marching along beside him as he hurried down the slope of Oak Hill. With her usually straggling hair tucked under a felt hat topped with a saucy feather that bobbled with every step she took, and a neat blue jacket replacing her customary apron, she looked very different from the untidy figure Leonidas was accustomed to seeing about his house. There was something almost jaunty about the way she swung her string bag, which contained her pocketbook, her rubbers, and the last of the summer squash from his garden.

Both of them automatically swerved for the shadow at the edge of the sidewalk as the sound of a police-car siren rang out through the clear autumn air.

"Didn't lose any time, did she?" Mrs. Mullet said conversationally.

"No. From my brief encounter with Mrs. Finger, I judged that she would not dally any. Mrs. Mullet, I've done my best to warn you that this expedition is definitely beyond the law. While I have experienced certain precarious moments before this evening, from now on, this is the—er—the—"

"McCoy?" she suggested.

"Exactly. I am now what Haseltine refers to as a hunted man, enmeshed—"

"In the toils of the law or something. I know. But with Lady Alicia standing by, he never comes to no real harm," Mrs. Mullet said. "Mr. Witherall, where did this fellow that got me with the cable-stitched socks kill this Finger? In your house, or somewheres else?"

"Whether or not he killed Finger," Leonidas said, "is a moot or debatable point. If that was a Meredith Academy deep freeze, as the presence of that tag might seem to indicate, I am inclined to think that the murder must have taken place at the Academy. After all, one would hardly kill a man in Pomfret, for example, and then laboriously transport his lifeless form all the way over to Meredith's Academy in Dalton—the mere transportation of lifeless forms is a perfectly frightful job anyway," he added parenthetically, "and one which troubles both Haseltine and myself. Sometimes we solve it by rolling a body in a rug, and delivering it to someone—which gives the consignee a horrid shock, and sometimes we walk the body between two men, pretending it's drunk—which shocks me. At all events, even if we ignore the practical difficulties of corpse disposal, why transport a body from somewhere else to Meredith's, and thrust it into one of the school's deep freezes?"

"Well, you can't never tell what some people will do," Mrs. Mullet said, "but as for me, *I* wouldn't go to all that work!"

"Nor would I. That," Leonidas said, "is what might be termed the body-in-motion angle. The other possibility is, of course, the freeze-in-motion angle."

"Like how?"

"Er—like—er—while the freeze was being moved from the school, the body was thrust into it. But I cannot think of any reason why anyone should have been transporting a Meredith deep freeze anywhere," Leonidas said. "Or why, if anyone were, he should pause, kill a man, put him in the freeze, and cause both to be delivered to me. The complexities of either of those angles are terrific. Providing, therefore, that the freeze belongs to the school, I think that he was killed at the school, put into the freeze at the school, and that the freeze was thereafter moved from the school."

"And even that," Mrs. Mullet said, "ain't exactly what you'd call *simple!*"

Leonidas concurred.

"Nothing to do with this," he went on, "has been simple. And even if anything has smacked of simplicity for two seconds, fate has at once turned me from the pursuit of it, and sent me reeling in two other directions. I am frankly beginning to feel very battered."

"Would it help any to tell me about it?" Mrs. Mullet asked sympathetically. "You know, Haseltine always finds the situation clear as sparkling crystal after he's summed it up for Lady Alicia—"

They both stopped for a moment as the police siren sounded beyond them on the next street.

"It's all right," Mrs. Mullet started up again. "They've gone past to the turnpike. Maybe I better walk on the outside, though, Mr. Witherall, and maybe you better turn up your coat collar so as to hide your beard. All right, now. Sum!"

Leonidas smiled. "At the police party I briefly attended tonight, Sergeant MacCobble asked me to sum up for him in a nutshell the problems of the postwar world. I had to tell him that I felt unable to comply with his request, and I feel almost equally unable to sum this up for you."

"Oh, sure you can! You could've summed up the postwar world for him in a nutshell, too, Mr. Witherall! Why, even *I* could!"

"Er—indeed?"

"Sure. It's *all* soy."

"Er—*soy?*"

"Soy beans. The minute they give them soy beans back to Henry Ford," Mrs. Mullet said seriously, "everything'll be *all* right again. Let him make his cars out of 'em if he wants to. Let him do just what he wants to with the things. Only give 'em *back* to him, so as I don't have to eat any more candy made of soy beans, and sausage made of soy beans, and wear stockings made of soy beans, and sit in old chairs made of soy beans! No, Mr. Witherall, I thought it all over, and in my candied opinion, the minute they stop fooling around with those soys, why the world'll go on all right again. Now, sum!"

Leonidas decided that he might as well try. They were, after

all, still a good mile from Meredith's, and if that police ca
picked him up before he got there, some practice in the re-
counting of his saga might prove very useful.

He began with the story of Matt and Shorty leaving the
freeze in his kitchen, despite his protests.

"Well," Mrs. Mullet commented, "if they told you that twice
about the guy in the beachwagon giving the freeze to 'em to
deliver to you, they were telling you the truth. Drunk or sober,
that pair's honest. I know."

"By the way, how *do* you happen to know them?" Leonidas
asked.

"They live next door to my sister's on Murphy Vista. Go on."

He told her all about Terry, Terry's letters to Finger, and
how he had discovered from her that Ernest Finger was Carlos
Santos.

"Well, I never!" Mrs. Mullet said. "Here I was thinking I'd
never heard the name Finger before today, and then it seemed
like everyone was named Finger! Well, well, so he's that crooning Santos, and the blonde girl's a suspect. I always *like* a blonde
suspect!"

"She might be one if I were writing her in Haseltine," Leonidas said, "but she is not, at least, a suspect in my opinion!"

"She's got a motive for killing him!"

Leonidas couldn't deny it.

He told her about the police party and how he had found
out from Anderson that Matt and Shorty were real, and about
the directors' banquet, and how he had met Sonia there.

"Sonia, my eye! Her name's Gerty, and none of that silly
Sonia nonsense!"

"Er—while Gerty was plying me with Mammoth Stuffed
Olives at the Minturn Club," Leonidas said, "I learned about
Bedford Scrim's relation to Honest John Scudder—"

"And didn't *I* try to tell you that myself?" she interrupted.

"I *said* you knew his uncle, but you just went gabbling on about him being born to hang, and hey nonny nonny, and such. And he's perfectly all *right,* Mr. Witherall!" she said earnestly. "Everyone in Dalton knows Honest John foxed the fellow, and framed him, and done him dirt!"

"Possibly, but the fact that he's John's nephew gives him some motive for exercising revenge on me," Leonidas said, "either on his own or his uncle's behalf. If his uncle forced Scrim to act as his secretary, his uncle may still have some hold over the fellow. Furthermore, he chased Terry and me. He pursued us!"

He told her about their dash to the bookstore, and how they had hidden among the biographies.

"M'yes, indeed, Mrs. Mullet, I find my mind keeps wandering to Bedford Scrim. Think how many times he came to the house today!"

Mrs. Mullet conceded the point. "Oh, how terrible," she said sadly, "I never noticed his socks!"

"I noticed his shoes," Leonidas said. "He had on two, and they were black, and Terry said the shoe she found was brown. Er—dear me, I quite forgot to tell you of that episode, didn't I? That occurred between the first invasion of the Haverstraws and the police party. Terry and I were hunting the brown shoe—"

"*What* brown shoe?"

Leonidas shook his head. "I warned you," he said, "that this summing up was nothing one undertook lightly. We will go back now to the desk-rifler, or your binder-upper, and the brown shoe Terry claims he left behind him."

He told her of his futile chase, and his interlude with Winston Abercrombie.

"Then there was the first Haverstraw invasion, and following that, Terry and I tried to find the shoe, which she'd dropped at the onset of the chase. While we were grubbing, Scrim came. He wore two shoes. Black. I—"

"Maybe he'd got another pair in his car!" Mrs. Mullet interrupted excitedly. "Maybe it was *he* lost the brown one, and then he come back and got it while you and Terry waited in the garden for the Haverstraws to go! And then he put on black ones to fool you!"

"Did you honestly ever know anyone," Leonidas returned, "who carried a spare pair of shoes with him—er—just in case he lost one of the pair he was wearing?"

"In *my* candied opinion, you can't never tell *what* people may do!" Mrs. Mullet said firmly. "There's no reason he couldn't have picked up that brown shoe after the Haverstraws went, and before you and Terry come back from waiting in the garden. Then he threw 'em both away, knowing someone could identify 'em, and put on his spare black ones! Count Casimir did something like that with neckties once in Haseltine!"

"I'm afraid, Mrs. Mullet," Leonidas said, "that you place too much faith in what transpires in Haseltine. Now, to continue. On my return from the Minturn Club, the Haverstraws invaded again. They'd also turned up at the police party, just before we left—did you know, by any chance, that Maude Haverstraw was a Carlos Santos fan?"

"Did I know! Oh, Mr. Witherall, with all you have to do these days, you don't know what goes on under your own nose! And if that doesn't give you two more suspects to work on!"

Leonidas stopped.

"Come now, Mrs. Mullet!" he said. "The Haverstraws can't be considered suspects!"

"In my candied opinion, they pursued you as much as Bedford Scrim, Mr. Witherall, and wasn't it Mrs. Haverstraw's own brother, that one with no chin that never amounted to

much, that you and your committee did out of a soft job when
you cleaned up the Water Works?"

"*What?*"

Leonidas found himself thinking suddenly of Maude's opening his front door, and her knowledge of when to give the knob
that little hitch.

"Sure, you never knew, but Mrs. Haverstraw had to give
him money so he could go to the west coast and get a new job,
and it burned her up! And isn't that a motive in there for getting back at you?"

"But—"

"Didn't Mrs. Haverstraw tell me once that Carlos Santos
meant more to her than anything in the *world?*" Mrs. Mullet
went on. "Didn't Mr. Haverstraw almost cry on my shoulder
one day when I was hanging out the sheets, and ask me what
I'd do if my daughter went chasing after a crooner, and screeching like a banshee every time he opened his mouth—Santos'
mouth, I mean. Not Mr. Haverstraw's."

"Possibly, but—"

"Didn't Mr. Haverstraw tell me he was getting to be a
desperate man about it all? And," she concluded with triumph, "wasn't it *me* taught Mrs. Haverstraw how to do that
cable stitch like the white socks, and she went and made Mr.
Haverstraw some because he loves knit socks, and she knew it
would please him so she could wangle the car out of him, so
then she could go see Santos?"

"I'm sure it's all true," Leonidas said as she paused for
breath, "but—"

"She could kill him from jealousy, like him not paying any
attention to an old—uh—well, to anyone like her. And Mr.
Haverstraw might've killed him because he got so desperate he
didn't know what else to do. There's your motives. And then—
that beachwagon!"

"Which beachwagon?"

"Don't the Haverstraws have that old beachwagon? And didn't Matt and Shorty say the guy gave them the deep freeze had a beachwagon? Oh, Mr. Witherall, for someone that can write Haseltine, you can be awful slow!"

"M'yes," Leonidas said as they approached the turnpike, "I'm afraid that my thought processes appear slow in comparison to Haseltine's. But remember that there is more. There's the Finger boy, and his one shoe. Remember we don't know what relationship may exist between Ernest Finger and these other Fingers!"

"Terry and the Haverstraws," Mrs. Mullet said, "Scrim and the Fingers. You got quite a few suspects, but when you boil it down, whoever bust in and tied me up is the murderer!"

"If he's also the desk rifler," Leonidas said, "that eliminates Terry."

"I never eliminate blondes," Mrs. Mullet said. "You can't tell about 'em. In my candied opinion, whoever tied me up is the murderer!"

Leonidas decided against attempting to discuss with her the fallacy of arguing post hoc, ergo propter hoc. After all, it hadn't moved Terry a whit. He tried another tack.

"Er—you said that you'd know the man, Mrs. Mullet. But you've seen the Finger boy, and Bedford Scrim, and Foster Haverstraw, and you didn't recogni—"

"But I seen them *before* I was tied up!" she interrupted. "Not after. I'll know which one it is when I see him again, don't you worry, Mr. Witherall! I'll know in my bones! No, sir, you can't get rid of me, because *I'm* the only person that really *saw* this man. Say, aren't those the school buildings around the corner? Isn't this Meredith's—"

This time it was a flock of sirens which split their eardrums.

Prudently, Leonidas drew Mrs. Mullet behind an oak tree as three prowl cars raced past on the turnpike.

"Busy as little bees, ain't they?" she commented as they stepped back to the sidewalk. "Well, we got as far as here without their finding us, and us in plain sight all the time. How you going to get in here, Mr. Witherall?"

"Professor Skellings," Leonidas said, "has an apartment in the main building. We'll just ring his bell. Up this path, here."

Although he could see a light in Skellings' study, no one answered his insistent peals on the old-fashioned hand bell.

"Huh!" Mrs. Mullet said ominously. "Something's amiss!"

"Er—I fear me, beauteous Lady Alicia," Leonidas returned, "that you err. Our friend Skellings is merely taking a bath, listening to his radio, and doing a crossword puzzle, all at the same time. We've lost him for hours that way."

"What you going to do? Where you going now?"

Leonidas drew his watch from his vest pocket.

"D'you see this gold key on the chain?" he asked. "I was presented with this once, in a ceremony so highly symbolic I rather missed its point. This key is engraved with a number of lofty sentiments in Greek, and it supposedly opens the main front door."

Somewhat to his surprise, it actually did.

Mrs. Mullet shivered as they crossed the threshold into the main corridor.

"Gloomy barn of a place!" she said. "Can't you put on a light?"

Leonidas found the switch, and snapped on the corridor lights.

"I think," he said, "that we'll not bother with Skellings. We'll go directly to the kitchens and see if a deep freeze is missing—hm. On the other hand, if he emerges from his tub and discovers that the lights are on, I suppose we'll only have the police on our necks that much sooner. M'yes, perhaps we'd best inform him of our presence, after all!"

But Skellings' little apartment was empty.

"Something," Mrs. Mullet's voice was dripping with what Haseltine customarily referred to as dire foreboding, "something is *amiss* on these premises! I don't care what *you* think, Mr. Witherall, but in my candied opinion, it's *amiss!*"

"To anyone as absent-minded as Skellings, anything is liable to happen."

Leonidas spoke with a lightness he didn't entirely feel. On the night before the school's reopening, Skellings ought to be there! Heaven knew the man had enough to do—and even if he'd managed to do it all, to attend to every last detail, he ought to be there in his apartment, preparing to sleep the sleep of the just and weary!

"Like," Mrs. Mullet demanded, "what? Like what would happen?"

"Oh," Leonidas waved his hand in a casual gesture, "oh, he's missed the last bus, or the last train from the city, or taken the wrong trolley. Er—suppose we just go on to the kitchens, and eliminate him from our thoughts."

Their footsteps echoed hollowly along the marble floors of the corridors, and somehow Mrs. Mullet's thudding heels gave Leonidas the impression that there was a small army stalking along, instead of just the two of them. He also found himself wishing a little irritably that she would not crane her neck as they passed by the door of each empty schoolroom, and peer in fearfully, as if she expected something with horns to pop out at her and say "Boo!" in a fiery breath.

"What a funny smell buildings like this always have," she remarked suddenly. "Wet mops, and people, and disinfectants, and old overshoes—what's *that?* What's all those?"

She stopped and pointed to a pile of packing cases and crates that reached to the ceiling and almost blocked up the west-wing corridor entrance.

"Navy matériel," Leonidas said, "which I was assured would be removed last week, without fail, and anyway today. Hm. I must write my good friend Coe-Chester, and ask him to have his old flotsam and jetsam speeded elsewhere!"

"Coe-Chester—he used to be the head of the navy school that was here, didn't he?" Mrs. Mullet said rapidly. "Wasn't he that admiral that used to play chess with you so much, and golf, and all?"

"M'yes, the one who looks like a freshly scrubbed bulldog," Leonidas said. "One night he informed me positively that he would surely and unquestionably continue in charge of the school for another year, and the next day he was ordered out to examine factories, which he knew nothing whatever about."

"What did he do then?"

The feeling grew on Leonidas that she didn't really care a fig about Coe-Chester, or what he did, and that she was merely talking in order to hear the reassuring sound of her own voice, rather as someone might whistle bravely in the dark.

"Oh, he examined," Leonidas said. "If Roderick Coe-Chester were ordered to mount a flagpole and stand on one ear, he would ascertain through the proper channels which specific ear was indicated, and carry out his orders to the letter until someone officially relieved him, or his ear fell off. He's now been sent to an unknown destination, but he telephoned me before he left and said that if I had a sola topee—er—a sun helmet, that is, perhaps I would come and see him some time. I gather—"

Leonidas broke off.

He, too, was gabbling on simply to hear the sound of his own voice.

It was absurd!

Utterly absurd!

Of course nothing had happened to Skellings!

He turned abruptly on his heel, and about-faced.

Then he stopped and turned back.

"Well," Mrs. Mullet said, "well, can't you make up your mind, Mr. Witherall? What do *you* think's become of your friend Skellings?"

"I'm sure that nothing," Leonidas began firmly, "nothing can have hap—oh, very well, Lady Alicia! Er—hist! Hist, I smell a mice, and something is direly amiss! We'll hunt for him, to the ends of the earth, if need be!"

They found Skellings half an hour later, in the very bowels of Meredith's main building.

He was locked in a small, closetlike cubicle that opened out of the boiler room, a spot Leonidas dimly recalled as the favorite cubbyhole of the school engineer back in the days when the Meredith heating system had required the constant services of an engineer.

He had been there, Skellings announced, since two o'clock that afternoon.

"Frankly, Leonidas," he said as he gratefully accepted a cigarette, "while I *don't* want to cast any aspersions on the character of our new French master, and while I yield to no one in my conviction that the fellow's had a sound, sterling background, and is academically capable in every way, I nevertheless—"

"Er—let us," Leonidas interrupted, "dispense with polite circumlocutions and get to the point, Harry. What, exactly, did Ernest Finger have to do with your being locked up in that miserable little chamber?"

"While I would not," Skellings said, "nor should I even care to try to prove that he was responsible for the act, I feel that the evidence, although admittedly circumstantial and of a flimsy nature, points—damn it, Leonidas, I don't understand that fellow! He came here quite early this morning, around nine, and he kept turning up in the oddest damned places!"

"Er—what d'you mean?"

"Why," Skellings said, "when I went up to the cupola—you know how we always check on that trap-door lock, so that the lads can't get up there and set the Founder's Bell ringing—why, there was Finger!"

"Up in the cupola?"

"Up in the cupola! Then I found him in the zoology stacks in the library annex, way in the back room! You know," he added, "there are always a few books we—er—keep out for the—er—more advanced students, and I was checking up on them. Not that facts, per se, are ever harmful, of course, but some of the younger lads might—"

"Harry, get on!" Leonidas said.

"Well, Leonidas, he simply turned up all *over* the place! Everywhere I went to check my list, there was that Finger! When I saw him disappearing down here—in rather a furtive fashion, I might add—I took the liberty of following him. Equally furtively. Not," Skellings said seriously, "not that I felt he was any—any Guy Fawkes, shall we say?"

"Harry, why should you feel he was a Guy Fawkes? What an odd comparison! Why," Leonidas said, *"why* in the world should you even remotely connect Finger with a gunpowder plot in your mind?"

"Why? Why, after all, Leonidas, there's been a great deal of bitter comment—arising solely from jealousy, of course—from individuals connected with other scholastic institutions which are still unable to open their doors because of continued service commitments, and—"

"Are you," Leonidas interrupted, "trying to insinuate that people assume that my friendship with Admiral Coe-Chester enabled me to wrangle Meredith's out of the clutches of the navy?"

"Why, certainly!" Skellings said. "It's the consensus, I should say. I know differently, of course, but some of the other school heads are very bitter about it—Halliday, for example. I wouldn't put it beyond Halliday to attempt sabotage. Halliday is entirely capable of subsidizing our French master, or anyone else, for that matter, for the purpose of causing injury to Meredith's. Therefore, when I saw Finger furtively creeping down here to the basement, I followed. Now, of course, whether or not there may have been other persons down here is a moot point. There may have been, or there may not have been. One cannot assume—"

"Will you," Leonidas sat down on a toolbox, "will you reduce this narrative to its very lowest terms, Harry? Did Finger lock you up, or didn't he?"

"Thinking I heard a noise in there," Skellings pointed to the cubicle, "I entered. At once the door was slammed behind me, and I heard the bolt shot home. As you may have noted, there are no windows, there are no pipes on which one might have banged for help, there are no implements with which one might have created a disturbance, or have attempted to force one's way out. So—"

"Wasn't you near crazy?" Mrs. Mullet demanded.

"No," Skellings said. "While the situation had its definite disadvantages—I hadn't my pipe, and the floor was rather hard—and while the thought of all my undone chores rather upset me, I knew that when Tony came to see to the boilers, I could make myself heard. Therefore I set tomorrow morning as the latest possible time of my release. Obviously there was no sense in my howling my head off for help unless I heard someone here. When I heard you, I made my presence known."

Leonidas stifled a smile at the thought of the dignified knocking by which Skellings had advised them of his whereabouts.

"Harry," he said suddenly, "what did you do in all that time?"

"Since the last few days have been rather a strain, and since I was quite tired," Skellings said, "I went to sleep."

"Er—did I remember to introduce you to Mrs. Mullet? How very remiss of me! Mrs. Mullet, this is Professor Skellings. You two have much in common, including a definite philosophic acceptance of fate. Harry, did you ask Finger what he was doing, what he was up to, why he was flitting from cupola to—er—post?"

"He said he was acclimating himself," Skellings returned. "Learning his way about the school. He was most evasive. I had at first a feeling that he was hunting something, but being unable to think what it could be, I then considered the possibility of sabotage."

"Mrs. Mullet," Leonidas said thoughtfully, "in your wanderings about my house, did you ever notice any bushel baskets of precious jewels? Er—rubies worth a king's ransom, for example, or emeralds as big as hens' eggs?"

"*What?* No! Of course not! What—"

"Harry, d'you know of any cache here at Meredith's where one might uncover a few Kohinoors, say, or some new formula for creating—er—soy beans from old carpets, or something equally revolutionary?"

"Why, no, Leonidas, what a bizarre idea!" Skellings said.

"I just thought I'd ask," Leonidas said. "Because the only conclusion I can possibly draw from Finger's scouring Meredith's from cupola to basement, and from someone else's prowling around my house and rifling my desk, is that there must, willy-nilly, be some object or objects of great value secreted somewhere, of which I personally have no knowledge. Now, let us withdraw to the kitchens!"

It was Skellings who stopped short in a passageway near the head of the basement stairs, and pointed in bewilderment to a blank strip of bare wall.

"Where's the deep freeze?" he demanded excitedly. "What happened to Freeze B? Leonidas, someone has moved Freeze B!"

"M'yes," Leonidas said. "So it was Freeze B!"

"I knew, I knew even though I explained everything to them very carefully, I knew those men would take the wrong things!" Skellings shook his head. "I tagged all our fixtures, but those men—"

"Er—what men?"

"Oh, navy men, and warehousemen, and moving men— they didn't arrive to remove things until this morning, Leonidas, and the place was a bedlam, a madhouse of people taking things out and putting things back. We were still moving the library, you know, and replacing the navy's bedding arrangements in the assembly hall with our chairs and settees. I must say in passing," Skellings sounded aggrieved, "that although I knew you were—er—with book, I did rather expect that you'd come and help! Freeze B," he concluded mournfully, "had *my* leg of lamb in it!"

"Er—whose haddock was it?" Leonidas inquired.

"Admiral Coe-Chester's. His own personal hoard. He presented it to me when he had to leave—oh, to think how I've saved points for that leg of lamb! Leonidas," he said suddenly, "if you know about the haddock—Leonidas, d'you know where Freeze B *is?*"

"Not at the moment," Leonidas told him. "I mean, I have an excellent idea of where it ought to be, but that freeze is captious, Harry. It gets about. And I truly regret to have to inform you that when I last saw Freeze B, Finger's murdered body was also among its contents. Now *don't* start asking me questions!

And under *no* circumstances ask me to sum the situation up in a nutshell for you!"

"But how—"

"If you absolutely must know all—I use the word 'all' very loosely," Leonidas said, "the Lady Alicia will oblige. Sum, Lady Alicia, while I survey the geographic possibilities here."

He went back to the head of the basement stairs, and then slowly returned to the passageway.

Finger, coming up from the basement, could without any difficulty have been set upon by someone lurking in the passageway. Had he himself been writing a similar scene in Haseltine, he would have located the stairs and the passage just the way they were. Had the original architect of Meredith's drafted a hundred thousand plans, he couldn't have devised a better passageway from which someone could suddenly jump on some unsuspecting victim coming up from the basement.

Of course, the murderer had had to face the problem of all those people milling around. To judge from Skellings' description, the place must have been teeming with incipient witnesses.

But with Freeze B sitting there so conveniently to hand, the murderer could have hidden the body in virtually the twinkling of an eye. He had only to lift the lid and put Finger inside.

Turning from the passageway, Leonidas started for the service entrance, perhaps a dozen feet away, and almost at once stumbled over something which went rolling away from him to hit against the wall with a resounding bang.

Leonidas snapped on the light, affixed his pince-nez, and stared down at a wheeled platform, a twin to the one Matt and Shorty had used.

Then he turned and called out to Skellings.

"Harry, what d'you call wheeled platforms? I've been trying all evening to remember the word."

"Dolly," Skellings informed him. "At least, the smaller ones, like all those the warehousemen left behind, are dollies. I've often run across them in crossword puzzles."

Leonidas walked on to the vestibule.

There were practically enough dollies stacked up out there, he thought, to remove all of Meredith's Academy, stick by stone.

"Harry!" he raised his voice. "Harry, was there a ramp laid on the back steps here?"

"*A* ramp?" Skellings said as he joined Leonidas. "There were ramps. Plural. There were boards laid down over the thresholds. There were duck walks outside. The place looked like a veritable anthill with all those men wheeling things in every direction!"

One more person wheeling one more thing, Leonidas thought, would be a drop in the bucket.

He returned to the passageway, walked through it to the adjoining pantry, and for several moments surveyed the walls, with their rows of bright copper pans.

Then he walked over and touched the knife rack.

"I suppose," he said to Skellings, who had followed him, "that you had no chance to check the kitchen things?"

"That's one task I completed," Skellings said with pride. "Mary, the housekeeper, and I checked the inventory lists early this morning. That's done."

"Er—these knives, here," Leonidas pointed to the rack. "D'you happen to remember if that rack was full?"

Skellings nodded. "I remember it in particular, because Mary had had the knives sent out and ground, and we checked them rather carefully to make sure all had been returned. Why— oh, I see! One is missing! Well, they were all there this morning! Leonidas, I can't make head nor tail of what Mrs. Mullet's been telling me—what happened? *How* did Finger ever get into that freeze, and up to your house?"

"It just happens," Leonidas said, "and I *do* mean it just happens, that I can tell you. After locking you up in the cubicle, Harry, Finger came up the basement stairs, and was promptly stabbed to death by someone standing in the passageway by Freeze B, someone who had previously taken a carving knife from this rack. He was at once popped into the freeze by the murderer, who then grabbed a dolly, whisked the freeze out the service entrance on the ramps so conveniently laid down, and loaded it on to his beachwagon—and that is that."

"What an incredible imagination you have, Leonidas!" Skellings said admiringly. "I assume, of course, that your answer is simply a fabrication of unbridled fancy."

"To me," Leonidas said with a twirl of his pince-nez, "it is simple fact."

"But Mrs. Mullet said something about two men named Matt and Shorty—"

"Ah, yes. The beachwagon was then driven to the corner of the turnpike and Linden Street, where the murderer thoughtfully smeared his face with grease in order to disguise himself—not a new twist at all," Leonidas said critically, "not very dazzlingly brilliant, on the whole, but apparently as effective in practice as Haseltine and I have found it on paper. Then he let the air out of a tire, and composed a sad story about having no spare. Then he hailed trucks, I suppose, until he happened on the pair named Matt and Shorty, who were only too happy to—er—pick up a couple of bucks by delivering Freeze B to my door. It is genius, Harry. Sheer genius. I'm frank to confess that Haseltine never thought of anything so exquisitely simple."

"So Finger was moved," a slow smile spread over Skellings' face, "—er—the moving—"

"M'yes, quite so. The moving Finger. Did he have a friend with him, Harry?"

"A friend? I'm afraid that I don't quite understand what—"

"If only he had been accompanied by a friend, to whom he introduced you," Leonidas said, "giving, of course, his right name and address, how spectacularly we could wind this up! What a Garrison finish! Mrs. Mullet," he added as she joined them in the pantry, "did you hear my explanation of how Finger got into the freeze?"

"I heard, and in my candied opinion," she said, "you're getting somewheres at last, Mr. Witherall. Like Gerty'd say, now you're cooking with gas. Mr. Witherall, what *do* you make of this, I wonder?"

"Please, Mrs. Mullet, *don't* let's go into that again! I summed for you once!"

"I don't mean this whole thing. I mean, if only your blonde was wearing one of these," she held something out toward him, "I'd say in my candied opinion the plot was beginning to thicken good!"

Leonidas whipped on his pince-nez.

She was holding out an orchid.

VII

It was a deep lavender orchid with a streak of royal purple.

Royal purple, like Terry's velvet wrap.

And Terry had worn three orchids, just exactly like this one, on her shoulder.

"Where," Leonidas demanded as he stared down at the flower, "did you find *that,* Mrs. Mullet?"

"Out there in the back hall, with them doilies, or dollies, or however you call them. It was just sitting there on top of one of 'em just as you go out the door. Now if your blonde girl was just wearing one—"

"She was. A corsage of them, to be exact."

"Aha!" Mrs. Mullet said. "Aha! Aha!"

"I never before realized," Leonidas said, "how very annoying that 'Aha-aha' habit of Lady Alicia's could be. She will have to be switched over to 'So!' or 'Indeed!' or even perhaps a refined 'Yeah?' "

"I like 'Aha!' " Mrs. Mullet returned. "You can put a lot *into* 'Aha!' And in my candied opinion, this orchid is something to 'Aha!' about! How'd it get here, Mr. Witherall, unless your blonde girl left it? Now, if *she* was here this afternoon—"

"I'm sure she couldn't have been!" Leonidas said with finality.

Then he remembered that of course Terry knew all about Finger's teaching at Meredith's. And what was it she had said when she'd told him of writing Finger that last threatening letter? Something about rushing to the head of Meredith's, and telling him that Finger was Santos. Of course, she had said that she wrote it. But suppose that she actually had come to the school and attempted to see the head? It wasn't impossible!

"But if she *was* here, and if she dropped this," Mrs. Mullet persisted, "then—"

"That orchid," Leonidas interrupted, "does not look as if it had been here since afternoon!"

"Oh, orchids last forever," Mrs. Mullet said. "That is, if you take care of 'em, and put 'em in the icebox at night. Gerty gets 'em from boys once in a while. She can make 'em look fine for weeks."

"Er—I'm sure she can," Leonidas said. "Still, I doubt if that particular orchid has been out there on top of a dolly very long. After all, Terry and I only became separated at the Minturn Club. Before then, she was with me. She was at my house even when Matt and Shorty brought the freeze the very first time!"

"Oh, these blondes!" Mrs. Mullet shook her head. "I don't know how it is they do it, but they just twist people around their little fingers! Now here's this orchid, and it's hers, and you know it's hers, Mr. Witherall, you know you do. And here you're almost choking to explain how it don't signify a single thing!"

"I am merely trying to point out," Leonidas said a little coldly, "that her corsage was apparently whole and complete when I saw her last. How she got here after we parted, or why she should come here, I cannot imagine!"

It occurred to him suddenly that perhaps Terry might have come to find him, and Mrs. Mullet promptly and uncannily echoed his thought.

"Bet she was hunting you!"

"But, Mrs. Mullet, how could she have got *in* here?" Leonidas demanded. "I'm sure *she* had no gold key on *her* watch chain!"

"Don't ask *me* how she could've got in! All *I* know," Mrs. Mullet said, "is what I *see,* and there's the orchid, and it's hers, and it's *here!* Maybe some door or other was left open."

"Oh, I think not!" Skellings said quickly. "Whether or not I was in evidence, the doors would have been locked. Mary is always very careful, and with new kitchen girls and strange cleaning women about, she'd have checked most conscientiously, I'm sure. Of course, Leonidas, there is *his* key."

"Er—whose key, Harry?"

"Finger's," Skellings said. "I gave him a master key last week. I don't suppose you noticed, Leonidas, if he had that key —er—on his person?"

"Aha!" Mrs. Mullet said. "Aha!"

"Because he had the key this morning," Skellings went on. "He used it when he came. If, however, the key is not now on his person, one might assume it had been taken by the murderer, who consequently has access to the school buildings. In fact, one might go so far as to say that perhaps suspicion might be attached to any outsider, to anyone not connected with the school, who now has access—" he broke off. "Do I hear some—"

"It's those police sireens," Mrs. Mullet said. "Well, well, it took 'em a long time to track us here!"

"But," Skellings turned anxiously to Leonidas, "they can't be after—"

"After me? M'yes," Leonidas said, "I'm sure they are. It was inevitable that someone would ultimately recall my connection with the school. You must stave them off, Harry."

"I? How?" Skellings asked helplessly.

"Be vague," Leonidas said. "Be—er—scholarly. Use the largest words you can think of. Use antidisestablishmentarianism, if you can think of a place to work it in. Say over and over again that you are at a loss to understand things. There's nothing more time consuming than being at a loss. If it's Sergeant Mac-Cobble," he paused as the front-door bell pealed, "discuss with him the problems of the postwar world. He finds them fraught with interest. In short, Harry, do anything but discuss me, or my being here. Good night! Come along, Mrs. Mullet!"

She picked up her string bag, Leonidas put on his Homburg and picked up his Malacca cane, and they departed by the service entrance.

"I suppose," Mrs. Mullet said, "that we circle, and backtrack, and all sorts of things like that, Mr. Witherall?"

Leonidas shook his head. "No Haseltining. I can frankly think of nothing more calculated to attract attention at this moment than the sight of you and me—er—backtracking. No, we're going to walk quite normally over to the turnpike, Mrs. Mullet, and hitch a ride."

"*Hitch?* On the *turn*pike? In plain *sight?*" Mrs. Mullet sounded profoundly shocked at such a suggestion. "But the *cops!*"

"We shall not attempt," Leonidas said, "to hitch a ride from them, I assure you. But it's necessary that I go to Pomfret, and while Pomfret is no great distance, it's a bit farther than I care to walk at the moment. Er—just how," he put his hand on her elbow and steered her down the driveway, "how does one go about the business of hitching a ride, Mrs. Mullet? I must confess that I have never—er—hitched before."

"You'll never have the chance to hitch now," she retorted acidly, "if you don't keep back in the shadows and out of sight, Mr. Witherall! Look here, we can't just *walk* past them two cars—look, *see* 'em?" she stopped and pointed to the prowl cars parked outside the school's front door. "See 'em, right there, right *ahead* of us?"

"M'yes, I see them," Leonidas said. "They're quite empty, too, if you'll notice. Under the circumstances, Mrs. Mullet, I feel we are not entirely justified in treating them like a couple of enemy pillboxes bristling with machine guns. Of course, if you really *wish* to wiggle past them on your stomach, you may. I, personally, intend to walk."

"This isn't *right!*" Mrs. Mullet said as they walked past the cars. "It isn't *right!* The cops ought to be chasing us, and we ought to be being chased, and—and—and all like that! Haseltine never just *walked* out of trouble like this, Mr. Witherall! Never!"

"He must try it some time," Leonidas remarked. "I frankly find it a most refreshing change. Now, let us cross the pike, and—er—hitch, if you'll be so kind as to tell me how one proceeds."

"I'll show you!"

Mrs. Mullet planted herself under the arc light across from the corner of Linden Street, where the police cars were still plainly visible.

As the headlights of a car appeared, she jumped out from the curb and waved her string bag violently at the speeding vehicle.

"Hi!" she yelled. "Hi—"

The sedan went sailing past them, and then it stopped and backed up with such urgent swiftness that Leonidas feared the driver intended to mow Mrs. Mullet down and grind her to bits under the rear wheels.

The front door burst open.

"Ma!"

"Gerty!" Mrs. Mullet said. "Well, well, *isn't* this nice! Get in, Mr. Witherall! Gerty, here's Mr. Witherall with me!"

"Hiya, Mr. Witherall—hey, Chuck, say hello to Mr. Witherall!"

"Hello," Chuck said.

"Er—how do you do?" Leonidas followed Mrs. Mullet into the back seat.

"Say hello to ma, Chuck!"

"Hello, Mrs. Mullet!"

"Well, well, Chuck!" Mrs. Mullet said. "How are you, Chuck? How are you, Gerty? You been all right?"

They were still discussing Chuck's health and how Gerty had been when the police cars left Linden Street and went screaming off up the turnpike toward Dalton Centre.

"Those cops!" Gerty said. "They're thick as flies tonight. All over the place—well, well, ma! How are you, anyway?"

"Fine," Mrs. Mullet said heartily. "I had a nice sleep today, Gerty. My imsomnia's pretty good today. They're after us, Gerty."

"Who?"

"The cops. Gerty, what do you think? Mr. Witherall's Haseltine! I mean, he's Morgatroyd Jones. He writes Haseltine!"

"No!" Gerty said delightedly. "No! Honest? Well, knock me down! You hear that, Chuck? Mr. Witherall's Haseltine."

"I knew," Chuck said.

"Oh, you never did!" Mrs. Mullet said. "Go on with you, Chuck! You didn't know! You *couldn't* know! Why, *I* didn't know, even, and there I been working in the same house with him!"

"I knew," Chuck returned.

"Er—how?" Leonidas asked.

"I knew," Chuck said, "when you look like Shakespeare. That's why I stared at you, see?"

"Indeed! And how did you—er—make the connection?" Leonidas inquired.

"General Carpenter," Chuck said. "He's inspecting one day, and he sees this Haseltine book in my stuff, and he stops and says 'Hah! Know the man writes that. Looks like Shakespeare! Hah!' Then he went and bawled me out I didn't have my shoes shined enough."

"Carpenter to the very breath!" Leonidas said. "M'yes, he's an old friend of mine. He was once police head in Dalton, you know. Life here was very different during the Carpenter regime, before he went back to the service."

"Was that when the cops was so polite?" Mrs. Mullet asked.

"M'yes. Carpenter wrote a little pamphlet," Leonidas smiled reminiscently, "which he compelled every man on the force to learn. It explained who paid them—er—d'you suppose we might get on to Pomfret?"

"Sure," Chuck said. "Why not?"

Five minutes later, after a ride which made his trip in the prowl car with MacCobble seem like a coast-to-coast trek behind a tired pair of oxen, Chuck drew up in Pomfret's main square.

"Seems funny driving regular, after a jeep," he remarked "Poking along. Where do you want to go, Shakespeare?"

"Er—to Ernest Finger's apartment. I don't know the address—"

"He means Carlos Santos', Chuck," Mrs. Mullet interposed, before Leonidas could add that a telephone book would doubtless supply the required information.

"Oh," Chuck said. "Sure."

He shot the car up a side street, turned, shot up another street, and stopped in front of a three-story apartment house.

"Here you are," he said.

"Look, ma!" Gerty said excitedly. "Look, ma! No lions!"

"Well, well," Mrs. Mullet looked out of the window. "So they went and took them lions away! Well, well! Looks a lot better!"

"Er—lions?" Leonidas felt a little bewildered. *"Lions?"*

"The stone lions out front," Mrs. Mullet explained. "They took 'em away. In my candied opinion, it's an improvement. More refined, like."

"Do I gather," Leonidas said slowly, "that you—er—that *you* are acquainted with—"

"With Santos? Why, I told you!" Mrs. Mullet said. "I told you, if only I'd known you meant Santos when you said Finger!

That's why Mrs. Haverstraw used to talk to me about him so much, Mr. Witherall—didn't you understand about that? I used to work for Santos. He was Tuesdays."

"Er—Tuesdays?"

"I went to him Tuesdays. So you see," Mrs. Mullet said, "I got a sort of personal interest in this anyway, as you might say. It isn't like he was a stranger we didn't know. We *know* him! Why, I've blacked his eye, Mr. Witherall! So's Gerty!"

Leonidas leaned back against the car seat, and drew a long breath.

"Why?" he asked at last.

"He tried to get fresh with Gerty," Mrs. Mullet said, "so I and she let him have it. Then I left, and gave you his Tuesdays. Say, Gerty, I forgot to tell you—somebody killed Santos today, and left him to Mr. Witherall's house. That's why the cops are after Mr. Witherall, see? Mr. Witherall's busy tracking down the villain right now, just like in Haseltine."

"Oh," Gerty said. "He's *tracking!* I see *now* why he couldn't tell me anything about you, if he's busy tracking. I get it! I wondered where you was, ma. I was worried."

"It so being that I'm the only one that's seen the murderer," Mrs. Mullet said with pride, "I'm helping him track."

"Ma, you really seen him?"

"I certainly did, and he's wearing white woolen socks with that pretty cable stitch—can she have the orchid to wear, Mr. Witherall, or is it too valuable a clue?"

"Orchid? Oh," Leonidas said as Mrs. Mullet held it out, "oh, yes. The orchid. I thought at first it was merely another spot floating before my eyes—er—in technicolor. M'yes, indeed, by all means give it to Gerty. Now, I wonder how we can get in!"

While he toyed with the notion of presenting the problem to

Chuck, Mrs. Mullet casually removed her pocketbook from her string bag, and drew from it a large bunch of keys.

"I forget which is his," she said as she gave the lot to Leonidas, "but you can run through and find it. Chuck, maybe you better stay in the car, so as to give us warning if the cops come, see?"

"Okay," Chuck said. "Faithful Frank."

"That's just what I was thinking!" Mrs. Mullet said. "You even *look* like Faithful Frank, Chuck, being so big and all! Well, let's get on!"

As Leonidas followed Mrs. Mullet and Gerty into the apartment-house foyer, he found that he was beginning to feel somewhat the way Terry had said she'd felt, back at the police party.

In two shakes there was going to be a loud bang, and he would be waking up on the gravel sidewalk over in Oak Hill, with Winston Abercrombie growling menacingly at him.

This was simply a case of slight concussion, that was all. He wasn't here, he wasn't in Pomfret, nonchalantly and with complete illegality setting out to enter the apartment of a man who'd been murdered and left in his kitchen in a deep freeze. He was merely lying there on the gravel with Winston. He had not picked up an entourage which included a marine who was identifying himself with Haseltine's Faithful Frank, a charlady who'd taken to thinking of herself as Haseltine's Lady Alicia, and a pert redhead in slacks and a sequined fascinator who thankfully was too busy admiring the orchid on her shoulder to select for herself any Haseltinean role.

"I guess you're awful busy thinking," Mrs. Mullet said. "Give 'em to me."

She took the keys from his hand, and after a few preliminary fumblings, opened a door to their right.

"There! I suppose," she added, "that you got your pocket microscope so you can get right to work?"

"Mrs. Mullet," Leonidas said as they entered the apartment and she switched on the lights, "I do feel that you should—"

He paused, wondering how best to make her understand that he, Leonidas Witherall, and Haseltine, the fictional lieutenant, bore not the slightest resemblance to each other. He would simply have to make it quite clear to her, he would have to drive it home once and for all, that the gallant lieutenant was only a paper thing, a creature built from words which mercifully managed to provide him with a certain amount of amusement as well as his bread and butter.

"The truth is," he looked at Mrs. Mullet and Gerty, both surveying him with glowing expectancy, and paused again. He almost couldn't bring himself to shatter their illusions.

"Or do you use special glasses?" Mrs. Mullet wanted to know.

"Er—I use my—er—special pince-nez," he said, and walked over to the Governor Winthrop desk in the corner of the living room.

The first thing on the desk top that met his eye was a typed list of names.

Good solid Meredith's Academy names, names of the boys whom Ernest Finger would have had in his classes tomorrow.

And beside each name was a careful annotation.

Leonidas picked up the list and studied it thoughtfully.

"M'yes," he murmured as he finally laid it down. "My suspicions that I mentioned to Terry were quite correct. Quite. Unquestionably, Ernest Finger *was* another Shurcliff!"

Mrs. Mullet and Gerty nodded knowingly at each other.

"Is that so?" Mrs. Mullet said interestedly. "What do you know about that! To think of me working for him all those months and never knowing he was a—well, well! I always say you can't tell what people'll turn out to be, can you? Uh—say, Mr. Witherall, just what *is* a shur—a what-do-you-call-it?"

But Leonidas was busy examining Finger's tooled-leather date book.

Under today's date, there were half a dozen brief items in Finger's cramped and strangely scholarly handwriting.

"Meredith's A.M.," Leonidas read. "Terry. Scrim. Haverstraws. Dinner—question mark? Dalton cops party, eight or nine."

"Aha!" Mrs. Mullet peeked over his shoulder at the page. "Terry—there's your blonde girl again!"

"There's also Scrim," Leonidas pointed out. "And the Haverstraws. Mrs. Mullet, did Finger, as Carlos Santos, know Maude Haverstraw? I mean, had they met? Did he actually know her?"

"He couldn't help knowing her, Mr. Witherall, with her almost living in his hair, as you might say! Sure, he knew her all right!"

"Mr. Witherall means did he know her *personal!*" Gerty said.

"Well, he didn't up to the time I left," Mrs. Mullet said. "Of course, she kept wanting me to snuggle her in here."

"Er—snuggle?"

"'Mrs. Mullet,' she used to say to me, 'if only you'd just snuggle me into his apartment!' But," Mrs. Mullet said practically, "what was the use? He'd only just have fired me for it, and it was easy work here. I must say for him, he was an easy man to do for. As quiet as you, Mr. Witherall, and nearly as booky. Only trouble I ever had was the time he got fresh with Gerty, and after that, I sort of wished I *had* snuggled Mrs. Haverstraw in on him for spite. It'd have served him right— what you going to do with that tin box?"

"This so-called strongbox," Leonidas said, "is not very strong, Mrs. Mullet. But because Finger took the trouble to lock it and to keep it hidden away in the bottom drawer, I have an irresistible urge to see if it doesn't contain letters. I wonder, now, if perhaps a can opener might not—"

"If a can opener don't fix it, an ice pick will," Mrs. Mullet interrupted. "You leave it to me. I'll attend to it."

"Thank you. Er—perhaps," Leonidas suggested, "you'd best wrap a cloth—"

"Oh, I know all about hiding fingerprints!" Mrs. Mullet assured him. "Come along to the kitchen and help me, Gerty."

After they departed, Leonidas experienced a distinct feeling of humiliation when he discovered that Terry's letters were not in the tin box, at all.

They were in plain sight on top of the desk near the Meredith lists, secured with an elastic band, and plainly marked with her name.

There was absolutely no reason for him to have missed seeing them the instant he entered the room, except that he had taken for granted the fact that such letters would probably be locked carefully away in a strongbox in some bottom drawer or other.

"Haseltine," he murmured to himself as the sound of hammering issued from the kitchen, "you're going to lose face, my lad!"

Slipping Terry's letters into his inside coat pocket, he rose and prepared to put an end to the destruction of the strongbox.

"In my candied opinion," Mrs. Mullet greeted him as he entered the kitchen, "you're right on the beam, Mr. Witherall! He's her brother-in-law!"

"Er—who," Leonidas demanded, "is *whose* brother-in-law?"

"Carlos Santos. Ernest Finger. He's Mrs. Finger's brother-in-law! It's all about it in her letters to him—how'd you *ever* know those letters'd be in this strongbox, Mr. Witherall?" Mrs. Mullet asked wonderingly. "How did you *know?*"

Leonidas sat down rather heavily on a kitchen stool, took off his pince-nez, and then quickly put them back on again.

"Oh, *ma!*" Gerty said reprovingly, "of course he'd know! Haseltine *always* knows! They're kind of exciting letters to read, Mr. Witherall. They're all about how she's sent him money even though he didn't exactly ask her for it, see?"

"Indeed!" Leonidas said. "Indeed!"

"Don't you want to read 'em yourself?"

"Er—no," Leonidas said. "Er—just tell me. I think that my eyes are a little tired. I keep seeing dogs. No matter," he added. "It's nothing serious. Just tell me about the letters, please."

"Well, she's sent him this money that he didn't exactly ask for but she sent him anyway, and she wishes he'd stop bothering her now her husband's away. They're all sort of alike. I mean, they say about the same thing. She sounds awful worried, and she sounds pretty sore with him, too. You got that one from Jay, ma? Read Mr. Witherall the end of that one."

Leonidas leaned back against the kitchen wall.

"Winston," he murmured, "see the cat. See the nice kitty, Winston!"

"What did you say?" Mrs. Mullet asked curiously.

"Er—nothing, Mrs. Mullet. I was merely—er—thinking aloud. Perhaps you'd read me the end that Gerty mentioned?"

Mrs. Mullet cleared her throat.

"It's not we meant to *pry* into these letters," she assured him a little anxiously. "We just couldn't help seeing what they said, though, on account of their not having envelopes. This one from Jay's the one you probably wanted, in my candied opinion. When I saw this last part, I said to myself *'Aha!'*"

"May I hear it?"

Mrs. Mullet cleared her throat again. "'If you don't stop taking advantage of father's position to scrounge money from mother, I'll use every legal means at my disposal—and they're plenty—to see that you don't bother anyone again.' *Threat,* see?"

"M'yes. Go on."

" 'You know,' " Mrs. Mullet continued, " 'that father is absent through no fault of his'—don't you think that sounds as if maybe he was in jail?"

"I shouldn't dare," Leonidas said, "to venture a guess. Er—please continue!"

" 'And you ought to know by now that he wouldn't care how much of a stink you raise anyway, even if mother does. So go ahead and raise it if you want to, but remember—I'll be around, from now on, to tackle you in person. Another letter to mother, and you'll find yourself in court. Another visit in person, and I'll break your neck instead of only your arm.' There!" she concluded. "Jay's already had *one* good fight with him, see, and broke his arm!"

"Aha!" Leonidas said. "M'yes, I think we might go so far as to place these letters in the 'Aha!' category. M'yes, indeed. For some reason, Mr. Finger is absent. During his absence, his brother almost—but not quite—blackmails Mrs. Finger. Apparently Jay is also away, and Mrs. Finger—er—falls, shall we say. Jay returns, uncovers the situation, and takes it firmly in hand. A vigorous young man, Jay Finger. Very definitely the bone-breaker type."

"He sure told Santos—I mean, Ernest Finger—where he got off at!" Gerty said.

"M'yes," Leonidas said, "in a not very thoughtful fashion. After all, if one has plenty of legal means at one's disposal, as Jay stated, one ordinarily utilizes them. One does not threaten to break necks. All of which leads me to wonder if Ernest Finger did not perhaps have something on his Dalton relations! M'yes, indeed!"

"Well," Mrs. Mullet said with satisfaction, "we got the Finger family all worked in and motived up. What do we do now?"

"Is there," Leonidas asked, "some rubbish-removal system in this building?"

"There's an incinerator out in the back hall."

"If you'd be so kind," Leonidas said, "as to put the strongbox in it, and return those kitchen implements to their rightful places, I will tuck these letters back in the bottom desk drawer for the police to find, and we will take our departure."

As they were about to leave, a few minutes later, Mrs. Mullet stopped by the hall door and dramatically pointed.

"Hist!" she said. "I mean, *look*, Mr. Witherall! Look!"

On the back of a tapestry-covered lounge chair, stabbed through the center with a purple-headed corsage pin, was another lavender orchid with a streak of royal purple!

"Well?" Mrs. Mullet said as Leonidas stared at it. "Well? Well, what do you think?"

Leonidas shook his head speechlessly.

"In my candied opinion," Mrs. Mullet said, "I'd say that blonde girl of yours sure gets around, don't she! What do we do with this one, give it to Gerty and pretend that it don't signify nothing either?"

Leonidas walked slowly over to the couch, and sat down.

"No," he said, "no, Mrs. Mullet, I rather think we will ponder this one."

"How in the world can she be getting all over the place, and into apartments and schools, and them all locked up, and—"

"Ma!" Gerty said sternly. "Ma, when Haseltine wants to ponder, he don't want the Lady Alicia nor anybody else asking him a lot of questions! You know that as well as I do!"

Leonidas hardly noticed them as they tiptoed with elaborate care into the kitchen.

First of all, he was thinking, those orchids were undeniably Terry's. That purple-headed pin clinched the fact. He remembered that pin. He'd noticed its unusual length, and the shape of the head.

Undeniably, Terry had been at Meredith's, and she had been here.

He could understand why she had come here. She had made no secret of her firm intention to retrieve the letters she'd written Ernest Finger.

But if she'd been here in the apartment, why hadn't she taken the letters? They were in plain sight!

That he had missed them at first, Leonidas thought, was entirely beside the point. He was interested primarily in the lists of the names of Meredith's pupils, and the notations on Finger's tooled-leather date book. To him, Terry's letters were secondary.

To Terry, however, they were of the utmost importance. They would have been uppermost in her mind.

The pince-nez swung violently.

Here was Terry. Here were her letters that she'd worried about for so long.

But she hadn't taken them.

Why?

"Idiot!" he said aloud. "She didn't take them because she couldn't take them! And she couldn't take them because she wasn't alone! Of course!"

He walked over to the lounge chair and stared down at the orchid.

There was something very poignant about that pin, stabbed through the bloom.

"Haseltine," Leonidas murmured, "sometimes I marvel that you were not cut off in early youth by the sheer force of your own crass stupidity!"

After all, he had only to put together simple facts, to indulge in a little simple arithmetic!

The orchid at Meredith's, for example, had been near the door.

And this orchid was near the door.

And Terry was not alone.

Terry was with someone. She was with someone to whom she couldn't explain about her letters. Someone in whose presence she didn't dare reach out and take those letters which had made her life so troubled.

But most important, she was with someone who was watching her every minute.

That, of course, was why she had left the orchids near the door! She hadn't any chance to leave them anywhere else. She didn't dare to let her companion know that she was leaving behind any trace, any clue to her presence!

"Uh—how you getting along?" Mrs. Mullet asked in a hushed voice from the kitchen doorway.

"I can visualize it," Leonidas said promptly. "She is at the school. She knows, she senses what Harry Skellings pointed out to us—that someone not connected with Meredith's who possesses a key may conceivably have taken that key from Finger's body. She thinks perhaps I will try to find her. She thinks perhaps in my search for Finger's murderer, I may come to the school. A little desperately, she tries to think what she can do to give me some inkling of the situation in case I should come there. The solution flashes to her mind. Quickly, she reaches up to her shoulder as she is led out the back door. She jerks an orchid from her corsage, and puts it on top of the dolly as she goes out."

"Gee!" Mrs. Mullet said. "Gee! It gives me a creepy feeling! What then?"

Leonidas shrugged. "I don't know what then, Mrs. Mullet. That's merely what I think happened over at the school. Now in the apartment here, Terry must really have been torn. How she wants those letters of hers, and she can't take them! And once again, her companion starts to lead her out. This time she's more desperate. This time she is positive I'll be here, because she knows I planned to come. In a stroke of what I can only call imaginative genius, she indicates her frame of mind by stabbing the orchid—come over here, Mrs. Mullet. Stand here."

"Here?"

"M'yes. I want to see if I'm right. Now," he reached out for the handle of the hall door, "I'm opening the door, and you're Terry, standing there. M'yes, exactly! While I'm busy with the door, you're facing me, but behind your back, you're busy stabbing the orchid into the back of that chair. I do not notice. To me, you're merely leaning back. I snap out the light—m'yes, that's it!"

"It sounds swell," Mrs. Mullet seemed deeply impressed. "Say," she added suddenly, "say, Mr. Witherall, who *are* you, anyways? I mean, who're you pretending you are?"

Leonidas smiled.

"I'm glad you asked that," he said. "I was just working up to the answer in my mind. Er—I rather think, Mrs. Mullet, that I am being Bedford Scrim."

"Scrim?" Mrs. Mullet said. *"Scrim?"*

"M'yes, I'm rather sure of it. M'yes—"

"But, Mr. Witherall, Bedford Scrim's no villain! I keep telling you, Scrim's all right! I know people that work at the mills and know him, and they *know* he's all right! He isn't a bit like his uncle. He's not like Honest John! Just because he sounds like a villain to you—"

"M'yes, Scrim," Leonidas almost appeared not to hear her protests, "m'yes, it works out so well! It fits so beautifully!"

"I'd like," Mrs. Mullet said, "to know how! Or even what. What fits so fine?"

"I lost Terry in Dalton Square," Leonidas said, "not very

long after Scrim had been pursuing us in the vicinity. Since Dalton Square is the logical destination for anyone cutting through Crowninshield's alley, I think we may assume that Scrim went there. M'yes, it's both possible and highly probable."

"So what?" Mrs. Mullet said. "What's his maybe going to Dalton Square got to do with your blonde girl's leaving orchids all over the place?"

"Perhaps Terry knew I'd gone to the Minturn Club," Leonidas seemed to be talking to himself. "Perhaps. It's possible. But I'm inclined to think I was dragged away so quickly by those muscular Wemberley bankers that for all the girl knew, I simply vanished into a puff of smoke and became a—er—a wisp of carbon monoxide in the square's traffic."

"The way you put things!" Gerty said admiringly. "Hear that, ma?"

"I hear all right, but what's it all got to do with Bedford Scrim?"

"Let us assume," Leonidas said, "that Terry is standing there in the square, definitely bewildered by my disappearance, and Scrim approaches. Scrim asks for me. Terry says blankly that she has lost me. Now she is in rather a trying position, because —owing to circumstances into which I shall not delve at the moment—she cannot exactly say that I am me."

"I don't get it!" Gerty said.

"The fact is not important," Leonidas assured her, "except in so far as it doubtless caused Terry a certain amount of embarrassment, which probably consequently caused her to acquiesce hurriedly when Scrim suggested that he would assist her in locating me."

"Is what you mean," Mrs. Mullet asked, "that you think she was *trapped* by Scrim?"

"No," Leonidas swung his pince-nez, "no. I should say, rather, that she accepted the spider's invitation without in the least realizing that she was the fly. I rather wonder," he added thoughtfully, "if Scrim quite realized that he was being the spider! I wonder if perhaps he wasn't merely trying to find me by way of Terry, and that once having taken up with her, so to speak, he became too suspicious of her to let her go!"

"Look, Mr. Witherall," Mrs. Mullet said patiently, "you'd ought to make up your mind! If it's Bedford Scrim that's the villain, though in my candied opinion he's as nice a fellow as they say, then what would he get suspicious of this blonde girl of yours for? You mean, he'd get to thinking *she* was the villain, which in my candied opinion it looks more like, even though every time she's got in somewhere I don't see how she could of got in, you keep saying she was *led!*"

"No," Leonidas said as she paused for breath, "I mean that Scrim began to suspect that Terry suspected him of being the villain. It's very possible. Just a minute or two before I lost her, she confessed herself very apprehensive of Scrim and his pursuing us. M'yes, he suspected that she suspected, and so he daren't let her go. And having myself had some slight experience with Terry in her limpet mood, I wonder if, once she became really suspicious, she'd let him *let* her go!"

He expected that his statement would bring forth a torrent of confused mutterings from Mrs. Mullet, but she accepted it in her stride.

"I get it," she said. "That's like when the Lady Alicia wouldn't leave Count Casimir even though she knew he'd blown up the airport, and was planning to blow up New York City. She loathed his very presence, but she wanted to stick to him so as Haseltine could find her and maybe foil Casimir, and all. I get it now! You mean, she left them orchids like a *trail!*"

"M'yes, in a sense."

"Why didn't she drop a note?" Gerty inquired. "Lady Alicia always does."

"If one is with a person," Leonidas said, "with whom one has a certain sense of being a hostage, shall we say, and of whom one is very definitely suspicious, one does not obviously and overtly leave billets-doux behind one." He looked at Gerty's face. "Er—Terry could hardly ask Scrim to excuse her for a few moments on the grounds that she wished to write an informative note to leave behind for me."

"But Alicia always does!"

"Regretfully," Leonidas said, "I never thought to deck Lady Alicia with an orchid corsage—although I'm almost sure I've used the adjective orchidaceous in describing her charms. It's an omission I shall certainly take steps to remedy. At some later date, Lady Alicia will most assuredly drip a trail of orchids, a veritable stream of the costly blooms, for the gallant lieutenant to pounce upon and 'Aha!' over. Now, Gerty, pick up your new orchid, and let's get on!"

Mrs. Mullet was strangely silent as they left the apartment.

"There's only one thing," she said hesitatingly as she paused at the foyer door, "only one thing—"

"Er—yes?"

"Well, I hate to say it, Mr. Witherall, but it's—well, it's all sort of made *up,* isn't it? I mean, there isn't real clues. Not that I don't mean," she added quickly, "that it isn't like Haseltine, Mr. Witherall! It's an awful lot like Haseltine. I mean, there isn't—well, *cop* clues. It's—well, it's like the papers. That's it, like the papers!"

"What papers, Mrs. Mullet? I'm afraid," Leonidas said, "that I don't quite understand."

"Oh, you know. Like when somebody says that an unconfirmed rumor from somebody that won't let 'em use his name says our armies'll without any doubt land in such and such a place on such and such a day," Mrs. Mullet said, "and the war'll unquestionably end on the sixteenth of this month at seven and a half minutes past ten. Like all those sort of things they keep cooking up out of nothing at all."

Leonidas smiled.

"Er—I see your point," he said. "M'yes, indeed. My—er—ratiocinations *do* have that—what shall we term it?—that touch of the paragraph troopers of the chair-borne command. M'yes, they do indeed!"

"Boiled down, Mr. Witherall," Mrs. Mullet said, "just how you going to prove any of this to the cops and especially about Bedford Scrim?"

Leonidas waved his Malacca cane in a casual gesture.

"That we have found out this much, that we have proceeded thus far without police interference, Mrs. Mullet, should be considered a good omen. No geese have honked menacingly, no thunder has sounded upon our left. Let us ignore the fact that some of our premises are—er—what did Skellings call them?—fabrications of unbridled fancy. Let us ignore certain obvious gaps. Let us look on the cheerful side. Let us—"

"Let's us remember," Mrs. Mullet interrupted a little acidly, "that you ain't got any proof of *noth*ing, Mr. Witherall!"

"In my heart," Leonidas returned, "I always knew that Bedford Scrim had to be a villain! 'Bedford Scrim was born to be hanged, Bedford Scrim is a crook!' M'yes, I feel like setting that little ditty to music, Mrs. Mullet, and caroling it—"

"Mr. Witherall," Gerty said. "Mr. Witherall!"

Leonidas ignored her tug at his sleeve.

"To the good citizens of Pomfret. I bask in a glow of undiluted optimism. I feel that between here and the car, we'll stumble on a patch of four-leaf clovers, a brace of horseshoes, a packet of bright pins with the heads turned toward us!" he opened the foyer door. "Come along, and let us—"

He stopped short.

The car had gone!

"That's what I was trying to tell you just now," Gerty said. "Chuck's gone! The car's gone! I looked, but I don't see any sight of it anywheres, either!"

"Four-leaf clovers!" Mrs. Mullet said succinctly. "Horseshoes! Pins, yet!"

"So Faithful Frank," Leonidas observed, "has failed us! So Faithful Frank has gone and let us down at—"

The rest of his words were drowned out by the wail of police sirens.

"My, my! In what sounds like our veritable hour of need," Leonidas went on as the sirens briefly paused, "Faithful Frank has—er—flew the coop! Alas!"

"They're black-and-white! They're Dalton cars!" Gerty said excitedly. "They're coming here!"

"And it's a dead end! You can't walk out of this!" Mrs. Mullet added gloomily.

"Lady Alicia," Leonidas said rapidly, "they cannot bother you and Gerty. You're safe—"

"Where you *going?*"

"Perhaps some day we'll meet again! Farewell!"

He darted to the alley next to the apartment house and disappeared down it as the Dalton police cars came to a stop at the front door.

Five seconds later, he was flat on his back after being subjected to a display of jujitsu such as Haseltine had never dreamed of.

VIII

TEN seconds later, Leonidas was being borne away like an old sack of meal on the shoulder of his unknown assailant.

A minute later, he was being roughly and unceremoniously dumped into the rear seat of a car.

"Now, let's see!" A flashlight beam was played on his face. "Gee! *Gee!*"

"Chuck!" Leonidas said weakly. "Chuck! Faithful Frank! *You?*"

"Gee, Mr. Witherall, honest, I thought you was him!" Chuck sounded miserably unhappy. "I thought you was him! Twice he'd snuk out of that alley and come back, and so of course I thought you was him coming back again! He had on a coat like yours, and a hat like yours, and he was just about your height! Gee, are you hurt?"

"I suppose it is logical to assume," Leonidas said as he slowly picked himself up from the floor of the car, "that sensation will ultimately return to my right arm. As to my shoulders, legs, neck, and left arm, I feel that the issue is in doubt."

"Gee!" Chuck's remorse deepened. "I hurt the tissue, huh? Bad?"

"Whatever harm you may have done to either the tissue or the issue," Leonidas said, "has been compensated for by your rapid removal of my person from those—er—premises. Chuck, what man were you jumping? Who was the object of your attack? What's been going on?"

"Well, a little while after you three went into Santos' apartment," Chuck said, "this beachwagon drove up slow, and turned around, and then went away. I wouldn't have given it a thought, but gee—gee, what a blonde was in that beach-wagon!"

"A blonde? In a beachwagon? Chuck, describe her!" Leonidas said. "What was she wearing?"

"Well—uh—Gerty's a nice kid, Mr. Witherall. She's my girl, and we're practically engaged, I think. But this blonde in this beachwagon, she was a slick trick! She was the slickest trick I ever seen except when Myrna Nestle come to camp to give her show. She had on an evening dress, and gee, her hair!"

"Who was with her?"

"I didn't get a look at first at the guy's face that was driving," Chuck said. "I hadn't no time for him. I wouldn't of thought about him or the beachwagon again, I guess, only a little while after it went away, it come back again, see? And then again it turns and goes away. The first time I just thought somebody'd got on to that dead-end street by mistake, see, but the second time I begun to think it was kind of funny. Suspicious, like. Gee, her hair! Gee, that blonde's hair!"

"M'yes, quite so," Leonidas said. "Quite so! Er—then what?"

"Well, then the beachwagon comes back for the third time! This time it parks down the street behind where I am, and this guy gets out and walks up to the Mildred—that's the name of them apartments where Santos lives—and goes in. I'm look-ing," Chuck said, "in the rear-view mirror to see if I can't get a glimpse of the blonde, and I can't, so I open the car door and stick my head out and look. Right away this guy comes out of the Mildred quick, like a fox. He's spotted me looking around, see, and he's all hot and nervous."

"And what," Leonidas tried to speak calmly, "what did he look like, Chuck?"

"He'd got on a black hat like yours with a high crown and a wide brim," Chuck said, and Leonidas remembered that Bedford Scrim had not been wearing a hat. "And a kind of light topcoat like yours. And a dark suit. At least, his pants was dark."

Bedford Scrim had been coatless. Bedford Scrim had worn gray flannels.

"Er—glasses?" Leonidas inquired hopefully. "Rimless glasses, or didn't you notice?"

"He didn't wear any glasses at all. He's sort of—well, he moved quick. I don't know how to say it to you," Chuck said a little helplessly. "He sort of bounced, like. He was like the guys I used to play football with on the Dalton Demons. Quick. Oh, and he took his hat off once. He's got black hair—"

Laboriously, under the patient prod of Leonidas' questions, Chuck ultimately brought forth a reasonably accurate description of someone who was very certainly not Bedford Scrim.

To Leonidas' way of thinking, the man sounded a lot more like the vigorous Jay Finger!

He drew a long breath.

"I see!" he said. "M'yes, in a small way, I see. Now, after he noticed that you were peering curiously back at his beachwagon, what did he do?"

Quick like a fox he had gone back to it, Chuck told him, and driven away like frantic. It was that time, Chuck further announced, that he had personally got hep to what was buzzing.

"While he's slamming the beachwagon around to make a quick turn to beat it out of there, I look and see his rear license plate's all muddied up, so as you can't see the numbers. Suspicious, see? So I get me an idea. I decide I'll drive over here to this street, and park, and then sneak back through the alley and watch to see if he'll come back again, and what he'll do if I'm not parked out front there getting him all hot and nervous. So I do, and he does. He comes back."

"And re-entered the foyer of the apartment?" Leonidas asked.

"He starts to, and then he spots the lights up in Santos' apartment, where you are," Chuck said, "so he comes down to the alley and looks up, sort of craning his neck. I thought once while I was watching that he was going to try climbing up to the window—he don't see me, see, because I'm behind some barrels."

"You seem," Leonidas said suddenly, "to know this place very well, Chuck."

"Oh, sure. Sure! Tuesdays and Saturdays was always my dates with Gerty, see? And on Tuesdays, I always used to come here and take Mrs. Mullet home. That was when I worked to the mills, and there was gas, and all," Chuck explained. "First I'd pick up Gerty from where she used to work to the Five-and-Dime, and then we'd come over here and pick up Mrs. Mullet. Tuesdays was stew," he added in nostalgic tones.

"Er—stew?"

"Mrs. Mullet always made me a nice beef stew for coming and getting her," Chuck said. "Gee, those was the days! I like what I'm doing now fine, out in the open and all like that, but I sure miss the gang at the mills and Tuesdays and stews and all."

"The mills," Leonidas said. "M'yes, the mills. Er—perhaps you know Bedford Scrim?"

"Do I know Bedford Scrim? We're pals!"

"Indeed!"

"Now there is a guy with a heart of gold!" Chuck said heartily. "Give you the shirt off his back, Bedford Scrim would. He's got brains, too. Only he don't let 'em bother him. If he sees me on the street, he says 'Hiya, Chuck!' just like when he worked in the loading room with me when he first got out of college. It don't matter to him he's general manager! No, sir, he's tops, Scrim is. Always doing things for people, too, just like his uncle. I always bet Bedford'd be mayor some day."

"Indeed!" Leonidas said.

"I tell you—"

While Chuck launched into an enthusiastic encomium on the virtues of Bedford Scrim, that dandy and democratic guy, Leonidas leaned back against the seat of the sedan and thought with irony of his four-leaf clover and horseshoe prophecy.

Chuck would without any question have recognized his old pal, Bedford Scrim, whether he wore flannels, a dark suit, or a bathing suit.

The man in the beachwagon *must* have been Jay Finger!

"Tell me," Leonidas said as Chuck paused for breath, "what was Jay—er—this bouncing fellow doing in the alley? Merely peering?"

"He was watching Santos' windows. Like a hawk," Chuck said. "I wonder to myself what he's up to, and finally I think, whyn't I go over and ask him? Casual, you know. Like, 'What you think you're doing here, bud?' or something like that."

"If you put such a question to me in that—er—casual tone, I should immediately take off from the ground like a helicopter," Leonidas said. "What was this fellow's reaction?"

"I never got the chance to ask him," Chuck said. "I start over to him, and I step on a board, and it cracks, and he jumps like he's been shot, and beats it. Right away he comes back like he was ashamed of himself for being so hot and nervous. Then somebody opens a window in the next apartment house, and he jumps out of the alley once again. I think to myself I'll put a stop to it, see, and grab him the next time. And I'm right there waiting for him, all set for him, only it's you that comes and not him—gee, Mr. Witherall, listen to 'em!"

He broke off and listened interestedly to the wailing police sirens on the next street.

"Having vainly scoured the vicinity for the miscreant," Leonidas murmured, "the police departed, at a loss to explain their failure. They confidently expect, however, to apprehend their prey in the near future. M'yes. Now I wonder—"

"Think they was after you, huh?"

"I see no reason," Leonidas said, "to think otherwise. Had they come for the purpose of thoroughly investigating Finger's —Santos'—apartment, they hardly could have completed their task in so short a time. Now I wonder, Chuck, how they might have suspected that I was there! After all, Dalton's finest are not psychic!"

"Well, anyways, they've gone," Chuck said as the wailings faded off into the night.

"M'yes. Suppose, Chuck, that we drive around and locate Mrs. Mullet and Gerty," Leonidas suggested. "They couldn't have gone far."

Chuck gave it as his opinion that they'd be waiting for the Dalton bus at the square, but a brisk tour of Pomfret's main square and the neighboring streets produced no trace of the pair.

"Gee, do you suppose the cops picked 'em up?" Chuck asked anxiously.

"I doubt it. I can conceive of no reason for their being taken into custody," Leonidas said, "even on one of those trumped-up charges of loitering, of which the Dalton police are so desperately fond. That might possibly have occurred over in Dalton, in their own district, had they found Gerty and her mother in suspicious proximity to where they found the freeze. But certainly not here in Pomfret! No, I think Mrs. Mullet waved her string bag at some driver, who obliged. Chuck, did you see the blonde girl again, after you moved your car?"

"Nope. I guess she was just waiting there in the beachwagon for the guy. I didn't even see the beachwagon again."

"Probably the fellow took a leaf out of your book," Leonidas said, "and parked out of sight. M'yes, he must have slipped out of the alley while Mrs. Mullet was discussing my—er—fabrications in the foyer. Probably the arrival of the police sent him packing."

"Gee, that hair!" Chuck said with a lusty sigh. "Gee! Say, you won't tell Gerty I said that blonde was a slick trick, will you? Gerty's awful jealous."

Leonidas assured him gravely that he would not bring up the topic.

"Gerty's awful quick on the trigger," Chuck went on. "She's like her ma. Either of 'em would as soon black a guy's eye as not."

"I trust you are not insinuating," Leonidas said, "that that pert snippet of a child has—er—blacked one of yours?"

"Both," Chuck said with pride. "She's a great girl. Where to now, Mr. Witherall?"

"How much gasoline d'you have?" Leonidas asked promptly.

"Not much. Maybe a couple gallons. Maybe three."

Leonidas thought for a moment.

There was, after all, little use in driving aimlessly around trying to locate that beachwagon.

And while he, personally, had no desire to return to Oak Hill, Oak Hill nevertheless would seem to be Jay Finger's logical ultimate destination.

If Jay and the beachwagon and Terry could be picked up anywhere, Oak Hill was the place.

"Oak Hill," Leonidas said aloud. "I—wait, Chuck. I don't wish you to drive there as though you were bearing the good news from Ghent to Aix. For me to be picked up at this point for speeding would be altogether too much of an anticlimax. Nor do I wish you to drive directly to my house. Take the back road up the hill, the road by the golf club. Park there, and we'll proceed on foot."

"We?" Chuck said. "We? You mean I can go along with

you and not just stay in the car keeping a sharp lookout like Faithful Frank?"

"Er—yes."

Even Haseltine, Leonidas reflected, had moments when the personal safety of Faithful Frank meant less to him than the comforting feeling that Faithful Frank's brawny form was at his side!

As Chuck drove toward Dalton at what he probably supposed was a funereal pace, Leonidas sat back and pictured the scene that would be now taking place over at Oak Hill.

Once before he had seen the Dalton police at the scene of a murder, and he had a very clear idea of what to expect.

There would be cars everywhere, an ambulance or two, and the mobile emergency unit that had been the pride of his friend Carpenter's life. Everybody on the force would be there, so would the reporters from the Dalton *Times*. All three of them. There would be photographers—professionals for the police and the press, and amateurs from all over the hill. There would be a state cop or two, slightly truculent and superior, lurking in the background.

The place would be a beehive of activity. The aroused citizenry would be milling around, burning with curiosity, but still apprehensive and resentful that such a thing should occur in their midst.

At this very minute, Leonidas thought with a smile, Stacey Abercrombie was probably sitting down at his desk in his dressing gown, starting a letter to the *Times* to demand why, in a neighborhood like Oak Hill, a respectable householder couldn't manage to get a little sleep. Stacey was always writing letters demanding to know why, in a neighborhood like Oak Hill, a respectable householder couldn't manage to achieve some simple end or other. It was Stacey's firm conviction that the rights of the individual, in this day and age, were slowly but surely being strangled—as he put it—as if by an octopus, and he invariably ended his plaintive epistles by insinuating that the whole situation was unquestionably some sinister outgrowth of the rising tide of bureaucracy, resulting from those fellows down there in Washington.

"Here you are!" Chuck said as he drew up by the golf club's sixth hole. "Okay?"

As they walked over toward Birch Hill Road, Leonidas found himself listening expectantly for the blare of the car radios which the police would surely have left on.

"Gee, it's awful quiet!" Chuck said. "Isn't it quiet, Mr. Witherall?"

Leonidas was forced to agree.

On Maple Street, near the scene of his encounter with Winston Abercrombie, Leonidas stopped.

"Chuck," he said, "something is definitely—er—amiss! We ought to hear some sound of all that from here! Suppose that you walk past my house, survey the situation carefully, and then report back here to me."

Five minutes later Chuck returned, and shook his head sadly.

"Gee, Mr. Witherall, *I* don't know how to describe it to you!"

"You mean the people and the police, and all the to-do?"

"Gee, no!"

"Er—what *do* you mean?" Leonidas inquired. "What's the matter?"

"Well, gee, Mr. Witherall, to tell you the truth, nobody's there!"

"Nobody's there? Oh, come, come, Chuck! Certainly even if people are not actually milling around, the neighborhood is aroused, the houses lighted—isn't One-forty, next to my house, a feverish center of activity?"

"Gee, the whole street's black as pitch and just as quiet as right here. You go see for yourself, Mr. Witherall, if it isn't true!"

Leonidas marched to Birch Hill and saw for himself it was gospel truth.

No lights showed at any windows, no police cars littered the street. Nobody milled anywhere.

Incredibly, everything was as quiet and peaceful as when he'd left!

Leonidas stood in the shadow of his lilac bushes and stared unbelievingly over at One-forty.

"Things pretty amiss, huh?" Chuck asked sympathetically.

"It's not possible," Leonidas said slowly, "that they—but of course Freeze B went sailing in that back door! Of course Matt and Shorty put it in there! Of course Mrs. Finger opened it! Of course—Chuck, we've got to get into that kitchen of One-forty and see if that freeze is there!"

"Okay," Chuck said simply. "How?"

"You go to that back door, Faithful Frank," Leonidas said grimly, "put your finger on the bell, and keep ringing till some-one comes. They'll have to put a light on. All I want you to do is to see if there's a deep freeze inside that kitchen!"

"What'll I say to who comes?"

"Ask politely if it's One-forty *Elm* Hill Road. Ask anything. Just go find out!"

Chuck's steps dragged when he returned some quarter of an hour later.

"I guess I'm not very good as Faithful Frank," he said. "I rung till I near bust my finger off, but I can't rouse nobody. And the bell rings all right. I could hear it chiming. I don't think there's nobody home."

"Chuck," Leonidas said, "Chuck, d'you see that elm tree by the side of One-forty? Can you climb that?"

"Could a duck swim?"

"Very well, Faithful Frank, listen! This is what you are going to do!"

Chuck listened, grinned, nodded, and within five minutes he was letting Leonidas in the front door of One-forty.

"Easy as pie," he said. "Duck soup. Window was unlocked, and nobody's home. Easy as—"

Leonidas blinked as the hall lights of One-forty suddenly snapped on.

In the first second of glare, he saw only the crates. Then, as his eyes became accustomed to the light, he saw barrels. Then boxes, tea chests, stacks of pictures, rolled-up rugs, piles of dishes, and seven floor lamps without any shades.

Then he saw Mrs. Finger, standing in the doorway of the living room, with a very businesslike-looking revolver in her hand.

"Lady!" Chuck said, "lay that down! That might be loaded!"

"It is," she said briefly, and turned to Leonidas. "Did you put him up to ringing the back-door bell just now, Shakespeare?"

"Er—yes." Leonidas saw no reason to deny it.

Mrs. Finger at once put the revolver down on a stack of books.

"Why *didn't* you come to the front door yourself?" she demanded. "Why *did* you have to frighten me to death, sending someone in uniform that looked like a cop to my back door? *Why* take years off my life pretending to be *bur*glars? And where *have* you been?"

"Er—to your brother-in-law's apartment," Leonidas told her.

"Oh, then you know about that angle! Look here, Bill Shakespeare, I won't have it! You can *not* do this to us! You've got to take that—that deep freeze back! We are *not* going to be arrested and involved with this thing! You take it back! It's yours! I recognized it, and I *know* it's yours!"

She hadn't called the police, Leonidas told himself as he gingerly edged over to a tea chest and sat down on it. She knew, and she had not called the police. She recognized the deep freeze, and didn't accuse him of being Ernest Finger's murderer!

"And right away!" Mrs. Finger added firmly. "At *once!*"

"Regretfully," Leonidas said, "I am unable to conjure up a set of circumstances in my mind which could convince me that such a move was justifiable. In short, Mrs. Finger, he's your brother-in-law. He was only—er—my French teacher-to-be."

"It's not my husband's fault," Mrs. Finger said, "that his father married a parlor maid in his dotage, and adopted her child! For the last thirty years my husband has put up with Ernest, and although I know this is the bitter end, it's just *too* bitter! You take him *back!*"

"But—"

"Let's be honest," Mrs. Finger said. "I don't for a moment think that you killed him, and neither Jay nor I did, either! If you won't take that freeze back, won't you at least join forces? I mean, if we can find out *who* did it, that would at least be *some* help! At least Jay and I wouldn't be dragged off to jail!"

With great care, Leonidas put on his pince-nez, and found that the barrels and the crates and the packing boxes still seemed to swim slightly before his eyes.

Then, out of the floating clutter, he found himself staring at a pair of white woolen socks, definitely knit with a cable stitch, that hung over the hall bannisters.

"Mrs. Finger," he said, "—er—will you answer some questions for me?"

"Answer questions?" Mrs. Finger returned. "To solve this hideous mess, I'd push a peanut with my nose across the Grand Canyon! You didn't run across Jay at Ernest's apartment, did you? He's out solving."

"Indeed!"

"He thought the very first thing to do was to go to Ernest's apartment—you see, there's just a chance Ernest may have kept some letters Jay and I wrote him," Mrs. Finger said, "and the police would never understand those letters. Never!"

"Ernest kept them," Leonidas said. "They're in the bottom drawer of his Governor Winthrop desk. Was he—er—blackmailing you?"

"If only he had!" Mrs. Finger said. "If only he actually had! But he didn't. He skirted the fringe, if you know what I mean. I—oh, I don't know how much you know about Ernest, or how much you may have found out, but I know what he's done to us, and I'm perfectly willing to come right out and say that in one sense, this hideous business is a relief!"

"Just what," Leonidas said, "d'you mean? If he didn't blackmail you—"

"In many ways, Ernest was brilliant, Shakespeare. He had great gifts. He was scholarly. But he just simply wasn't honest. On the other hand, he didn't have the nerve to be good and dishonest, if you see my point. He'd love to have been a Raffles, or a Robin Hood, but he didn't have the nerve, or the courage. A psychologist explained it all to Ted—my husband. Ernest had all these talents without the drive to use them decently. But he didn't have whatever it took to use them in a wholeheartedly bad fashion, either. What it's really meant," Mrs. Finger said, "is that Ted and I have spent years getting Ernest out of petty, nasty, *little* messes. Things that couldn't just be glossed over and ignored, and things that weren't big enough for him to be labeled a crook."

It sounded, Leonidas thought, rather like the sort of thing Terry had tried to tell him about Ernest Finger.

"Er—Ted Finger," he said. "Theodore Finger. Is he the—"

"Oh, yes, he's in politics," Mrs. Finger said. "He's that one. That's the trouble. Now that he's in the army—"

"He's Old Gore-face," Cupcake's voice floated down from the second-floor landing, where she had apparently been listening with interest. "He's the general who took all those islands. Old Gore-face."

"Darling, please! We can't help what the papers call daddy! Actually, Shakespeare, Ted's very sweet, and in civilian life he just quietly manufactures bedsprings. This Gore-face business followed him out of the last war—he thought he'd lived it down."

"Er—I see," Leonidas said. "Now—"

"Ted wants awfully to be governor, or senator, or something," Mrs. Finger went on, "and with his being a hero and all, it seemed so easy!" She paused. "You see, it's because of Ted's ambitions that I sent Ernest money last year. He didn't exactly ask me for it, he just wrote me a lot of pitiful letters after Ted left, telling me all the terrible things his draft board said he had the matter with him. I wanted Ernest out of the way. I didn't want him popping up during all that Gore-face publicity, and saying he was Ted's brother, and bringing up his own somewhat sullied record. That sort of thing has always haunted me. Ted pretends it doesn't bother him, but it really does. I suppose I shouldn't have been so soft about Ernest, or written him. But with Jay overseas, and Jimmy missing in action at that time, I was slightly frantic."

"Jimmy's my other brother," Cupcake called down from the landing. "He got back walking through two jungles. He's a pilot. He—"

"Darling, mother's dis*tract*ed!" Mrs. Finger said. "I know you won't stay in bed even if I tie you in, but please *do* be still! Where was I?"

"You were being frantic," Leonidas said, "with every reason, I should say. Tell me, why was Jay wandering around my house earlier tonight?"

"He wanted to see your niece," Mrs. Finger said. "That blonde simply hit him in the face like a ton of bricks. Frankly, she's one of the most beautiful creatures I ever saw!"

"A blonde!" Chuck spoke for the first time since Mrs. Finger had surprised them in the hall. "Gee!"

"Chuck, I forgot all about you!" Leonidas said contritely. "Do move a few crates and sit down."

"If he can move that packing case, I'll give him a vote of thanks," Mrs. Finger said. "Yes, Jay was going to trump up some excuse to call on you again, but your house was dark, and you didin't seem to be there."

"Er—why," Leonidas played with his pince-nez, "why did he—er—wear only one shoe?"

"Oh, dear, did he forget again? I hope you won't mention it. It's his new leg, you know. He keeps forgetting his shoe, and we try not to call it to his attention. He walks with all his old bounce. You know," she added hesitatingly, "today is his birthday."

"Indeed?"

"He's been so despondent after coming home and finding his girl had married a Four-F. That's why I decided so suddenly to move to another state. I might add," Mrs. Finger said grimly, "that I had no idea that Pomfret was *any*where near Dalton till we drove through it yesterday. I'd almost forgotten about Ernest, I was so busy worrying about Jay. I did hope that a good shake-up like moving might take his mind off himself."

Gazing impartially around him, Leonidas saw her point. The cluttered mess at One-forty was enough to take anyone's mind off anything.

"Cupcake and I'd moved about a bit following Ted around," Mrs. Finger continued. "We felt that while we were reasonably hardened to the process, it might really *do* something for Jay."

"But it—er—didn't?" Leonidas felt sure he could guess what such a state of confusion would do for him, personally.

She shook her head.

"He was completely gloomy. Utterly morose. I—well, this sounds idiotic, Shakespeare, but I'm telling it to you for a reason. Both Jay and Ted have always gone around saying, when anyone asked them what they wanted for their birthday, that—"

Leonidas knew suddenly what was coming, and he felt the corners of his mouth begin to turn up into a smile.

"That all they wanted," Mrs. Finger went on, "was a beautiful blonde with violet eyes. It's been a family joke for years. So when Jay looked so sad, even with moving, I yielded to a sudden impulse, and called up the first model agency I found in the phone book this afternoon, and asked for a blonde. I explained to the girl who answered all about Jay's service, and his leg, and his birthday, and his girl marrying the Four-F, and all."

"Did you," Leonidas said, "by any chance use the phrase 'a matter of life and death'?"

"Perhaps. Probably. I don't really remember. I'd have said the house was on fire if I'd felt the fact was likely to be useful in getting Jay something that would make him laugh, and snap him out of that ghastly mood he was in. Anyway, the girl finally agreed to take on the job of being a birthday present, and I sent some money around by messenger, being far too busy to go myself, and I had orchids sent the girl, too. I thought I might as well do the job up brown. Well," Mrs. Finger said, "the long and short of it is, when I saw that blonde in your kitchen, with the orchids on, I thought there'd been some mistake, and *she* was Jay's present. That's why I gabbled so, and stalled. I wanted to find out about that blonde!"

"M'yes," Leonidas said, "I see. You were not, as I thought, vitally interested in the contents of Freeze B."

"I didn't care a snap of my fingers—" she stopped. "I didn't care a whit, Shakespeare. I only wanted to know who the girl was, and you simply wouldn't introduce her, or give me any hint. If only your niece had worn a lavender ribbon bow, as I specified in my order—"

"You'll find it," Leonidas interrupted, "over in my breadbox. And I'm very happy to have that part of this affair satisfactorily explained, for Terry's sake. Now, will you listen, please, while I recount my—er—saga?"

It seemed to him, as he rapidly summed up his adventures, that the oftener he told them, the simpler they seemed. Some of the fuzz was disappearing. Outlines were beginning to show. Things, to his pleasure, began to make some sense.

But when he finished, Chuck was looking at him in a frightened way, and Cupcake was sitting in front of him with her mouth wide open and her eyes half-popping out of her head.

"Between us," Mrs. Finger said thoughtfully, "we have not just lived through a day apiece. We could write one of those big fat novels and call it 'Our Eons.' Oh, I must tell you—between what you refer to as their invasions, those awful Haverstraws called on me. Killing time, as they truthfully said. I don't know how they go about the job of moving, but my clutter seemed to bother them dreadfully. They poked into everything and asked a million questions—you know, just a short visit from the Haverstraws ought to count as a full day."

"But," Leonidas said feelingly, "how true!"

"They saw a typewriter in the bathtub, and they decided," Mrs. Finger said with a grin, "that I was a writer."

"Er—are you?"

She shook her head. "I don't even know where the typewriter came from. I don't think it's ours, even. I think the movers just left it as a token of their esteem, or something. No, I'm no writer, but after today, I'm going to try to write something like a Haseltine story—would you know Haseltine, I wonder?"

Before Chuck could say what was on his lips, Cupcake opened her mouth.

"'*Has*-el-tine!'" she bellowed out. "'HAS-EL-TINE to the RES-cue!' Like on the radio."

"Shush, darling! Have you any more questions to ask me, Bill? I hope," Mrs. Finger added, "that you don't mind my calling you Bill. I frankly feel that in a sense, we've been through a lot together. Bill, you didn't kill him, and Jay didn't, and I didn't, and I'm sure Terry didn't. And the Haverstraws *couldn't* have. That would simply be too ridiculous. In books, it's always the person you never contemplated—what about Mrs. Mullet, I wonder? Or her daughter?"

"Hey!" Chuck said. "Hey!"

"Be fair, Chuck," Leonidas said. "After all, they once had a fight with Santos! And, as you yourself said, they're both quick on the trigger. Not that I think for one moment that either of them is guilty," Chuck relaxed visibly, "but one must consider all possibilities. No, Mrs. Finger, we come back to Bedford Scrim."

"Hey!" Chuck said again. "It wasn't Bedford in that beachwagon over in Pomfret! I guess I'd of known if it'd have been him!"

"It was Scrim whom you first saw in the beachwagon," Leonidas said, "with the blonde. Rather, it was Bedford Scrim whom you didn't see, because you had eyes only for her. Both times."

"But I *did* see him! I mean, I seen the driver!" Chuck protested. "In the alley, and—"

"M'yes, you saw the driver of beachwagon number two," Leonidas told him. "What you thought of as the third trip of beachwagon number one was, in reality, a different beachwagon altogether. That was Jay Finger in his first trip in beachwagon number two. I—er—trust that I make myself clear?"

"You mean there was two beachwagons," Chuck said. "Sure, I get it. But how do you know?"

"I guessed," Leonidas said simply. "If you recall, you didn't see the girl in the beachwagon that parked behind you. That was because it was another car, and she wasn't in it. That was Jay—"

"I wish I knew where Jay *was!*" Mrs. Finger interrupted. "What a lot of people we've lost by the wayside, haven't we? Terry, and the Mullets, and Jay—probably Jay's run out of gas—"

They stiffened as something crashed in the kitchen.

"All right, mother, only me!" Jay called out. "Just tumblers. Not the Lowestoft or anything!"

They sat and listened to the thuds and clatters as he apparently with great difficulty picked his way through the litter from the kitchen to the front hall.

"What a road block you could have set up, mother, without half trying! This damned mess—" Jay stopped as he saw Leonidas and Chuck. "Oh."

"That's him!" Chuck said excitedly. "That's the one I seen, Mr. Witherall! *That's* him!"

"Friend," Jay inquired, "or foe?"

"Allies, darling," his mother said. "It's all right. I mean, nobody's discovered Ernest yet, like the police. And Bill Shakespeare here's found out an incredible amount, and had the strangest things happen to him. Did you get our letters? Bill says they're in the bottom drawer of Ernest's desk."

"First," Jay said, "there were people around. Then it turned out I couldn't pick locks. Then I ran out of gas."

"It was only Bill and his friends, darling!" Mrs. Finger said. "You shouldn't have been so surreptitious!"

"But damn it, mother, you don't seem to realize how serious this all is!"

"Don't I, darling!" Mrs. Finger returned. "Don't I, just! And the blonde—"

"Say!" Jay turned suddenly to Leonidas. "Your niece—"

"Have you seen her?" Leonidas asked quickly.

"Yes. It was the most amazing thing! I went into a diner over in Pomfret to phone you, mother, and ask for advice and instructions—that was when I finally realized I'd never in a million years ever pick that apartment-door lock. I tried the window, but I couldn't make that. Remind me to practice getting into windows, mother. I'm sure there's just a trick to it. Anyway, she was there at the counter with a man—"

"Wait!" Leonidas said. "Did he wear—"

"Let me!" Chuck said, and proceeded to give his own description of Bedford Scrim. "There, now! Did the man look like that?"

"If he were your brother," Jay said, "you couldn't have described him better. Right down to the Navy E in his lapel."

"Honest?"

"Honest."

"Gee!" Chuck said. "Gee! Gee whiz! I guess you was right, Mr. Witherall! That's him! Say, the blonde girl was all right, wasn't she?"

"Never looked better, I'd say," Jay told him. "Well, of course, Shakespeare, I started to speak to her, and she just looked at me as if she'd never seen me before in her life. Absolutely dead-pan. Cut me dead. Well, then I phoned you, mother—"

"But you didn't, darling! I mean, the phone never rang!"

"It seems we're out of order, or not connected, or something," Jay said. "I left the phone and went to the counter and had a cup of coffee. In a few minutes, she and the man left and— this is the amazing part! As she went by me, she dropped this at my feet—wait now, I've got it right here. No, it must be in the pocket of my coat! Well, anyway, what do you think? It was—"

"An orchid?" Leonidas asked. "M'yes, I thought as much. You see, Terry—"

There was a crash in the kitchen, and then a scream that turned the five of them to stone.

IX

THE second scream, more piercing and horrifying than the first, had the effect of setting them all into motion simultaneously.

As one, Mrs. Finger, Cupcake, Jay, Leonidas and Chuck all started for the kitchen.

But only Cupcake managed to wriggle her way between the crates and boxes and barrels and all the rest of the clutter in the hall.

Before Leonidas had achieved even two yards, what with Chuck trying to shove past him on one side, and Jay trying to push past him on the other, and Mrs. Finger trying to hurtle past both of them, Cupcake was wriggling back.

"Mother," she said excitedly, "mother, guess *who!* Guess! *Guess!*"

"Maude Haverstraw," Leonidas said. "It *was* Mrs. Haverstraw, wasn't it? M'yes, I recognize the sound of her muffler—there goes her car!"

"Mrs. Haverstraw!" Mrs. Finger said. "Mrs. Haverstraw—what would that woman be doing in the kitchen? Cupcake, are you *sure* it was Mrs. Haverstraw?"

"You couldn't miss *that* hat, mother!"

"But what was she doing in my kitchen at three o'clock in the morning?" Mrs. Finger demanded. "What was she *doing* there?"

"Not what she *was* doing there," Leonidas said, "but what she is now about to do, is our major concern. Er—I think, after those screams, that we may assume she knows in full the contents of Freeze B."

"*What* was she doing in my kitchen at *three* o'clock in the *morn*ing?"

"I can't imagine," Leonidas said, "but she knows! And within five minutes, the police will know. Within two more minutes—frankly, alas is the only word I can think of at the moment. Alas! Just plain alas! Oh, if that freeze had the wings of an angel—of course, you haven't got one! That would be asking too much!"

"An angel?" Mrs. Finger stared at him.

"A dolly. In this miscellaneous assortment of," Leonidas indicated with a gesture the clutter in the hall, "of stuff, have you a dolly?"

"Hush, Cupcake, darling," Mrs. Finger said, "he doesn't mean yours! We've got that platform thing with the wheels that those drunks left when they left the freeze—if Jay and I had been able to get inside your house, we'd have trundled that over—"

"Chuck!" Leonidas said. "Jay! Hurry!"

Two minutes later, Freeze B was once more en route, from One-forty back to Forty.

At his back door, Leonidas paused.

"If you," Mrs. Finger's voice cracked, "if you say you haven't a key—"

"I haven't! I haven't!" Leonidas felt that his voice was going to crack, too. "I left so hurried—"

"It's all right, Mr. Witherall!" Mrs. Mullet emerged with Gerty from the shadow of the lilac bushes. "I got your key right here! Gerty and I, we been waiting here for you, and I declare, I didn't know *what* to think when I seen that thing coming through the gateway and up the path, and—here you are!"

"I got it!" Chuck said. "I got it, now. Beat it back, Jay! I hear the sirens!"

"Hurry, Mrs. Finger!" Leonidas pushed her out of his kitchen. "Scuttle, Cupcake! Rush!"

With their noses pressed against the glass of the kitchen window, Leonidas and Chuck and the Mullets watched the precipitous flight of the Finger family back to One-forty.

Chuck let out a gusty sigh of relief.

"Gee, they made it! Just! Gee, what luck you thought of putting all the lights out before we left, Mr. Witherall! Nobody'd guess they wasn't all in bed and asleep—say, Gerty, how'd you get back here?"

"We hitched," Mrs. Mullet said simply. "Took us some time because the man went around Wemberley way—there they are!"

They watched the police come, watched the upstairs-bedroom lights flash on, then a downstairs light, and finally the light over the front door.

"There's Mrs. Haverstraw with 'em!" Mrs. Mullet said. "Gerty and me seen her and heard her car leaving—that's why we kept out of sight in the bushes. We didn't know *what* was going on! Was it her that snitched, Mr. Witherall? Did she snitch to the cops?"

"M'yes," Leonidas said. "Maude—er—snitched. I should have known it was inevitable!"

"Can't we get out so as we can *hear? I* want to hear!" Mrs. Mullet slipped out the back door before Leonidas could stop her, and Gerty and Chuck followed.

Leonidas restrained his impulse to go with them. He was better off where he was.

Besides, he needed a brief lull in which to do some serious reflecting!

The trio was shaking weakly with laughter when they finally returned.

"If you could of *heard* what Sergeant MacCobble told Mrs.

Haverstraw!" Mrs. Mullet said in a choking voice. "If you only could of heard! Nobody never told Mrs. Haverstraw anything like that in her whole life before!"

"He told her to go home to her kennel," Chuck said, "and mind her own bones—"

"He told her—he told her to—" Gerty collapsed in a spasm of giggles.

"And MacCobble was awful apologetic to Mrs. Finger," Mrs. Mullet said. "Right from the start. He said they'd been informed there was a murdered body in a deep freeze in her kitchen, and he'd tried to get her on the phone to check up only she wasn't connected, and he was sorry he had to investigate—you could tell he didn't believe any of it, himself!—and she *didn't* have a body, did she?"

"How did Mrs. Finger cope with him?"

"She was fine, just fine!" Mrs. Mullet said with admiration. "I'm getting to *like* her! She said merciful heavens, she had a *lot* in her kitchen, and goodness knew she'd found a typewriter that the movers had simply left in her bathtub that wasn't hers, but she was *sure* she didn't have a body *any*where, and certainly not in a deep freeze on account of her never even *own*ing one, and gracious goodness *wouldn't* the police come in and make *sure!*"

"That Jay," Chuck said, "he'd put a uniform coat over his shoulders, and say, he was a *major!*"

"And when MacCobble seen the coat," Mrs. Mullet said, "he started in calling Jay 'sir'—oh, if you'd only heard what he told Mrs. Haverstraw when he found there wasn't any freeze or any body or anything!"

"He said—" Gerty began, and collapsed again.

The three were still helplessly giggling when the Finger family trooped back.

"This night," Mrs. Finger said, "has taken twenty years off

my life, and nothing'll convince me that the law isn't going to grab the few months remaining to me—Bill Shakespeare, this is desperate now! There's *no* other word for it! *This* is *desperate!*"

"M'yes," Leonidas agreed. "M'yes, indeed. As I watched you —er—foil the minions of the law in what Mrs. Mullet assures me was a most masterly fashion, I've been contemplating the ironies of fate. I have been asking myself why, at this moment, when the situation is fraught with desperation, why should fate decree that the situation should have resolved itself into two very simple problems!"

"Two?" Mrs. Finger said. *"Two?* You mean two million, don't you, or are you just poor with figures?"

"Er—two. Just two. There are really only two things," Leonidas told her briskly, "which we really need to know. First, what possible connection or relationship or bond may have existed between Ernest Finger and Bedford Scrim. And last, what *do* I possess of value which I don't know about!"

"Bill, what d'you mean? What are you talking about?" Mrs. Finger demanded.

"Ernest Finger was searching something at Meredith's when Scrim killed him," Leonidas said. "Whatever it may have been, Ernest had not found it when he was killed. Scrim did not kill him for it. Obviously. Because Scrim later searched this house—"

"That was when he tied up Mrs. Mullet?" Mrs. Finger asked. "And when you chased him out of your study, and he'd rifled your desk, and all?"

"M'yes. I suppose," Leonidas said reflectively, "we may assume that the bond between Finger and Scrim was the thing they sought. But what it could be—things of value, Mrs. Mullet! Things of value! Think, now! Haven't I things of value or vital import that I don't know about? Think!"

"Well," Mrs. Mullet said, "well, I don't know about things

of value, but things that're important—say, did you ever look at all them telegrams, Mr. Witherall, that kept coming all this morning and this afternoon? Maybe you'd be meaning something of vital import like them?"

Leonidas shook his head. "Those telegrams are merely from my publishers, Mrs. Mullet. I am always sent them at this point in—"

He stopped short.

Smith and Beston always prodded him with telegrams. Invariably. But it was not Smith and Beston's custom to stop prodding until the latest overdue Haseltine was safely in their hands!

And the telegrams had stopped. None had arrived since Mrs. Mullet was thrust out of his study, before four o'clock that afternoon!

Turning abruptly on his heel, he practically flew to his study, picked up the top yellow envelope in the little stack beside the Shakespeare inkwell, tore it open, and read it.

Then he opened the others, one by one, and read them.

Then he looked up at the group eagerly watching him, and smiled.

"Well?" Mrs. Finger said impatiently. "Well! What *are* they?"

"Lady Alicia," Leonidas said to Mrs. Mullet and swept her a courtly bow, "Lady Alicia, you—er—get a raise. These telegrams are not from Smith and Beston. They are from my good friend Admiral Coe-Chester. Some pink-faced aide of his—or as he puts it, 'Some infernal beardless child, doubtless a refugee from the insurance or bond business'—left his personal file behind at Meredith's. Admiral Coe-Chester, having just arrived at his tropic base, has just discovered the omission. He hopes, in a rather forcefully salty way, that I'll find the damned thing and put it in a safe place, since it contains carbons of some important letters, and his own personal notes on certain factories that he inspected. Admiral Coe-Chester felt that I could doubtless locate the missing file with greater celerity and ease than some official who knew nothing of the school. Ah, how simple!"

"How *what?*" Jay said.

"Simple. Among the factories he inspected," Leonidas said, "were the Dalton mills. Bedford Scrim is the general manager of the mills—oh, how dull of me! You said he wore a Navy E in his lapel, Chuck, a fact I missed completely!"

"What's it got to do with all of *this?*" Chuck demanded.

"The mills have been engaged in producing certain materials for the navy," Leonidas said. "You know that. And before he left, Admiral Coe-Chester told me that his inspections were less of checkups than surveys for future conversions and changes. If Scrim, for example, could find out that certain quotas had been filled, that certain conversions were to take place—well," he took off his pince-nez, "had *I* known that the navy intended to leave Meredith's, had I any advance inkling of their intentions, much time, toil, trouble and worry would have been saved! M'yes, indeed! Among other things, I should not have been compelled hurriedly to hire Ernest Finger as a French teacher! To a far, far greater extent, similar advance information—even a hint!—would have profited Bedford Scrim. A few days' or a few hours' warnings would have given him the jump on his competitors! M'yes, indeed!"

"But how in the world would Scrim have known that this admiral's file was left behind?" Mrs. Finger asked. *"He"* didn't get sent telegrams, certainly!"

"Admiral Coe-Chester is an impatient man. When I neglected to answer his first message, he sent a duplicate. Then another. Then, as he says here in one of these later messages, he sent a telegram to the mayor, asking him to locate me at once. Now," Leonidas said, "the admiral is an admittedly brilliant man. But he is also absent-minded. He furthermore categorically refuses to be involved with political issues. In short, he started sending telegrams to Honest John. He forgot that Honest John was with us no more."

"Honest John was a former mayor?" Jay asked.

"M'yes, and also Scrim's uncle. You see, Admiral Coe-Chester knew Honest John. He sat next him at innumerable banquets. He stood beside him to review any number of parades. He enjoyed Honest John as a companion in his many extra-curricular duties, and he was frankly entranced by Honest John's fund of stories. I never troubled to explain to Coe-Chester that his favorite Dalton raconteur was being investigated by the Good Government League, because once when I started to discuss our so-called government, he stopped me and said that he was beyond politics."

"I still don't see how Scrim *knew!*" Mrs. Finger said.

"I think it's rather clear that in his uncle's absence, his tele-grams were delivered to Scrim," Leonidas said. "I also think that Coe-Chester's messages to me stopped because Scrim sent some reassuring answer to Coe-Chester, in my name. After killing Finger, Scrim still had to get the file, you see, before I did. Hm! My complete lack of any vigorous action in locating the file at once must have puzzled our friend Scrim consider-ably!"

"But how did Scrim and Ernest get together?" Jay wanted to know. "I mean, how does Ernest hitch up with all of this?"

"As Honest John's former secretary," Leonidas said, "Scrim doubtless knew many people. Now suppose that you, as Scrim, are faced with the information in Coe-Chester's telegram to your uncle. You—"

"But would Coe-Chester have told the mayor?" Jay inter-rupted. "Would he have told him about the file?"

"Not intentionally. Not if he'd suspected his message might

fall into the hands of a manager of the mills! Of that," Leonidas said, "I am very sure! Probably Coe-Chester didn't even know that Honest John had a nephew, let alone one in such a position."

"Then how—"

"Probably, Jay, Coe-Chester barked at some underling and told him to send telegrams to the mayor, the while impatiently maligning me for not answering his messages. 'John Scudder, Dalton. Unable contact Witherall at his house. Most imperative you locate him immediately wherever he is. Inform him he must secure file accidentally left at Meredith's labeled Personal-Confidential containing most vital reports. Reply.' Something like that would be all Scrim needed. After all, *he* knew Coe-Chester had inspected his factory, and other factories, and had a very good idea what for, I've no doubt."

"I suppose so," Jay said. "I suppose that's how it would probably have to work out. But what about Ernest?"

"M'yes. You're Scrim, let us say, and you have this telegram. You know what it would mean to you to get a look at that file yourself, to see if it contains what you suspect. What is your reaction? You can't just stomp into Meredith's Academy this morning, and start hunting! You can't take the chance of waiting to burglarize the place at night. That might well be too late. You wish violently that you knew someone connected with the school who—aha! You have it! Santos! Finger! He told you the other day he was going to teach at Meredith's! At once, you telephone Finger and ask him—"

"*Did* he, Mr. Witherall?" Mrs. Mullet interrupted, "did he *really?* Or is this just a lot more that you're making up?"

"It's fancy, Mrs. Mullet, but I'm so very sure I'm right! My first telegram came about six this morning. Say that Scrim got his uncle's a couple of hours later, around eight. M'yes, it all works out! Skellings said that Finger came to the school early, before nine. Scrim had phoned him, and he'd even noted Scrim's name down on his desk pad. M'yes, indeed!"

"But if Scrim called Ernest to help him get into the school," Jay said, "then why did he kill him? I mean, what was his motive, particularly if Ernest hadn't found the file? I could understand if Ernest got it, and then Scrim killed him for it. But this confuses me!"

"Darling," Mrs. Finger said soothingly, "you didn't know Ernest! You simply didn't *know* him! We kept him from you chil—"

"Didn't I break his arm?"

"Yes, darling, you saw him that time, but you don't understand. He double-crossed Scrim, of *course*. That's why Scrim had to kill him."

*"Moth*er!"

"Darling, *I* know Ernest! He'd gladly and willingly have entered into a scheme to get that file. It was intrigue, which he loved, and Scrim would pay him money, which he loved, and there wasn't much chance of his getting caught, which he loved! Then all the glowing possibilities probably began to occur to him. He realized he could make more money showing the letters to other mills or factories. Probably he at once demanded more money from Scrim, on the threat of exposure—don't you think so, Bill? Don't you think that's what happened?"

"M'yes," Leonidas said. "Something on that order. Probably a very definite threat of exposure—it could have been very pointed, too, with Skellings snooping around after him! And I'm sure he demanded more money. M'yes."

"Where is it?" Mrs. Mullet demanded suddenly. "Where *is* this file? Where is this stuff of the admiral's, anyway?"

"Oh," Leonidas said, "it's in the trunk in my car. It's one of those pasteboard-box affairs that looks like a ledger. I put it in the car a good ten days ago, and forgot it along with everything else."

"But where'd you find it?"

"In a drawer of the headmaster's desk at school. I noted the 'Personal-Confidential' label, and Coe-Chester's name, and instinctively felt it shouldn't be left lying around. How well," Leonidas said cheerfully, "how well this has worked out!"

"Well?" Jay inquired. *"Well?"*

"M'yes. Now, I wonder," Leonidas seemed to be thinking out loud, "how things happened at the school! Doubtless Finger slipped Scrim in, and thrust him behind some handy door while he hunted for the file—I'm sure, with all the hurly-burly going on there today, he felt no particular necessity for secreting him very deeply. M'yes. Then Finger proceeded to goad Scrim with demands for more money, and with threats of double-crossing him."

He wondered suddenly if Skellings' rushing to the basement after Finger might not have appeared to Scrim, lurking behind his door, as something rather sinister. Could Scrim have imagined, in a moment of panic, that Finger intended to tell Skellings all?

"Ah, well," he said aloud, "that's all conjecture! At least we know the connection between Scrim and Finger, Scrim's motive for killing him, and of course, Scrim had a personal grudge against me on his uncle's account, I assume."

"And me always thinking he was such a swell guy!" Chuck said. "Gee!"

"Others have held similar opinions," Leonidas said. "Even the Wemberley bank director thought he was a fair-haired young man, led astray unwittingly by his wicked uncle. My, what problems poor Scrim has had today!"

"You," Jay said plaintively, "keep saying things the wrong

way! You don't mean what problems Scrim's had! You mean, what problems *we've* had, and have got!"

Leonidas shook his head. "No, I mean what problems Scrim has had. Think of his waiting and waiting for that body to be found! Think of the tension!"

"Say, what did he keep coming here for?" Mrs. Mullet demanded. "To get the admiral's stuff from you?"

"Probably that was his primary purpose," Leonidas said, "although I'm sure he had some excellent trumped-up reason for seeing me. I also think he assumed that his presence here during the arrival of the freeze might somehow add to whatever alibi he had thought up. Later this evening, I think his sole purpose in coming was to precipitate the discovery of the freeze."

"Why'd he want it found?" Mrs. Mullet asked. "I should think the longer it wasn't found, the safer for him!"

"On the contrary, the quicker it was found, the better. The longer he had to wait, the more alibis he would find necessary. And the minute the freeze was discovered here, he would be rid of me," Leonidas said. "I suppose he thought the coast would be quite clear for him to hunt that file, after the police led me away. M'yes, what a ghastly, nerve-racking time he's had! Even my original greeting to him this evening must have been genuinely upsetting, when I insinuated that I was not Witherall at all! Dear me, the poor fellow!"

"All I can say," Mrs. Finger announced, "is that while I grasp your general trend, I don't pretend to understand some things, even yet! *What* was Mrs. Haverstraw doing in my kitchen just now? I mean, Jay says he left the door unlocked, so that's how she got in, but what was she *doing* there?"

"I am quite willing to wager," Leonidas said with a smile, "that Bedford Scrim stage-managed that."

"What?"

"M'yes. Scrim," Leonidas said, "has been waiting to have that body found, as I've just pointed out. Waiting and waiting and waiting. Now, Maude Haverstraw is well known as Dalton's most violent Santos fan—er—you know about his crooning, I assume? M'yes. Well, if one called Maude Haverstraw in the dead of night and told her that Santos would meet her in the kitchen of her old home, say, one could be very very sure that Maude would at once fly to meet him. Er—is that a reasonable assumption, Mrs. Mullet?"

"Say, she'd dived off the deck of an ocean liner and swum to shore to meet him personal!" Mrs. Mullet said. "She'd get up off her death bed to! I told you so!"

"I can't believe it!" Mrs. Finger said flatly.

"I can. I know Maude," Leonidas said. "I know Scrim wants that body found. I think—m'yes, I think he's getting a little desperate, too! Now I wonder," he added, "if the police don't know about this, I wonder why they pursued me to Meredith's, and to Finger's apartment! I wonder!"

"Look," Jay said. "Clues. I mean, I hesitate to bring up the topic, but have you *any* clues? Or *a* clue? Have you anything tangible to go on at all?"

"Oh, yes, indeed!" Leonidas said. "We're quite sure that the murderer should have in his possession Finger's key to the school. He should also have disposed of a very tangible pair of shoes, one of which Terry—"

"I keep *worrying* about her, Mr. Witherall!" Mrs. Mullet said. "If Scrim's got her in his clutches, he may kill her, you can't tell! You know Haseltine always says murders are like olives. After the first, the rest come easy. I think we should ought to rescue her!"

"I'm considering that," Leonidas returned. "I'm considering

many things, Mrs. Mullet. Hm. *I* can't do it, because Scrim has been suspicious of me from the very start. He's suspicious now of Mrs. Finger and Jay—"

"Why?"

"He knew the freeze was in your house. He must have known, to have sent Maude there. Obviously he's been keeping watch on things. He's been around here. M'yes, and he saw Chuck, even if Chuck didn't notice him in front of Finger's apartment. He saw Mrs. Mullet here, he tied her up. Hm. Gerty, does Scrim know you?"

"I worked in the mills once, for a little while. But," she smoothed down her sweater, "I did my hair different. I don't think he'd known me. He was working for his uncle then, anyway."

"Hm. And he doesn't know Cupcake. Hm!"

"What," Mrs. Finger demanded, "what goes on in your mind?"

"Scrim had very little time," Leonidas said, "very little time between the departure of the Haverstraws and the arrival of Terry and myself to grub for that shoe. M'yes. He had very little time in which to find it, and very little time, considering his quick return, to do much about disposing of those brown shoes. I wonder, what would one do with a pair of brown shoes on Oak Hill, if one wanted to dispose of them in a hurry?"

He looked questioningly at the group. The Fingers were eyeing him skeptically, Chuck looked blank, and while Mrs. Mullet and Gerty were obviously thinking very hard, they were as obviously arriving at no conclusions.

Only Cupcake seemed to follow his train of thought.

"You'd put 'em in an eagle's nest," she said. "Or a hollow tree. Haseltine would, anyway."

"M'yes," Leonidas said. "M'yes. I think myself that Scrim would leave them somewhere and retrieve them later. He had no time to hurl them in the river, as I originally suggested. And people are so amazingly quick to pop up just at the moment one hurls anything anywhere. Hm. He displayed such inventive genius in disposing of a body, I wonder what he would have done with those shoes? A hollow tree—m'yes, it should have appealed to him. A hollow tree is so exquisitely simple!"

"There's a perfectly elegant hollow tree by our garden," Cupcake said. "I found it this afternoon."

"M'yes, I know it. Slip out, Mrs. Mullet, and see if there is a pair of brown shoes in the hollow tree, will you? Oh—don't bring them back, by the way! Just check up on them."

"You keep talking," Jay said, "as if you actually expected to find those shoes there!"

"I shall be very surprised," Leonidas said, "if they are not there. They have to be there. Cannae virtually depends upon their being there."

"*What* does?"

"Cannae." Leonidas spelled it. "C-a-n-n-a-e."

"Oh, I know that!" Mrs. Finger said. "It's something I missed at school, I might add. I picked it up from listening to Haseltine with Cupcake. After the gallant lieutenant's been buffeted around by fate till he's all but a pulp, he thinks of Cannae, and he just solves everything!"

"What *are* you talking about, mother?" Jay demanded. "What *is* Cannae, anyway? What's it got to do with all of this?"

"Cannae," Leonidas said, "is the historic battle between the Romans and the Carthaginians, fought in Apulia in the year 216 B.C., in which the small, weak army of Hannibal cut the incomparable forces of eighty-five thousand proud Roman legionnaires to pieces—"

"Shreds," Cupcake interrupted. "Haseltine always said *shreds.*"

"M'yes, to shreds. In that," Leonidas continued, "by means of an ingenious strategical concentration, it caught the enemy from the flank with cavalry, and surrounded him. Clausewitz and Schlieffen of the Prussian General Staff elaborated the idea of Cannae into a general theoretical doctrine, and then compressed the doctrine into an exact strategical system. Blitzkrieg, in short, without latter-day elaborations. Er—that is Cannae."

"And if you actually wrote Haseltine," Mrs. Finger said, "you couldn't reel that off any better!"

"He does," Mrs. Mullet said as she rejoined the group in the study. "He *does* write Haseltine—didn't you know? The brown shoes are right there, Mr. Witherall."

"He writes Haseltine! Bill, you *do?* I felt instinctively when you were improvising that niece story about Terry that I was in the presence of a genius!" Mrs. Finger said. "Cupcake, meet Morgatroyd Jones! Have you thought Cannae all out?"

"Mother!" Jay said. "Listen, I don't like to be a wet blanket, but this crazy mad business *needs* a few wet blankets tossed over it! Look, there's Ernest out in that freeze. There's that blonde girl with that murderer, and you—"

"Hush, darling!" Mrs. Finger said. "Remember you've been away from civilian life for some time, and you've lost track of things like Haseltine! How does it go, Bill? Your Cannae, I mean?"

"I've decided," Leonidas said, "that it is only fair and proper for us to appeal to the same covetous feeling in Scrim which led him into this originally."

Walking over to his desk, he drew out a pad of telegraph blanks.

"Going to send him a telegram, eh?" Jay asked with irony.

"M'yes. A telegram from Admiral Coe-Chester," Leonidas said, "informing him that the aide who originally misplaced the 'Personal-Confidential' file has now been located, and states that same is in trunk of Witherall's car."

"But he'll know it's a fake! You can't—"

"We'll mark it delayed," Leonidas said, "and list its time of origin as early this afternoon. Yesterday afternoon, that is. m'yes."

"No idiot on this earth would accept as genuine a screwy-looking telegram in handwriting—"

"Half of those in that pile by the inkwell," Leonidas coolly interrupted, "are handwritten, and—er—screwy-looking. I accepted them as bona fide, knowing that the telegraph office is woefully shorthanded. Scrim will do the same. Let's see, now. This must be carefully worded. 'Using any means at your disposal secure file at once from Witherall's car trunk in his apparent absence. Counting on you. Coe-Chester.' M'yes."

"How," Jay inquired, "do you expect to deliver it to Scrim, who's wandering around in his beachwagon? Who'll deliver it, you, I suppose?"

"Gerty," Leonidas said. "He doesn't know Gerty. We—er— went through that. M'yes, owing to the manpower shortage, Gerty will be the messenger girl."

"How simply peachy!" Jay said. "Dropping upon him, no doubt, by parachute?"

"No, she takes Chuck's sedan. Hm. Scrim has seen it, but—"

"Oh, disguise it!" Jay said. "Disguise it! Put a crest on the door! Give it a paint job! Don't carp about little details like that!"

"We'll add Cupcake," Leonidas said. "Even though you work at night, Gerty, you do not neglect your child—d'you understand?"

"Sure," Gerty said. "I keep her right by me, don't I, Cupcake?"

"It's amazing," Leonidas gave Jay no chance to comment, "how the presence of a child or a dog adds an aura of veracity to a situation. The last murderer I caught was a dog lover, and very nearly foiled me in consequence."

"The last—you don't mean you've done this sort of thing before? Not *really?*" Jay demanded.

"Er—really." Leonidas finished writing the telegram, folded it carefully, and inserted it into one of the envelopes from his own stack of messages. "Now, we'll phone police headquarters!"

"Goody!" Jay said. "All we needed! All we—"

"Hush, darling!" Mrs. Finger said. "I want to *hear!*"

"Say," Leonidas said, "headquarters? Western Union. Say, I got a wire here for Honest John Scudder that's important, see, and I want to deliver it to Bedford Scrim. Yeah, it's urgent, and I think somebody in the family ought to get it and phone it to him. Had another one like it today. Yeah, that's it. That's right."

Jay shook his head sadly.

"I tried to get Scrim, sure," Leonidas went on. "That's the trouble, see, he's out. They say he's on a date. That's right. He's in his beachwagon, and he's somewheres around Oak Hill, they think, and say, what I wondered was, could you ask your prowl car to pick him up and tell him there's a vital wire for his uncle I'm trying to get to him? Sure, he'll understand. If you could pick him up and tell.him, see, I'd have my girl wait for him on the corner of Fruit and Elm. She'll drive there in her car, see, and it'll save him the trouble of coming to the office. Yeah. Then he can sign for it, too."

After going over the situation once more, Leonidas thanked headquarters, and hung up.

"There!" he said. "Headquarters knew that was bona fide

because I said he could sign for it. Signing is another veracious touch. Now, they'll pick up Scrim, Scrim will proceed to Fruit and Elm—got that, Gerty? That's where you and Cupcake will be waiting. You give him the wire, have him sign," he crossed over to his desk, "in this mangled notebook, and forthwith return here."

Jay sat down and crossed his arms. "I thought," he said, "I'd heard everything! I thought—"

"Darling," Mrs. Finger said, "I do wish you'd hush! Scrim will come here at once of course, won't he, Bill? You'll leave the garage unlocked, I suppose?"

"M'yes, but with the padlock in place," Leonidas said, "and of course we'll leave the car keys conveniently in the ignition, so that he may open the trunk without difficulty. As he leaves with the file, he will doubtless pick up his shoes in the hollow tree. At that point, Chuck will take over."

"And the dear good police?" Jay said sardonically. "How are you going to hand him over to the dear good police? Thought *that* one out? Thought out what's going to happen when they find the freeze, and learn—"

"Hush *up!*" Mrs. Finger said. "You're going to feel such an idiot, Jay Finger, when this works out! How long should it take, Bill? Half an hour?"

"I'd say," Leonidas said thoughtfully, "Chuck should be taking over in half an hour, m'yes."

Almost half an hour later, Chuck was pinning Bedford Scrim's arms behind him as he reached for the brown shoes in the hollow tree.

"Splendid, Chuck!" Leonidas said. "Into my study with him, quickly! Hurry him—"

"I got to carry him," Chuck said. "He's wilted. Gee, was he ever surprised! The look on his face!"

"Hurry! Maude Haverstraw ought to be here any minute!" Leonidas said.

"No!" Jay said. "No, that *can't* work out, Shakespeare! I give you credit, Scrim bit! But she won't bite again!"

Twenty minutes later, Maude Haverstraw was displaying the body of Carlos Santos to the Dalton police in Leonidas' kitchen.

"*There!*" she said. "I *told* you I saw it—I told you! I—Leonidas," she turned to him as he entered the kitchen, "what does this mean! Who—"

"Ah, MacCobble!" Leonidas said. "I'm very glad to see you!"

"Say, Leonidas, what goes *on* here?" MacCobble demanded. "What *is* this? Who done it? And say, where you been? We made you Honorary Police Chief at the party, and we wanted you should know! We hunted you all over, wherever anybody thought you'd be—"

"Er—why Pomfret?" Leonidas inquired.

"Pomfret? We never went there for you! We went there for *him!*" MacCobble pointed to the freeze. "Some of those Santos fans wouldn't leave till he come, so we went over a couple times for him—say, what *is* this? Who *done* it?"

"Bedford Scrim," Leonidas said promptly. "He's in my study, writing a full confession. You may just possibly have to make him write it over, because he's in rather a—er—state."

"You mean," MacCobble said in a dazed voice, "you mean that this murder is all *solved?*"

"M'yes," Leonidas said with a smile. "All that remains for you to do, MacCobble, is to have someone—Matt and Shorty, for example—remove this freeze for you, and to convey Scrim to a cell. I'm delighted to be Honorary Chief, and if I do say so myself, I feel I've made rather a good beginning! And now, I'm sure you've a lot to see to, and so have I. Er—I have a book to finish!"

Mrs. Mullet pounded on Leonidas' desk.

"Mr. Witherall, it's after half-past eight, and you haven't been to *bed* yet!"

"Neither," Leonidas returned, "have you. Er—how *is* everyone?"

"Well, Chuck and Gerty're eating breakfast, and Mrs. Finger and Cupcake've gone home to bed—I'm getting to *like* them, Mr. Witherall!" Mrs. Mullet said. "They grow on you."

"And Terry?"

"She's with Jay. She said she thought he ought to get some of his birthday present—honest, wasn't she just like the Lady Alicia, saying she didn't mind being with Scrim, or his threatening her, on account of her *knowing* you'd rescue her? They've gone," she added somewhat unexpectedly, "to steal her letter out of Finger's mailbox."

"*What?*"

"Yes, that letter of hers seemed to worry her, so," Mrs. Mullet said, "I gave her his mailbox key I had. In *my* candied opinion, she and Jay are going to get *on!*"

"Indeed!" Leonidas said. "And the freeze?"

"Oh, Matt and Shorty took it away. I wish you could've seen their faces, Mr. Witherall, when they seen what was *in* it! Shorty, he turned to Matt and says, 'Matt,' he says, 'leave us never move no more freezes!' Is it done?"

"Er—is what done?"

"The book, of course!" Mrs. Mullet said impatiently. "Did you finish? Gee, you did? How's it end?"

" 'Bathed in the refulgent glow of the setting sun,' " Leonidas read from the manuscript, " 'Haseltine clasped the Lady Alicia to his manly bosom.' A band plays, and cymbals crash. Thank heaven," he got up from his desk and picked up his cap and gown, *"that's* off my mind for a while!"

"Where," Mrs. Mullet demanded, "d'you think you're going now?"

"To the grand reopening of Meredith's Academy," Leonidas told her, "and I trust Jay Finger remembers it, because he's the new French teacher. Mrs. Mullet, when Smith and Beston start sending me telegrams again, will you remind me of the next Haseltine's title?"

"What is it?" Mrs. Mullet asked eagerly. " 'The Moving Finger,' *I* bet!"

"Er—no," Leonidas returned. "Not 'The Moving Finger.' Nor 'Deep Freeze.' But—"

"But *what?*"

" 'Dead Ernest,' " Leonidas said simply. "Good morning, Mrs. Mullet."